PROLOGUE

———• •———

Her blood felt warm on Cassius Ashmore's hands. He looked down at his wife of twenty years in his arms, his expression full of horror. The sky above darkened, the silvery stars disappearing into the murk of the night. The old buildings slowly closed in on them in the narrow street, smothering them in brick and concrete. Cassius pressed his hand against the stab wound in her abdomen.

'Eliza,' he breathed. Her eyes were fervent as she stared up at him. She squeezed his arm as she attempted to heave herself up, her lips moving to form incoherent words. Even at the brink of death, Eliza would not go easy, which only deepened the pit of despair forming within Cassius. He screamed for help, screamed until the cords within his throat almost snapped, yet he couldn't even hear his own voice. His fingers had become slick with blood, dripping down his knuckles onto the cobbled stone.

'Do not leave me, Eliza, *please*,' muttered Cassius, pain

slashing the lining of his throat. He pressed his gliding hand deeper against the wound, as if he could stop the tendrils of life from escaping out of her. Her breathing turned shallow, the colour draining from her face. A sound drifted from her lips. Cassius leaned closer to listen, thick tears falling onto her cobalt dress as he tried his hardest to shut out the roaring in his head and listen.

'I will not,' she managed in a rasped voice. There was blood on her lips. Cassius could not tell if it came out of her mouth or from his hands. There was too much of it, colouring the world before his eyes a devilish scarlet. He screamed, and yet, nobody heard him. As he looked down at her again, her eyes started to fall shut.

'No, Eliza, hold on, please,' pleaded Cassius, shaking her by the shoulders. She stared up at him, her eyes conveying a deeper sadness than anything he had ever seen before. Her raven hair fell over her shoulders, blood dripping off the ends; a goddess of despair in her own right, until the last of her breath escaped her lips and she fell silent forever.

CHAPTER I

Morality

The sky above hung still and lifeless. It had blackened into hues of obsidian, plunging the alleyway into darkness. The light of the main street was only a faint shimmer in the distance, fading the longer he looked at it. A carriage charged past a street away, the sound reverberating in the stillness where Gabriel Ashmore waited, just opposite the Tower of London. The castle's domes slashed against the sky, illuminated by the distant slivers of the moon cast down upon the earth. He marvelled at something so ancient, something which had seen the fall of great men, fed itself with centuries worth of blood and tears staining its stones.

He took the Erebus out of his pocket. The black powder felt like a heavy weight against his broad palm; Gabriel could picture its darkness even through the fabric of the pouch, darker than the parts of the ocean where light

hadn't penetrated for millennia, a composition of onyx and eternal hell. Suddenly, boots squelched on the wet and muddy ground, nearing him as the seconds ticked by. He turned around and was met with a man who stood before him. He had pulled his hood up, hiding his features. Everyone he delivered to did so. The edges of his coat were dirty and frayed, and so was his voice as he spoke.

'Have you got it?' The hoarseness of his voice vibrated in the air around them like a broken instrument. He cracked his neck, fumbling with the hem of his shirt, as if something were trying to worm itself out of him. Overcome by addiction. A faint outline of who he used to be before. Gabriel despised this, despised the immorality that was everywhere in London, the immorality he helped spread; but he had no choice. No choice but to merely watch as the city succumbed to the dark instincts that lined each street.

'Payment first,' he said with a firm voice, holding out his hand. Gabriel's demeanour was calm against the man's frantic manner. He'd done this at least a hundred times, so much he'd almost become numb to it. The man's shaking hand dove into his pocket without question, his head twitching up and down. The man's hood slid back, revealing a face as white as snow, dotted with droplets of cold sweat, and – Gabriel's heart skipped a beat, eyes widening – covered in ghastly black slashes. No, veins. They spread under his skin like cobwebs, slightly raised as if tar would come spilling out of his blood at any second. They bundled around his darting eyes, turning them into black pits.

'What happened to you?' breathed Gabriel, his brows furrowing. The man didn't speak a word as he reached out

2

and handed Gabriel the coins, waiting for the Erebus. 'What happened?' Gabriel repeated, more forcefully this time. The man only stared at him, head twitching, shoulders hunched. Gabriel eventually dropped the pouch in the man's hand and watched him scurry off. It must have been the darkness of the powder that tainted his blood. Gabriel did not stop to fathom how that could be possible. There was simply no point; he had stopped questioning the integrity of what he was doing a long time ago. He needed the money and people needed the Erebus. The new craze. The city's new menace.

CHAPTER II

The Lost Visitor

The house was colder than the early winter air outside. Gabriel slammed the door behind him, almost making the house rattle. It was big, but old. Inherited from his father's father, a decaying jewel planted right on the edge of Belgravia. A remnant of a by-gone age of wealth and status, a useless and forgotten palace. Restoring it would cost a fortune; a fortune Gabriel didn't have. He walked through the foyer into the parlour. Images of the man, the darkness of his veins, his blood, filled his head. There was something wrong, he could feel it, but he pushed it aside, letting the memory fall away. He was too tired, too exhausted. Always too tired, too exhausted. He halted. His eyes fell on the lit fireplace, its flame engulfing the wood in its scarlet and amber brilliance. The curtains had been drawn open and the sky spilled into the room like tar. Gabriel drew in a sharp breath as his eyes fell upon his

grand piano. It stood in the corner of the large room like a skeleton. His fingers itched to play its keys again, hear the melodies he could produce, feel it engulf him. But he couldn't. Not anymore. There were multiple copies of *The Illustrated Police News* on one of the coffee tables, with the usual headlines speaking of a record increase in theft and burglary, and another one mentioning multiple murders. Gabriel frowned as he picked the paper up, starting to read the column before a familiar voice sounded behind him.

'What time do you call this?'

Gabriel's shoulders tensed up. 'Hugo.' He turned around, standing face to face with an exact copy of himself.

'Hello, brother.'

'What are you doing here?' asked Gabriel with a set jaw, his green eyes staring into replicas of his own. He hadn't seen his brother for a whole year. Despite being twins, Gabriel felt more distant from Hugo than ever. But Hugo seemed different. More put together. His dark brown hair was combed back, his eyes no longer lined with dark circles and the identical sharpness of his features less prominent. The light coming from the fire cast a deep shadow upon his bone structure, making him appear ghost-like. Gabriel wondered just how alike they looked in the eyes of others. They didn't in his.

'Business,' Hugo replied as he hitched his trousers up at the knee, sitting down on the armchair by the fire. His deep navy trouser fabric gleamed as he moved, contrasting against Gabriel's worn-down attire. 'Where is father?' His tone was vacant, as if he were trying to distance himself from Gabriel. Gabriel didn't blame him.

'Upstairs,' answered Gabriel tightly. Bitterness always seemed to creep into his tone as he spoke to his brother, like a parasite worming its way into a willing victim. 'When did you come in?'

'Just this evening,' said Hugo with a sigh. 'The city is worse than I remembered it. How do you live here?'

Gabriel laughed bitterly. 'You used to live here.'

Hugo hesitated before he spoke. 'You do not look that great.'

'Many thanks, brother.'

'No, I mean, that scar,' Hugo said, pointing at Gabriel's face.

'A small fight.' Gabriel caught his reflection in the dark window, the thin white scar running from the end of his eyebrow to his cheekbone stood out like a livid marking. He had got it six months ago, whilst wandering the streets past midnight. He had encountered a pickpocket with a glass shard as a weapon, but the only thing he had managed to obtain from Gabriel was a broken arm.

'Are you in some kind of trouble—'

'Stop,' said Gabriel sharply.

'I could help you, Gabriel—'

'I do not need your help.'

Hugo scoffed. 'Why do you insist on speaking to me with so little endeavour of civility?'

'How amusing you think yourself deserving of civility.'

Hugo sighed, his nostrils flaring. 'It is unfair of you to—'

'Unfair?' said Gabriel, his voice cutting through Hugo's like a blade.

'Yes,' he snapped, 'it is unfair of you to just dismiss everything—'

'You know what is unfair?' hissed Gabriel, his jaw clenching as he spoke, all of his previous calmness stripping away. 'Adelia's cold and dead body. So far in the ground you would not even hear her if she would scream out. That is what's *unfair*.' Blood throbbed in Gabriel's temples, pulsing through his carotid artery.

Hugo's face twisted into something displaying a whirlpool of grief and anger, the two emotions fusing together into one. He steadied his voice before he spoke.

'You cannot possibly blame me,' he said slowly, as if the words were poison in his mouth.

Gabriel scoffed. 'Yes, I *am* blaming you, Hugo.'

'I did not *kill* her, Gabriel,' retorted Hugo, his voice heavy with an emotion Gabriel could never seem to figure out.

Gabriel let out a deep breath before he spoke. 'You may as well have.'

Hugo's shoulders tensed, as if he were composed of brick. 'She was *my* sister as well,' he hissed, rising from the armchair. He faced Gabriel, looking into the eyes of his brother.

'She might have been your sister, but you were never her brother.'

'I am cold, Gabriel.'

Adelia would always say that if she fell asleep with him there, the night ghosts couldn't get to her. And so, every night, Gabriel sat on the side of her bed, until her eyes were closed

and her consciousness had long gone. Sometimes she would reach out her hand in the middle of the night, reaching for the one that gave her life, reaching for something soft and thin; but instead, she would be met by Gabriel's calluses, the roughness of his skin. In the beginning, the unfamiliarity woke her up, causing tears to well up in her eyes at what she had lost. Now, her eyes remained shut and her hand eventually fit in his, and those imperfections were no longing alarming, instead they became the things she sought out when the torments kicked in.

'I shall fetch you another blanket,' he said, heaving himself up. Adelia tugged at his hand.

'Because you would not *allow* it. You have always kept her away. I was never good enough, never *worthy*—'

'Shut your mouth, Hugo.'

'Can we go sit in front of the fire?'

'Yes, of course.' He lifted her up; Gabriel was strong enough, even two years ago, but it didn't matter as Adelia felt awfully light, even for a three-year-old, as if he were holding a stack of feathers in his arms. He walked through the pitch-black house, down to the parlour. They couldn't afford to keep the gaslights on.

'Do you remember why we keep the lights off at night?'

'Tell me again,' said Adelia, a faint, sleepy grin tucking at the corner of her lips.

Gabriel smiled. 'In this house, an ancient magic exists at night.' Gabriel could see the shine in her eyes, illuminated by the shards of moonlight spilling through the windows,

as she looked up at him. A replica of his. 'Magic pulled from the deepest source buried deep within the layers of the earth, something which even ancient Gods were envious of. However, that magic must be protected. Light has the potential to harm its power.' He pointed at the window. 'See those stars in the sky?' Adelia nodded eagerly. 'That is where they sleep. Now, when there is light, their brightness is diminished. We can no longer see them, and their power could grow dormant. That is why we must keep them off, in order to protect that magic and so we may always see them.' Gabriel was determined for Adelia to never know of the economic troubles they had, how every day was a fight for survival. And so, he made up stories, so he may turn direness into joy.

Hugo laughed bitterly. 'Oh, yes. I had almost forgotten how you used to silence me, exactly like you are doing now. It appears you have not changed one bit, have you, brother?'

The fire in the parlour had almost died down, weak flames flickering absently. Gabriel put Adelia down on the sofa, wrapping her blanket around her. He put in a few more logs, careful to spare some. They were running out. He didn't know where his father was. Perhaps he was locked away in his study, or he had disappeared somewhere and would return in a few days, refusing to tell them where he had gone.

As the fire took hold, Gabriel sat down next to Adelia, making sure her feet were tucked in.

'Remember that you will never be alone,' said Gabriel. 'I will always be here.'

'What about Mum?'

Gabriel swallowed. 'She is here as well. A part of her. She will always watch over you, Adelia. You must remember that.'

Adelia nodded, just as her eyes started to flicker shut. Gabriel let out a deep breath.

The door banged open. Gabriel whipped his head towards the entryway. Adelia was already fast asleep. He instinctively reached over to her, pulling her into his arms. He scoffed at what stood before him.

Hugo stumbled into the parlour, his clothes dripping with sweat, his eyes absent as he avoided his brother's glare.

'I did not silence you,' hissed Gabriel. 'Whatever happened, happened because of *you*. It happened because *you* could not control yourself. Now, depart.'

'Not again,' said Gabriel, ice dripping from his voice. 'Get out.'

'I only had a few,' slurred Hugo, approaching Gabriel before tripping over the carpet, landing headfirst onto the floor.

'She is sleeping. For God's sake, get out,' hissed Gabriel as he shot up, tightening his grip on his sister.

Hugo glanced at Adelia, her pale face cushioned against his brother's chest. 'You always keep her away from me,' Hugo said as he reached out for her, before being shoved away.

'What on earth do you think you are doing? I can smell the alcohol on you, are you mad?' growled Gabriel. Hugo

groaned as he looked up at Gabriel, hatred pouring from his bloodshot eyes.

'Why all this derision, Gabriel? Are you scared she shall prefer me over you? I was always her favourite brother, you know that,' sneered Hugo.

'You are drunk, you do not know what you are talking of. Depart now.'

Hugo chuckled, his features twisting into pure contempt. 'I think I do. You are just desperately trying to cover up the fact you are just as futile as Father. Maybe if you could actually manage to find work—'

'Get out.'

'This is still my house—'

'Hugo, get out,' hissed Gabriel, with a tone so venomous it completely silenced his brother. Before Hugo could say anything, Adelia started to stir in his arms, her eyelids twitching. Gabriel's attention dropped away from Hugo. 'Hey,' he said softly, as he sat back down. 'Everything is fine, go back to sleep,' he whispered.

Hugo looked at the two, a bitterness forming in his throat. And so, he marched out of the room, stumbling out onto the street yet again.

Hugo glared at Gabriel. 'You never gave me a chance. Not one bloody chance.' Gabriel remained silent as his brother made his way towards the door and disappeared into the darkness of the night.

CHAPTER III

─────· ·─────

Cracked Dreams

Gabriel woke up gasping. He heaved himself upright, his back wet with sweat. His head ached. Images from his dream wavered before his eyes, and then slipped from his mind before he could even process them. He put his head in his hands. There was a moment everything went black, somewhere in between sleep and consciousness. Right after it, he'd wake. Often, it became the time he longed for the most.

Sweat dripped down his forehead as he leaned against the wall. It used to be worse. Nights he would wake up screaming. He'd always dream of their deaths. He looked out the window, at the city drenched in darkness.

Hugo had stormed out earlier, just like he always did. Gabriel suspected he was passing the night away at some pub, attempting to wash down whatever he was feeling. And yes, it'd work for some time – Gabriel knew, he did

it for a while too – but it'd all come back up to the surface eventually, and that the pain would be twice as bad.

He got out of bed and walked into the hallway. The vast space looked even lonelier at night. The many chambers lining it were empty, plagued by dust and shadows, except for his mother's. Her wardrobe remained full, glass perfume bottles still glistening under the glow of the chandelier, her bedsheets changed each week as if she would return from her grave at any second. Gabriel remembered wreaking havoc upon it not so long ago, obliterating each bottle into tiny shards, throwing out her gowns, ripping off her sheets whilst screaming at his father that she would never return.

A faint source of warm light came from the library. Gabriel paused before it, peering through.

His father was sat at his oak desk, scribbling frantically into an old book, accompanied by a nearly empty bottle of whisky. Pouring out his sanity bit by bit, writing things Gabriel could only imagine. But at that moment, looking at his father, Gabriel wanted nothing more than to have somebody to talk to. To be told lies of how it would all be okay, half-promises speaking of the prospect of better days. Even to sit and sob whilst his father comforted him with empty words. But Gabriel knew he'd never have that, knew a relationship like that wasn't destined for him. He knew he could never overcome his anger, his hatred towards his father. He knew he could never forgive him abandoning them when they needed him the most. And so, he didn't enter the library and reach for his father. Perhaps things would've been different if he had. Perhaps Gabriel could've

bled the madness out of him with love, but Gabriel had no more love left to give.

*

Gabriel hadn't been to the East End in months. He walked along the cramped streets under the pitch-black sky, amongst beggars fast asleep by the side of the road, dodging the mud upon the cobbles as he entered Chinatown. All the houses around him were covered in dirt, cracked and damaged and infested.

His head ached awfully, in a way it hadn't for a long time. His head seemed to cloud with memories, flashes of days past. Every time he blinked, right before his eyes.

He didn't want to go there. He'd sworn he'd never do it again. But this night he ached differently, as if the pain had taken on a different form. He wanted to forget. Just for a moment. Just for a bit.

He looked around the street before slipping into an alleyway, where the hidden entrance was located. He knocked on the door, hard enough to bruise his knuckles. He rubbed his temples as he waited, leaning onto the damp wall behind him. The muscles in his back ached. The handle twisted and the door swung open, spilling an orange light out onto the alleyway followed by a strong, familiar smell, similar to vinegar. A short, Chinese man with raven hair stood before him.

The man narrowed his eyes as he stepped forward. 'Gabriel? Is that you?'

'Yes, Sing, it is me,' replied Gabriel shortly. The man's

full name was Ah Sing. Gabriel thought Sing was easier. Others called him John.

'Have not seen you in a while,' said Sing.

'Bring me what I usually have,' said Gabriel as he walked in. It was the same as he had left it, all those months ago. It felt like an eternity. Discoloured mattresses were sprawled on the floor, covered in abandoned shawls and other items of clothing. It was a quiet night; the room only contained a few men and prostitutes. Opium dens were becoming emptier and emptier since the Erebus appeared on the market. The beige wallpaper had ripped, leaving the spine of the building staring back at him. 'And an additional one.'

'That is too much, Gabriel. It can kill—'

'Just do as I say,' snapped Gabriel. He couldn't bear to listen to anyone. Not now. Sing sighed, finally reaching behind the counter. Gabriel threw himself down in an empty corner as Sing returned, three full pipes of opium in hand. Gabriel handed him five shillings, part of what he took from the black-veined man just a few hours ago.

'Prices have been lowered,' stated Sing, he pointed at a frame hanging above the counter. 'Only four.'

'It has always been five.'

'Not since the Erebus...' he muttered in a disgruntled tone. 'Been driving our customers away.'

'Can't always have it good, it seems.'

Sing met Gabriel's eyes. 'I had been pleased you were not returning anymore, Gabriel.'

Sing had been one of the only people Gabriel had spoken to when Adelia died, alongside drunken words to prostitutes he only half remembered. Sing had listened

to him, had been kind, but Gabriel knew he never really understood. None of them did.

Gabriel held out his hand. Sing sighed before handing him the pipes. Gabriel knew he was a hypocrite. Condemning the Erebus, but then shamefully indulging in a similar poison. But the hurt was stronger than the shame.

'Leave,' said Gabriel as he put his head back and two of the pipes in his mouth. 'Please.' He closed his eyes as he drew the smoke into his lungs. Sing's footsteps receded into the distance, until nothing filled his ears but the sound of his pumping blood. He took another long puff, and then another and another until he lost track, until his senses had become numb and his mind occupied with a blissful emptiness.

The hours passed by like seconds, and the seconds passed by like hours. Reality seemed to fragment in between consciousness and unconsciousness. Figures and shadows passed him by, drowned out by whispers. A black sun loomed in the corner of his vision like some sort of reckoning. It didn't matter. None of it did.

CHAPTER IV

The Aftermath

'Gabriel, are you all right?'

Gabriel stumbled into the parlour, throwing himself onto an armchair. The room felt hot. Too hot. Heat radiated off his skin. His head was spinning, the room only a blur of colours. A figure stood before him, a hue of darkness. Was he breathing? He barely felt his chest rise up and down. The figure spoke again, but this time Gabriel didn't hear anything. Only echoes of noise, muffled as if he were underwater; drowning.

He felt something sting his cheek, an almost pleasant pain prickling his skin.

'How much have you had? *Gabriel?*'

He couldn't remember how he got home. Was he home?

He shivered suddenly. He was wet. Drenched in cold water. His consciousness returned for a few moments, his

vision less distorted. He could see a replica of his own face, staring at him anxiously.

'Hugo,' he breathed, his lungs heavy. He saw another outline. Someone else. A girl. A small girl with dark hair. And then it started to fade. Gabriel wanted to scream out, but he didn't have enough oxygen in his lungs. He couldn't breathe.

'Gabriel, not again, just wake, *please.*' Hugo's voice was shaking, and all of a sudden, Gabriel was ten again.

He was crouched beside his brother, hiding somewhere. The attic. They were hiding in the attic. Gabriel had his hand over his mouth, trying to stop himself from laughing. It didn't work. He had tears in his eyes. He felt Hugo's presence beside him, his shoulders softly brushing his as they moved up and down with laughter. He felt his cheek sting again. 'We mustn't let Mummy find us.' Then there was silence. Ear-deafening silence. Where is Mummy?

He slipped into unconsciousness yet again.

*

Daylight shone into his room, harsh and unforgiving. His head ached awfully. He had no idea how he got into his bed last night. All he knew was that his body ached and his mind felt numb. He stared at the ceiling, the crushing weight of guilt slowly suffocating him.

'Oh, thank God,' a voice exclaimed beside him, letting out a deep breath. 'You awoke.'

Gabriel didn't stir. 'How bad was I?' His voice was hoarse.

Hugo sighed. He was sitting in an armchair in the corner of Gabriel's room. He hadn't slept all night. He swallowed before answering. 'I thought you were dying, Gabriel.'

Gabriel inhaled sharply, his eyes prickling. He pushed it all aside. 'Well, you were mistaken,' he said finally. He got up out of bed. The room spun for a few seconds before he steadied himself on his nightstand. His limbs felt like lead, his mind hazy and muddled.

'What happened? I thought you—'

'You thought *what* exactly?' sneered Gabriel. 'What did you think?'

'I thought you did not do that anymore.'

'I do not. *Did* not.'

Hugo looked at him with sympathy, any bitterness of the previous night gone. Gabriel detested it so much he wished to punch the expression from his brother's face. 'Has it been worse lately?' Gabriel ignored him as he pulled off his shirt, his back drenched in sweat. 'You cannot be doing this anymore, Gabriel.'

'Quite comical of you to say that, is it not, brother?'

Gabriel wasn't looking but he was sure Hugo flinched. He grabbed a new shirt from his wardrobe and put it on, each heavy muscle in his body aching with the movement.

'I am certainly not drinking like before.'

Gabriel nodded his head at him as he put on his shoes. 'You tell yourself that. Perhaps one day you shall start to believe those lies.' He spoke harshly, uncaringly. Each word like a precisely aimed blow in his brother's face.

Hugo paused before speaking, as if gathering his energy. 'Where are you going?'

'None of your business,' said Gabriel as he walked out the room. Hugo's footsteps followed behind him, hesitant but determined.

'You need to rest. You simply cannot go out and do things like this.'

Gabriel ignored his brother, his head pounding with every step he took, his lungs screaming out with every breath. Gabriel stopped dead in his tracks. His father stood at the bottom of the stairs. His eyes were wild and bloodshot, his dark, greying hair dishevelled, his silk dressing gown wrinkled and old. The stench of whisky radiated off him, a scent that had grown awfully familiar to Gabriel.

'Is that you, Gabriel? Are you finally home?' He was looking at Hugo.

Gabriel could feel Hugo tense up behind him as he descended from the stairs.

'No, Father, it is me,' his voice was filled with confusion. 'Hugo.' Their father had always been able to tell them apart. 'Your appearances are like night and day,' he used to say to them.

'Who?'

Hugo swallowed hard before answering. 'Hugo.'

Cassius frowned, the wrinkles deeply embedded within his skin. A product of years and years of wasted thought. He didn't seem to notice Gabriel, who stood a few steps away from his brother.

'Where were you, Gabriel?'

He cleared his throat before answering. 'Father, it is *Hugo*, not Gabriel. You spoke to me last night.'

'Do not keep going out at night,' Cassius muttered. 'It disturbs me.' His eyes slipped off to something in the distance, something that wasn't quite there.

'For God's sake it is *me*, your son, *Hugo*!'

'Stop,' said Gabriel, grabbing his brother's arm and turning him away from their father. 'He has not seen you in a whole year. What did you expect?'

Cassius looked at them blankly. 'Your mother is waiting. I ought to go.'

'What?' said Hugo, his voice breaking as he spoke. He stared at his father with despondent eyes. The sight of it tugged at something Gabriel had buried deep within him.

'Mother is dead, Father,' said Gabriel matter-of-factly, repeated so many times it almost didn't hurt anymore. It was only a distant memory, something he sometimes convinced himself didn't quite happen. She had been killed on the street by a thief, leaving his father screaming beside her blood-soaked body. Gabriel turned to Hugo, his voice tight. 'Sometimes he...' A muscle in his jaw twitched. 'Forgets.'

Their father remained silent, his face a blank canvas before he walked back up the stairs, leaving Hugo staring after him.

CHAPTER V

A Stranger

The afternoon wind bit at his skin like cold fire. People bustled past him as he headed to Pickering Place, the sound of carriages and hooves bouncing off the large buildings. His brother's voice still rang in his ears. Gabriel watched the bustle of pedestrians: lawyers rushing off to their offices, a blacksmith wiping coal off his apron, newspaper boys with their dirty and ripped attire attempting to attract the attention of the people around them, shouting of daily happenings. In the distance, he could hear Christmas carols being sung. Wreaths adorned the front doors of the shops he passed by. Their juniper berries contrasted against the dark green pine branches, red like blood.

He never knew who he was going to meet. He picked up the Erebus from Whitechapel, alongside information regarding meeting points, and of course, the money he

received. Most of the time, he delivered the Erebus to individuals. Sometimes, he delivered it to shady pubs and opium dens. He had been pulled into it by someone he had come across in the city, two years ago. A foolish decision arisen from hopelessness. Although his father used to be an important merchant, he never went back to work after Gabriel's mother was murdered. Instead, he chose to wallow in his despair day after day, letting his sanity evaporate into thin air, until even that was not enough and he spent every last shilling they had on petty distractions: drinking, gambling and betting.

And thus, abandoning his studies, abandoning his aspirations and dreams, Gabriel did what he had to do to keep those he loved alive.

He was late. He winced at the sound of the carriages rushing past. His head still ached, alongside every other part of his body. The large buildings, mainly theatres and music halls, rose up around him like ancient colosseums. Gabriel remembered going to the Vaudeville Theatre with his mother, just the two of them. He could still smell the perfume she wore that day. Floral, lingering in the air around them as they walked, the feeling of her silk glove against his hand. They watched *The Tempest*. Gabriel remembered the backdrop upon which they had painted an island: the sapphire blue of the sea melting into the sky, the waves foaming on the beige sand, the calm presence of towering palm trees rustling in the air. He'd imagined being engulfed in that moment, feeling the warm sand between his toes, the breeze against his skin, a great ship with gleaming sails

waiting in the distance. But those times were long gone, and so was the Gabriel that once hoped. Hope had become futile now, nothing more than a poisonous disappointment.

He came to a halt and looked around the large road, before quickly slipping into Pickering Place. He looked down the empty alleyway. There was mud on the ground, squelching with each step he took. His muscles burned like acid every time he moved.

There was nobody there.

'Great,' he muttered under his breath as he ventured further into the alleyway. The large stone buildings towered around him. The damp scent of mud and moss wavered off the walls, mixed with something else. Something like strong copper. Gabriel sniffed the air again and turned the corner, steadying himself on the brick wall, and then stopped dead in his tracks. Slumped against the side of the wall was a man. Dark veins ran beneath his skin like a map of hell, and a knife stuck out the side of his neck. Pure black blood oozed out of his wound, puddling around him. His glazed eyes were wide open. Gabriel took a step back. His body stiffened. A horrid sense of déja vû washed over him. The previous night was only a blur, mere shadows in the dark, nothing but disjointed flashes returned to him, and before he could piece it all together in his head, a man slipped out from the house next to the body. Gabriel swore as he stepped back. The man immediately halted at the sight of Gabriel. He seemed to be in his early twenties, the same age as Gabriel. He had unnaturally light grey eyes held by narrow lids, which stared into Gabriel's own. His light brown hair was wavy and neat, and his attire, consisting

of a rather ornate red vest, gleamed even under London's grey skies.

'Oh, hello,' he said calmly, a posh accent lining every letter he spoke. He pushed his round glasses further up the bridge of his nose before he dusted down his grey coat and took off his shiny leather gloves, extending his hand out to Gabriel. Gabriel ignored it and stared at him with a frown, his eyes flickering to the dead body between them. The man looked at the body, as if he had only just seen it. 'Ah, that is certainly not a very pleasant sight. I shall… move.'

The pouch in Gabriel's pocket felt heavier than ever as he eyed the man. Was he the murderer? Had he killed a man in cold blood? *No, it couldn't be*, Gabriel thought. *He would have already fled.*

The man had now moved away from the body, holding his hand out yet again. 'My name is Alexander. Alexander Wakefield.' After several seconds, he let his hand fall down after Gabriel refused to shake it. 'This probably appears most odd.'

Gabriel could see him in more detail now. Unusually sharp cheekbones with freckles speckled upon his nose, as if he had suffered a strong sunburn. His thin lips were naturally quirked sideways, as if he were constantly on the verge of a grin. Gabriel thought he looked odd, like he didn't quite belong to this world.

'It does indeed,' answered Gabriel coldly, eyeing the man up.

'Well, I am investigating a string of murders. Or so they appear to be,' Alexander stated, enthusiasm lacing his words.

Gabriel furrowed his brows. 'A string of murders?'

'Yes,' he answered, looking down at the body. 'How come you find yourself here?'

'Just passing,' lied Gabriel. His voice was hoarse.

'In a hidden alleyway?'

Gabriel ignored his question. 'Who are you?'

'I have already told you.'

'No, I do not mean your name,' snapped Gabriel. 'Why are you here?'

'Then you should have asked *that* instead. As I informed you already, I am investigating a series of connected murders.'

Gabriel narrowed his eyes. 'Are you certain that is not something you made up to cover the fact you have indeed killed this man?'

Alexander raised his eyebrows, looking at Gabriel with a shocked expression. 'Pardon?'

Gabriel crossed his arms over his chest. 'You heard me.'

'Me? A murderer?'

'It is certainly not far-fetched, seeing as you are present at the crime scene. Although you do not look the part.' Gabriel looked Alexander up and down. 'You rather look like you belong in the circus with that vest.'

Alexander scoffed, before quickly looking down at his red vest, which was overwhelmingly decorated with golden stitching. 'This is Italian fabric! And you are at the crime scene too!'

'After the man was *already* dead,' retorted Gabriel. 'And your Italian fabric looks awful.'

'It does not.'

Gabriel glared at him. 'I do not speak lies.'

'You clearly are now.'

'Are you always this irritating?'

'I do not know how to answer that, in all fairness. I rather think highly of myself,' stated Alexander, putting his hands in his coat pockets. He looked Gabriel up and down, as if contemplating something. 'Perhaps you are the connection.'

Gabriel stared at Alexander with an uninterested gaze. 'I have no idea what you are talking about.'

'Four people found dead, all in different places across London,' stated Alexander, leaning onto the wall. 'All murdered. God, do you not read the papers?'

Gabriel resisted the urge to curse. He hadn't been. The past few days had been a haze. 'How does that imply they are connected?' he asked tightly.

'Well, what is there to be noticed on the body?' questioned Alexander, with an odd sort of excitement in his voice yet again, before continuing, 'The veins, obviously. And the rather grim blood.'

'Do not forget the massive, bloody knife protruding from his neck,' muttered Gabriel, screwing up his nose as a gust of wind carried the stench of fresh blood through the air.

'And guess what the other bodies also had? The same exact veins.'

Images of the man he saw last night flashed before Gabriel's eyes again, this time in more detail, and all Gabriel heard was the pounding of his heart, felt the dread flow through his blood and rush to his head. Was it the

Erebus? What connection did the killer have with it? Had he unwillingly facilitated all of this? The thought made his head spin, which was still throbbing due to his ungodly venture of last night.

'Are you with the police?' asked Gabriel bluntly. He needed to make sure Alexander wouldn't pose a problem to him later on.

Alexander chuckled unexpectedly. 'No.'

'Where are the actual police?' demanded Gabriel, looking down the empty alleyway.

'Well, they will be here in approximately...' Alexander pulled out a golden pocket watch. 'Ten minutes.'

Gabriel clenched his jaw. 'How on earth do you know that?'

'I have bribed one of the officers in charge. Therefore, I get to investigate before the police do, on the condition I leave before they arrive.' Alexander smirked, proud of his achievement.

'Well, good luck with your morbid investigation.' Gabriel turned away from Alexander. 'You shall need it.' And without another word, he made his way out of the alleyway.

'You have not told me your name!' Alexander called out from behind him, his voice echoing.

Gabriel ignored him as he turned the corner, heart pounding out of his chest.

CHAPTER VI

The Offer

Gabriel walked along the Thames, his limbs burning with every step he took. He knew he should rest. But he couldn't. He never did. Resting only made the memories worse.

He didn't want to think about everything he had just found out, but it kept nagging at him, like a half-spoken truth striving to break through the surface. Was a murderer targeting Erebus addicts? Was a part of it his fault? The sun had started to set, the sky coloured in soft hues of orange and pink, swirling together like paint. The temperature was dropping rapidly as they moved through December. A flyer stood crumpled beneath his feet, advertising the Conservative Justice Party. Gabriel looked at the charismatic face of Benedict Granville, leader of the opposition.

Change must come. Aid us in returning England's glory.
Good luck with that, thought Gabriel.

He walked upon Westminster Bridge, looking down at the river below him. His head was spinning, his legs numb. The silhouette of Westminster Palace and Big Ben was only a blur to him; the tumult of the city causing painful vibrations like knives to the brain. He let out a deep breath, pushing himself to walk on, as if nothing had happened, as if everything was just fine.

Evening had fallen upon him. He dragged himself along, slowly but steadily. From time to time, for a fragment of a second, the ancient buildings around him seemed to sway and twist like a wicked optical illusion.

He had reached the front of his towering house, feeling a dose of relief rushing through his blood. Just as he put his hand on the doorknob, he heard a strangely familiar voice behind him.

'What a lovely house you have.'

Gabriel almost jumped as he turned around. He cursed. 'Are you serious?'

'Yes, of course I am. It is extremely splendid, although it may need—'

'You followed me?' hissed Gabriel.

Alexander shot him half a grin. 'Yes. I did.'

'May I ask why?' Gabriel snapped, any patience he ever possessed quickly disappearing. He should have noticed it, should have realised somebody was tailing him, but his mind was foggy, slow.

'Well, I am trying to solve a series of murders,' said Alexander casually. 'And I need help.'

'Why on earth should you come to me?'

'Because you know something.'

'Find someone else,' said Gabriel. 'And do not *ever* follow me again.' He turned away, pushing the door open.

'And if I did not know better, you would be my primary suspect,' Alexander called out from behind him. 'I think the police would take a particular interest in that.'

Gabriel's posture stiffened, his nostrils flaring. He lifted his hand from the doorknob, the blood pumping loudly in his ears. He slowly turned back to Alexander, his stare as hard as ancient stone.

'*What?*'

'You heard me. You were there, at the scene of the murder. A hidden alleyway, with no other living soul present. You were looking around as if you came to do something, so clearly you did not just happen to walk in on it. You tensed up even more when I talked of the *other* murders. Now, some people would, but you do not strike me as the type of lad to get squeamish at the mention of murder, so you must know something of it.'

'Are you threatening me?' hissed Gabriel, stepping closer to Alexander.

Alexander slowly took a step back. 'No, I meant—'

'Because if you are,' Gabriel's eyes drilled into Alexander's, 'I will make you wish you had been stillborn. Is that clear?'

Alexander swallowed hard, a faint colour creeping into his cheeks. He cleared his throat before answering. 'Yes, very clear. And very vivid.'

'Now tell me, *Alexander*,' said Gabriel, spitting out Alexander's name like it was dirt in his mouth, 'why would

you follow a potential murder suspect? What would stop me from killing you as well?'

'Because I do not actually believe you are the murderer. But you can help me.'

Gabriel narrowed his eyes, looking him up and down before asking: 'Why do you even care about this?'

Alexander opened his mouth to speak, before closing it again. He eventually said, 'Accompany me to the Theatre Royal on Drury Lane tomorrow. I hear they shall be performing *Richard III*.'

'I beg your pardon?'

'I have heard it is a rather splendid performance. It would also give me an opportunity to answer any other questions you might have, because at the moment I am rather cold and it is quite late.' Alexander looked around the quickly darkening street as he put his hands in his coat pockets.

Gabriel scoffed. 'I do not believe I have ever heard of anything more dreadful,' he said, as he turned away from Alexander and slammed the door shut.

CHAPTER VII

———— • • ————

The Acceptance

Gabriel had no intention of going to the theatre. He had become numb to the indecency that came with the job a long time ago. He had left every part of his morality with his sister, but somehow it kept pestering him. He felt it crawl on his skin as he lay awake in his bed, staring at the ceiling. He could see it looming behind his eyes as he listened to his father's frantic footsteps coming from the library. He could just hear the man out. There was no harm in that. He did not need to agree to anything.

He sighed as he listened to his father's ramblings, drifting through the walls towards him. He could feel the house's emptiness like a hole in his stomach. Sometimes, when it was late enough and Gabriel was tired enough, he could hear his mother's voice, Adelia's laughter, Hugo's chatter and his father's sanity. They were like ghosts that

haunted him, taunting him every second of the night. He closed his eyes eventually, forcing himself to drift away.

✻

Gabriel's shoes squelched on the pavement as he made his way down Drury Lane. It had rained recently. The air smelt of metal, and shadows pooled on every corner of the street. He walked past the Cock and Magpie Tavern. It cast an orange glow onto the street, alongside the sound of men and women laughing, and Gabriel smelt the aroma of beer as people opened its doors to step inside. He had spent the morning resisting a drink. His body still ached, worse than before. The formal attire was uncomfortable, his tie seconds away from strangling him.

The Theatre Royal came into view; an enormous, beige-coloured palace. There were ladies in extravagant dresses of all colours, accompanied by immaculately attired gentlemen reaching out their hands to help as they carefully stepped out of their carriages and entered the theatre. Pushing through the crowd of people gathered before the building, Gabriel looked around for Alexander. He saw him eventually, right by the grand doors, leaning against a large pillar with a pocket watch in his hand. Alexander looked up, his eyes shining under the gaslight.

'Ah, there you are. I was afraid you would not come.' He put the watch back into his pocket. He was dressed similarly to Gabriel, except everything he was wearing seemed like it cost ten times more. The smell of perfume wavered in the air, coming from a group of ladies standing

on the other side of the doors. Some shot Gabriel and Alexander discreet glances, arousing a grin from the latter.

'Do not flatter yourself,' said Gabriel.

'Why not?' Alexander shot back.

Gabriel let out a cold laugh. 'Because those women are more interested in your money than you.'

Alexander shrugged. 'Everybody is more interested in money. One learns to get used to it after a while.' He opened the door. 'After you.'

They found themselves in a private gallery, right by the stage. The walls were painted a fresh golden colour, which seemed to illuminate the balcony from within. *Mother would have been delighted to see the actors in this much detail*, Gabriel thought. He pushed the thought away, willing his mind to forget all those times he had visited the place with her, although her missing presence weighed heavily on him. Alexander hitched his trousers up as he took a seat, gesturing for Gabriel to do so as well. The golden frames of the chairs matched the interior of the theatre, with the plush material soft beneath him. He watched as people filled the seats below them, women slightly lifting their skirts as they squeezed through, their husbands subsequently raising their eyebrows at the act. Gabriel noticed the other balconies fill up as well, with important-looking men and their female companions whose only duty was to look beautiful. They talked busily amongst themselves, probably about business, whilst the ladies chattered about matters that Gabriel guessed to be a lot less important.

'Do you come to the theatre often?' asked Alexander as he took off his leather gloves. His hands were neither thin nor broad, his fingernails neatly trimmed.

'No,' replied Gabriel shortly. His eyes fell on his own hands, broad and rough with multiple cuts he couldn't remember getting.

'Well, this is quite a magnificent play,' started Alexander as he looked down upon the last group of people shuffling in. 'I have seen it a multitude of times.'

'I did not come here to talk of plays.'

Alexander chuckled. 'Of course,' he answered. 'I enjoy your straightforwardness, Gabriel. It is a skill many are yet to possess.' Everyone was seated now, all sound quietening down to low voices and whispers as the curtains slowly started rising. 'I forgot to mention this last night, but I would like you to know I shall be compensating you finely if you decide to aid me with the investigation.'

'Are you trying to bribe me?'

'Of course not. See it as a weekly wage.'

'What makes you think we would even be qualified for such a thing?' Gabriel remarked as he watched the actors come into view. 'The police can do it themselves.'

'That is exactly the problem.'

'What?'

'They shall not. I have spoken to an inspector from Scotland Yard and he has confided to me that they have no leads whatsoever. And moreover, the Peelers are anything but effective anyway – too afraid to even venture into the darker parts of the city, meaning these murders shall remain unsolved,' said Alexander, passion rolling off his

tongue. 'I have already investigated the victims. Mostly lower-class individuals. Their families would not be able to urge the investigation even if they wished to. Moreover, those ghastly veins remain unexplained. Do we really want such a madman roaming the streets of our city?' Alexander was perceptive, Gabriel could give him that. And what he said had reason to it, which drew Gabriel further into the mystery he was already an involuntary part of.

'Why would the government not wish to investigate these murders?'

'Because they fear they won't be able to succeed and therefore prove their incompetency. Ironically, it is exactly this refusal to act that is leading to their loss of support. I suppose they hope to pass them off as mere accidents, of some sort. Scotland Yard appears to not be cooperating with them either, making everything even more difficult. The opposition, the Conservative Justice Party, is rising in popularity, promising to address these issues in rather controversial ways.'

The actor's voice suddenly became louder, drawing them both into the performance.

'And therefore, since I cannot prove a lover,
To entertain these fair well-spoken days,
I am determined to prove a villain,
And hate the idle pleasures of these days!'

Gabriel remembered seeing the Conservative Justice Party's pamphlets around the city and their articles in the newspaper. He had actually found himself agreeing with

their ideals, their harsh and unapologetic measures aiming to root out criminality once and for all. Their controversial ways, as Alexander mentioned, included repealing the Judgment of Death Act of 1823, which allowed the judges to pass lesser sentences for the 200 offences that had carried a sentence of death. Gabriel found this to be radical himself, but as he read further articles written by members of the party, he started to see the utility in their proposition, although he would not support the measure himself.

'Why do you wish to undertake this?' asked Gabriel, glancing back at Alexander.

Alexander looked surprised at his question for a split second. 'For everyone's safety, of course—' he started.

'No. Tell me the real reason.'

Alexander cleared his throat before answering, pulling at his bow tie. His gaze shifted from the stage to rest on Gabriel. 'I desire to be a detective,' he said boldly.

Gabriel raised his brows. 'A detective? You just deemed them useless yourself.' Gabriel knew they were. He tried to hide the distasteful look on his face, but he couldn't ignore the taste of venom in his mouth when he thought of them. They had done nothing to find his mother's killer. Instead, they had simply told his father these things happen sometimes and that they should have been more careful. Just another unfortunate event.

'I wish to make a difference. Be a true detective. Strive for justice, actually make a true effort to solve crime.'

'Why not just *join* the police force then?' remarked Gabriel taciturnly. 'It would be easier to make a difference there.'

'No,' said Alexander, shaking his head. 'I do not trust them. There is something amiss. I wish to find out exactly what it is and actually *solve* these murders. Moreover,' he started with a smirk, 'at Scotland Yard I would not have the pleasure of your distrustful company. It keeps things rather rousing.' Gabriel scowled at him. 'So, that leaves the long-awaited question... shall you join me?'

CHAPTER VIII

New Beginnings

Glints of moonlight spilled in from the window like silver blood. Gabriel let himself fall onto his bed, his muscles burning at the impact. He almost groaned at his own impulsiveness. What exactly had he agreed to? He was fairly certain Alexander was telling him the truth, but somebody like Gabriel could never be too careful. He hadn't even told him of his involvement. He had never told anybody. He thought about saying no, but then the awaited future flashed before his eyes: days of monotony, of despicable deeds, of hatred and regret and death, and all of a sudden, the investigation seemed like a welcoming prospect. Perhaps it would help ease his guilt. Perhaps it was a chance to set things right. He looked out the window, the outline of the tall houses like shadows around him. Thoughts preoccupied his mind, but he couldn't form them. They remained in his head like fragments, like shattered

glass he couldn't piece together, like half-truths, never spoken. He lay awake, letting the adrenaline drain out his body, only to be replaced by reviled memories.

'You have taken it?' hissed Gabriel.

'Yes, how else was I meant to buy my drinks?' slurred Hugo, steadying himself on the railings of the stairs. Beads of sweat glistened at the nape of his neck, red blood vessels visible in the white of his eyes. Gabriel took a hefty step forward.

'That was the last of the money. Do you have any idea what you have done?'

Hugo scoffed. 'Father has been spending it just the same.' He wiped at his sweaty brow and continued speaking in the same despicable, sarcastic tone Gabriel had grown to loathe more than anything. 'Moreover, I imagined we had more. Guess not.'

Before Gabriel knew it, his hand had moved from his side and struck his brother. Hugo staggered back, his hand clutching his cheek. As his eyes met Gabriel's, indignation burned within its pupils. Gabriel stared back at him, shocked at the vehemence of his hit.

'I hate you,' spat Hugo, before storming up the stairs, not to be seen again for days to come.

Gabriel's head pounded as he opened his eyes. The sun hadn't come up yet; he couldn't sleep like usual. Sometimes he felt like bashing his head into a wall. Splitting it open. Having everything come out. Maybe then the memories would stop. The nightmares, the thoughts. The regret.

*

Alexander didn't live very far away. Gabriel read over the address he had given him again as he walked. The streets were slowly filling up, more carriages riding past, more people rushing off to attend daily troubles. Alexander lived in Kensington, only a short journey away from Gabriel's own house.

Gabriel halted before number twenty-five. The house before him had five floors, rising up to the sky like an ancient palace. Owners bustled around the entrance: flocks of colourful skirts, gleaming suits, leather cases in hand.

He knocked on the front door. A few seconds later, a short, old man appeared before him. He had lost most of his hair, his cheeks hollow and his lips naturally pursed.

'Mr Ashmore,' he said by a way of greeting. Displeasure bore the sour features of his face, sporting a permanent displeasure towards the world. Before Gabriel could respond, Alexander appeared behind him, looking as though he had been running.

'Cyril, I had thought I said I would be welcoming Mr Ashmore.'

Cyril turned to face Alexander, his features softening only a fraction. 'My apologies, Mr Wakefield, I just did not believe it right for the master of the house to greet his guests at the front door.'

Alexander smiled uncomfortably. 'Alas, I am here now. Mr Ashmore and I shall be perfectly fine.'

Cyril nodded as he took a step back, positioning himself against the wall, his hands folded behind his back. Gabriel

cleared his throat, shifting by the door. Alexander's gaze fell on him.

'Oh, my apologies; do come in, Mr Ashmore.'

Gabriel entered the house, walking into the foyer. A great staircase stood to the left of him, composed of gleaming oak. A large Christmas tree stood beside it, adorned with red jewelled baubles and tinsel. The sight of it sent a sharp pain through Gabriel's chest. Portraits of stern-looking men decorated the walls on the right, their golden frames contrasting against the red wallpaper. Alexander noticed his observation.

'My great grandfather,' he said. 'He insisted on these ghastly portraits.'

'Yes, they are indeed quite ghastly,' said Gabriel dismissively.

Gabriel saw Cyril's expression out of the corner of his eye, and despite thinking it not possible, his features had soured even more.

'He was equally horrendous himself,' said Alexander, rubbing his chin as he looked up at the painting. Harold William Wakefield, the engraving beneath said. A narrow-faced man with large, bushy eyebrows and wrinkles lining every inch of his face. Two grey eyes under sagged lids burned lividly, shooting the painter a glance of the greatest displeasure. 'He lived an unnaturally long life, so I had the misfortune of being acquainted with him for quite a while. Do not take it lightly when I say he haunted me in my nightmares.'

'Well, good he is now only a portrait.'

'Yes, although at the moment, I am contemplating

whether I should just take it down. Prevent it causing even more misery.' He raised his eyebrows. 'Perhaps I could replace it with a dashing one of me.'

'I believe that shall make the matter worse.'

Alexander laughed heartily, contrasting against Gabriel's monotony. 'Ah, pity, I had imagined myself quite flamboyant on there. And, Cyril, do not look at me like that. You knew him yourself; he was unequivocally awful.'

Cyril's pursed lips moved from side to side before he finally answered. 'It would be improper to lie, Mr Wakefield, yet I do not wish to cause disrespect to the dead.'

'Are you afraid he shall hear you?'

Cyril's thin lips quirked up at the ends, only for a fraction of a second, before returning to their usual displeased appearance.

Alexander led Gabriel to a grand study, in which bookshelves lined most parts of the spacious room. A rush of warmth spread through his bloodstream at the sight of them. He looked around: to the right, a roaring fireplace with two leather armchairs before it, reflecting its hues of amber and scarlet onto the polished wooden floor. Above them, a mezzanine, filled with even more books. Right before him, large paned windows looked out onto the street, and finally, a large oak table in the centre of the room, the type which Gabriel imagined medieval kings utilised when planning elaborate wars, with various papers and pens spread upon it.

'How large is your book collection?' asked Gabriel as he walked amongst the shelves, carefully sliding his fingers over the spines. He couldn't help but feel a certain dislike towards Alexander and towards this room. It was obvious

it was used frequently, most probably being the place where his family gathered. Gabriel could tell from the scratches upon the wooden flooring beneath the table, the many armchairs spread around various corners of the library, the worn-down spines of the books.

'I am afraid I have not counted. I believe it should be exactly a thousand, if nobody has stolen one, of course. This study also serves as the main library.'

'*Main* library?' asked Gabriel as he pulled out a leather-bound book. The work of Tennyson. 'Are you implying there is more than one in this house?'

'Yes. The second one is located on the upper floors.'

'God, no wonder you are so stuck up. Portraits of dreadful dead great-grandfathers and multiple libraries.'

'Not any more than you,' countered Alexander. Gabriel ignored him as he walked back towards the table, leaning forward to examine an annotated map of London. Alexander moved towards him. 'Ah, that is the map upon which I have plotted all the murders.'

'Any pattern?' asked Gabriel. He kept his tone casual, although within his mind, a storm was raging. What if somehow the killer framed him? Gabriel knew nobody would believe somebody like him, even if he contested his guilt.

'No,' sighed Alexander. 'The locations in which they were killed appear tremendously unsystematic, and so do their manner of deaths. The first victim,' Alexander pointed at an area around Temple, reading the annotation, 'Thomas Graham, was pushed out of his own window, breaking his neck. Samuel Hall had his skull bashed into a wall in

Whitechapel. Quite horrific and rather difficult. The medical examiner stated the killer must have done it about five times for the victim to actually reach the point of death.'

'God,' muttered Gabriel.

Alexander pointed to Marylebone. 'Lewis Robinson was strangled by his own tie, in an alleyway right next to a pub named the Anchor. Rather a feeble way to go, but alas.'

Gabriel scoffed. 'Is death by tie not adequate enough for you?'

'I think death by tie would fail to suffice for anyone.'

'Yes, you are quite right. How dishonourable of the victim for allowing himself to die in such a manner.'

Alexander continued, ignoring Gabriel's remark. 'And the last victim – one very familiar to you – Nicholas Ward, was stabbed in the neck. None of these locations or manners of death correlate to one another.'

Gabriel nodded, clenching and unclenching his fists by his side. 'Thus, all of them male, with only their blackened veins in common. What about their professions? Social lives?'

Alexander shook his head. 'Nothing. I have already conducted research relating to it. All unskilled labourers, with only their class in common.'

'Well, perhaps that could be of some importance.'

'That they are all of the working class?'

'Yes,' answered Gabriel, leaning onto the table.

'So, you believe it plausible our killer may have a certain… aversion to those of lower classes?'

Gabriel snorted. 'If you could call murder an "aversion". What about the crime scenes?'

'I have been to all of them and have found nothing to link anybody to the murders. Whoever killed these men left behind no evidence, except for the knife on the body found last night.'

'There is your first lead, then.'

'Well, there is a slight problem with that. The knife has been taken into evidence.'

'I am certain you can bribe a Peeler to give it to you.'

Alexander leaned back on his chair. 'I tried. It appears they have been given strict orders to hide it away. But,' started Alexander, holding up a finger, 'before you lose all hope and re-evaluate your choice of participation, we do at least have one lead. The blackened veins. Caused by none other than that new opium variant named Erebus. Even samples were found on two of the victims: Lewis and Thomas.'

Gabriel's jaw clenched. Of course, he'd know of the Erebus.

Alexander continued. 'Our killer has targeted obvious drug addicts. A horrible one at that.' He met Gabriel's hard gaze. 'Have you ever tried it?'

Gabriel frowned. 'Of course not.'

'I have heard that those indulging in it never truly recover. Some say it tastes of sugar and death, a rather—'

'Quit wasting our time with inconsequential matters,' snapped Gabriel. Gabriel remembered the first time he had been in contact with the Erebus. He had never indulged in it himself, of course, but he lay awake at night staring at the silky, black powder.

Alexander raised an eyebrow. 'You are rather rude.'

'And you are rather vexing.'

Alexander shot him a glance of dislike, before continuing, his voice less animated than before. 'It is plausible our killer may have a sort of vendetta against it.'

Gabriel's heart was beating loudly in his chest, yet his expression remained a statue of stillness. A shadow moved in the corner of his eyes, then it disappeared again. What was he doing? It had been foolish of him to come here. Smoke rose from the table. Gabriel blinked. Alexander was pouring himself tea, his lips moving incoherently.

'Pardon?' asked Gabriel, swallowing away the tension in his throat.

'I said, the most obvious lead is, therefore, the Erebus. We ought to find out if there are any peculiar connections between the victims and the drug that go beyond addiction.'

Gabriel let out a controlled breath. 'What about the victims' personal lives? Their family members or friends may know more. Perhaps they were threatened prior to the incidents.'

Alexander took a sip from his tea. 'Yes, I believe that is a good place to start. Although, I must mention that it appears as though the killer, whom there might as well be multiple of, has selected these individuals in a completely unsystematic manner in regard to personality, with the only connecting element the Erebus.' He rubbed his temples with his fingers. 'Anyway, I could be wrong. We shall have to see.'

'Jack the Ripper's victims were chosen unsystematically, too. Perhaps our killer merely enjoys the act of murdering people,' stated Gabriel, as nonchalantly as he could.

Alexander rose from his chair, his hands clasped behind his back as he moved towards the bookshelves. He stared

intently at it, as if the answer to the investigation would present itself on the spines of the books. After two full minutes of awkward silence, in which Gabriel contemplated simply leaving, Alexander turned to face him, eyes shining brightly. 'Thomas Graham's wife.'

Gabriel frowned. 'Excuse me?'

'A Peeler had told me how the first victim's wife had been making quite a scene at Scotland Yard. If anybody would be willing to talk to us, it'd be her.'

Sweat dripped down the nape of Gabriel's neck. The room felt hot, too hot, as if the roaring fire would reach out and devour him whole. What if Graham told his wife about him? What he looked like? What he sounded like? Would she recognise him? He wiped his forehead. He'd be playing with fire. All it would take is one word, and then they would lock him away. An easy victory for the government, at a time when they so desperately needed success. They wouldn't even think twice about it.

He couldn't risk it.

'We ought to get started tomorrow,' said Alexander, leaning upon the edge of the table.

Gabriel blinked, swallowing hard. 'No. I cannot participate in this foolishness.'

Alexander frowned; his eyes filled with the surprise of disappointment. 'Pardon me?'

'This is a waste of time. You are not a detective, nor am I.' He marched towards the door. 'I refuse to spend my time entertaining your imprudent fantasies.' And with that, he slammed it shut.

CHAPTER IX

A House of Woe

Mist obscured the front door, making the edges of the frame blur and fall away. Gabriel entered the house, taking off his coat, and then he paused. The usual silence, the absolute silence that enveloped the house in its entirety, was absent. He already felt the annoyance prickle at his nerves, making his skin itch.

As he moved through the foyer and into the archway of the parlour, he noticed an orange flicker on the wooden floors. He looked up at the figure sitting on the sofa, head in his hands. He did not need to see a face to know who it was, he had known it ever since he stepped foot in the house.

'Why are you here?' asked Gabriel coolly. Hugo didn't stir.

'It is my house as well,' he answered. He then looked around the parlour. 'No Christmas tree?'

Gabriel's nails dug into his palm. His brother's return was nothing less than a nightmare to Gabriel, a sick dream he could not wake from. He tasted a bitterness in his mouth, a bitterness at the fact he had neglected them all. Hugo then turned around, and Gabriel noticed a fresh scratch on his cheek. The blood upon it was a vivid scarlet. 'Had a scrap?'

Hugo gritted his jaw, hesitating before answering. 'Father,' he muttered.

'Nothing you do not deserve,' stated Gabriel, turning away from his brother.

'He isn't himself, Gabriel!' exclaimed Hugo from behind him.

Gabriel halted. 'He has not been himself for three years now.' He turned to face Hugo, who was now stood by the doorway. 'But you wouldn't know that now, would you?'

'I do—'

'This is nothing new,' hissed Gabriel. 'You decide to show up after a whole year, with the expectation everything would miraculously be normal again. Well, everything has only gotten worse, and you are not helping. On the contrary, you are making things worse. Now depart.'

Hugo sighed heavily, before speaking again. 'I miss it, Gabriel,' he said in a quiet voice.

Gabriel felt a cold chuckle come out of his mouth, his brows twisting together into a hateful expression. 'You miss it?' he repeated. He laughed again, unable to stop himself, as if hate and wrath had completely taken over his soul. 'Got a bit lonely in Liverpool? Not enough prostitutes to get you through the night?'

Hurt flickered across Hugo's features and Gabriel found himself proud of it. He continued, spilling out a year's worth of repressed emotion – emotion he had kept to himself for so long. 'Did you miss it when you left us? When you abandoned Adelia and Father just because you were too weak to come to terms with Mother's death?'

'I had always been closer to her than you,' stated Hugo, his voice pained. 'You do not understand. You are just riven with resentment of me.'

'Yes, correct, I do not understand,' spat Gabriel through gritted teeth. 'I cannot understand how you would abandon us, waste *our* money on drinks, brothels, whatever other filth you got up to. Moreover, I am certainly not riven, I am quite simply and plainly repulsed by you.'

'Really, brother? What would you call your ventures nowadays then?'

'I never did any of that when she was still alive!' snarled Gabriel. His voice bounced off the walls, coming back to himself like a stranger's.

'And Father? Is he not alive?'

All of a sudden, Gabriel's hands found themselves on Hugo's neck, slamming his body into the foyer wall. He could hear his brother wince, his hands tightly wrapped around Gabriel's own. 'Shut your mouth,' Gabriel breathed, his face burning with anger. 'You have no idea what I do for him. What I did for all of you.' A gurgle escaped Hugo's lips, his face reddening as he clawed at Gabriel's hands. Gabriel released him then, blinking rapidly. Hugo slid down to the floor, coughing and heaving. Gabriel stepped back, the adrenaline and anger slowly evaporating out of him as his

chest moved up and down rapidly. He felt nauseous, as if he would vomit any minute. He avoided Hugo's eyes as he turned away, dashing up the stairs.

*

Goosebumps formed on his skin as he lay in his bed. The sky darkened, casting deep shadows into his room. He couldn't remember how much time had passed; it must have been several hours. The desire to return to the East End had taunted him this entire time, like a seduction of a lover, longing to cast the afternoon's memories from his head. Perhaps he could forget them if he smoked enough of the opium. But he knew that was wishful thinking. He knew it wasn't possible.

He ignored the cramping of his abdomen, the blur in the edges of his vision. He thought of the man he met. Alexander. His odd demeanour, his trusting nature. His desperate attempt at making one feel welcome. It made Gabriel dislike him even more. When he awoke, his room was still populated with shadows. He rubbed his eyes, blinking until his vision cleared. He heaved himself up, sitting at the edge of his bed. These were his nights: short and restless. Up each time at the crack of dawn, like clockwork. He wiped away the fog on the window and looked out onto the deserted street. Weak light had started to come through. There was snow on the ground, covering the dirt and imperfections in a perfect layer of purity. More fell from above, spiralling freely until they landed on the ground. Gabriel shut the curtains. He had deliveries to

make. Ten of them, in total. Most of them to individuals, a few to businesses in the East End. Most of these businesses were opium and drinking dens looking to maximise their profit. Sing's opium den, the one Gabriel visited, was one of the few which did not supply the Erebus. Sing was greatly against it, finding the substance foul and immoral.

He stepped into the hallway, heading towards the stairs, before he halted. A faint sound came from down the end of the long hallway. He turned and saw the door of his father's study, down the long hallway. It stood ajar, casting a flickering light upon the wall opposite. He turned away, taking one step down the stairs, and then he stopped. He glanced back towards the hallway, and before he knew it, he stood before the door. He slowly pushed it open, stepping inside.

The wood creaked beneath his feet. Cassius was sat in a large leather chair behind his grand oak desk. The walls of the room were covered in bookshelves, filled to the brim with old volumes. On the right side was an extinguished fireplace, filled with crumpled paper. His father was fervently scribbling on parchment yet again, whilst mouthing words Gabriel could not make out.

'Father.'

'Father.'

Cassius's head shot up, his eyes meeting a copy of his own. His lips glided into a smile. 'Ah, hello Gabriel. What are you doing still up?'

A seven-year-old Gabriel stood barefoot in the dark hallway. His pyjama trousers dragged on the floor. His

fingertips were cold as he gripped the doorframe, staring at his father with wide eyes.

Cassius frowned. 'Have you had a nightmare?'

Gabriel nodded so slightly that anyone else would not have noticed it, but his father did. He gestured for Gabriel to come in, and so he stepped into the room, immediately engulfed by the warmth coming from the softly burning fireplace. His father's face was illuminated by burning candles. Gabriel peered upon his desk, his eyes wandering over the book upon it. Cassius pulled Gabriel onto his lap.

'What did you dream of?'

Gabriel hesitated, fidgeting with the hem of his sleeves. 'I dreamt that I was left all alone. I could not find you or Mummy. Even Hugo was gone.'

Cassius raised his eyebrows. 'Well, what a silly dream! We would never leave you all alone, my dear Gabriel. Not until we are very old, at least, but even then, you shall always have your brother by your side.' He scooted forwards on his armchair.

'What are you reading?' asked Gabriel as he watched his father's eyes land upon the pages of the book.

'A history of Delphi. Do you know what that is?'

Gabriel shook his head. 'You never told me about this one.'

'Delphi was an ancient town, which the Greeks considered to be the centre of the world.'

Gabriel frowned. 'How?'

'Well, it is said that Zeus released two eagles, one from the east and one from the west, and made them fly towards the centre of the world. The eagles met at Delphi. According

to legend, the god Apollo founded his own oracle at Delphi, an oracle which was consulted regarding very important decisions throughout the ancient classical world.'

A faint smile crept upon Gabriel's lips. 'But surely that is not true, Father? Are they not just myths?'

Cassius shrugged. 'Who says it is not true? What harm comes in believing? Men nowadays are far too concerned with facts that they forget what brings pleasure to life. It really is no different to religion; everyone puts their unfaltering faith in it, whilst none of it is truly factual either.'

'Does God not exist?'

Cassius chuckled nervously. 'Now, now, boy, I did not say that. Do not go around telling anyone such things.'

'I believe God likes me very much,' started Gabriel with a smug expression on his face. 'But he is not very fond of Hugo.'

Cassius laughed abruptly, before asking: 'Whatever has Hugo done this time?'

'We were playing a game and he cheated.'

'Well, next time, you ought to cheat right back. There is honour in fairness and honesty, of course, but one cannot win against a lying opponent, unless you lie back. Remember that, Gabriel.'

Cassius's head cocked up, staring up at Gabriel. They had the same eyes: a steady green, passed down through generations. 'Gabriel,' said his father.

'Yes, Father. How are you doing?'

Cassius furrowed his eyebrows together in confusion. 'Fine. Why would you ask me such a question?'

'I just wished to know how you were, that is all.'

'I am perfectly fine.'

Gabriel sighed, before asking: 'What are you writing?'

Cassius looked down at the notebook in which he was writing and snapped it shut. No answer. Gabriel bit the inside of his cheek.

'Would you like something to eat?'

'It is late, silly boy.'

'It is morning, Father.'

Cassius frowned, turning to look out the windows behind him. He then opened his notebook again, continuing his scribbling.

Gabriel swallowed the blockage in his throat, looking around the room. His eyes fell on the fireplace. 'Do you wish for me to light a fire?'

Cassius reached for the glass of liquor upon his desk. 'Leave me.'

Gabriel had learnt not to flinch in response to his father's rudeness, yet some days it took everything within him not to. He always wondered why his father gave up on them so easily, why he let himself slip away. He wondered if it was truly madness, or if he simply did not care enough.

CHAPTER X

—— • •——

The First Lead

He still had a few hours to kill before his first delivery. He poked at the burnt logs in the fireplace and loaded in new ones. He looked through the cabinet for sandpaper matches, before realising they had run out. Gabriel sighed as he opened the bottom drawer, taking out the old equipment. He struck a piece of iron against some flint, holding it over the tinder in the box. Nothing. He struck it again, and again, until his hands started to ache, and then finally, the tinder ignited. He blew upon it, until it glowed sufficiently enough. The tinderbox smelt strongly of sulphur, biting at Gabriel's nostrils. He kindled a match, which he placed in the centre of the log structure he had assembled. He watched as the fire took hold and eventually engulfed the logs.

He ate breakfast, a large portion of porridge with bacon, although he did not feel hungry. He never did.

Gabriel found himself standing in the middle of the parlour. The grandfather clock ticked loudly through the house. The smell of fire and wood circled his nose. He always had trouble passing the time, every hour moving slower than the last. He tried to shut out his thoughts, the thoughts that were always present, lingering in the back of his mind until they caught him off guard and lunged for him. He never could. They ate away at him.

Good, thought a part of him. He didn't deserve peace.

Gabriel gathered his coat and hat, desperate to exit the house. The fire, despite barely warming the parlour, made Gabriel's skin feel hot, filling the house with the lasting smell of smoke. He could visit the library, continue his reading. He marched through the foyer and then his eyes fell upon the door. Gabriel stopped. The door stood ajar; despite the fact he always kept it locked. Gabriel frowned as he stepped towards it. He had made certain there was only one key left, one key which he possessed. He was convinced it was the work of his brother, although Gabriel wasn't certain how on earth he had managed to find that key. He stepped inside the room. It was empty, except for a piano, stood in the centre. Dust had gathered upon it, like a fine layer of snow.

Gabriel's fingers involuntarily fluttered by his sides. He neared the piano and brushed his hand against its mahogany wood. Dust sprang into the air, floating around him. He slowly lowered himself upon the stool and lifted the fallboard from the keys. Something fell to the ground. At first glance, it appeared to be a note of some sort. Gabriel bent down to pick it up.

His breath caught in his throat. It was a picture. A picture of a woman.

Her dark eyes stared back at his own, her gaze razor-sharp. Her raven hair was put up, save for a few curls that tumbled down her exposed shoulders. She wore a necklace, a silver locket. Gabriel had given it to her.

He felt his heart ache as he looked at the picture, yet he could not bring himself to put it down. If he closed his eyes, he could almost hear her voice, the richness of her laugh. And then suddenly, a banging sounded through the foyer.

Gabriel flinched at the sound, quickly hiding the picture in the inside pocket of his blazer. The noise occurred again, and Gabriel realised that somebody was knocking on the front door. He made his way to the entrance, already furrowing his brows at whoever had decided to disturb him. He swung the door open. And then he swore.

'Good morning, I was just on the way to visit Mrs Graham. Care to join?'

'What on earth are you doing here?' hissed Gabriel, stepping outside and closing the door behind him.

Alexander shrugged, taking off his top hat. 'I am merely seeing if you wished to join me.'

'Had I not made myself clear yesterday?'

'Perhaps you have changed your mind,' stated Alexander nonchalantly. 'Anyhow, she lives north of Temple Station. Somewhere around...' Alexander took out a crumpled piece of paper from his coat pocket, 'St Clement Danes,' he read out. 'Now, I know the place is rather unpleasant, but I do not think it shall take very long.'

'No.'

'Is that your final answer?' asked Alexander. 'I am certain Mrs Graham will be lovely company, surely you would not wish to miss out on that.'

'I said no,' Gabriel said adamantly. 'Don't ever come to my house again.' He turned his back, opened the door and stepped inside, until Alexander's voice sounded from behind him.

'Whatever work it is you do now, I shall pay you double that.'

Gabriel halted. He knew he could use the money. Put it into the house, get his father medical help. Then, after he had done those things, he could start thinking about university. He had obtained a scholarship from Oxford, three years ago, to study Jurisprudence. Yet, he had never told anyone. He wouldn't be able to go anyway, so it would have been futile. But perhaps, if he could sort out everything at home, he would have the chance.

Gabriel slowly turned back around, his body stiff with annoyance at the irresistibility of Alexander's offer.

Alexander raised an eyebrow, twirling his hat on his finger. A part of Gabriel wished to punch the smug expression off his face.

'Triple,' said Gabriel. 'And I get paid daily.'

Alexander chuckled. 'Triple? You, my friend, seem to be set on stripping me of my money.'

Gabriel shrugged. 'You can afford it.'

Alexander pressed his lips into a thin line, contemplating Gabriel's counter-offer for several seconds, before holding out his hand. 'Fine.'

Gabriel shook it.

Mrs Graham's house was located in a cramped alleyway on Vere Street. Gabriel rubbed his hands together as they stepped out of the carriage. The snow crunched beneath his shoes. He inhaled deeply, the cold air burning its way through his nose and throat.

'Vere Street,' muttered Alexander, before tucking the piece of paper back into his pocket and started heading towards their destination. Gabriel silently walked beside him.

'Could you not find some keen junior Peeler to aid you with this investigation?' asked Gabriel.

'It is interesting you mention that because I have, indeed, tried that. Alas, it was a fruitless attempt. They all seem to be – reluctant, somehow, over at Scotland Yard. I tried speaking to a few people, but they rejected my offer immediately, telling me to not come back if I knew what was good for me.' Alexander chuckled before continuing. 'And because I do not wish to get arrested, I have been left with no other choice but you.'

Gabriel shot him a glare.

'Although you are a fine choice, of course,' added Alexander quickly. 'Rather exemplary.'

'Oh, shut up,' muttered Gabriel before marching ahead.

They halted before a wooden, worn-down door.

'It ought to be here,' stated Alexander.

'Well, knock, then.'

Alexander looked at Gabriel with an expression of mild annoyance, before knocking upon the door. He stepped back, hands folded behind his back. They waited for several

seconds, until the sound of footsteps could be heard. The door opened, revealing a pale-faced woman. She wore a thin, cotton dress with sown-on patches and a dirty apron. Her brown hair had wildly fallen down her shoulders, and she had soot upon her cheekbone, which she quickly wiped off. She put her hand on her hip, eyeing Gabriel and Alexander cautiously.

'Good morning, Mrs Graham,' started Alexander, shooting her a wide smile. 'My name is Alexander Wakefield, this is my partner, Gabriel Ashmore. We wished to ask you a few questions regarding your late husband's death.'

She narrowed her eyes. 'Are you two Peelers?'

Alexander hesitated before answering. 'Sort of. May we come in?'

She looked both men up and down again, assessing whether they were harmless enough to let into her home. Whereas Alexander maintained a smile, Gabriel stared back at her with a blank expression.

'What do you two wish to know?'

'We are investigating your husband's murder, Mrs Graham. And quite a few others, for that matter. We believe there is a murderer on the loose, targeting even more people. Therefore, it is of critical importance you provide us with any information you may know regarding your husband's activities leading up to his death.'

The woman's stare was bitter, and as Gabriel looked into her eyes, he could tell she had seen worse things than they could imagine. The world's experiences had hardened her, shaped her into what she was today. Yet, despite the layers she had built around herself, Gabriel saw her bottom

lip tremble. She nodded, as if unable to form the words she needed to, and stepped aside.

The corridor they stepped into was so narrow they had to move in a single file. The woman led them to the parlour, which was a small room containing only a sofa, an armchair and a bookshelf. She gestured for them to sit down.

'Anything to drink? I'll have to make it myself since I don't have any maids at home, like you two probably do.'

Gabriel's eyes narrowed, but Alexander spoke before he could.

'Oh, no, thank you, Mrs Graham, that is very kind.'

Gabriel shifted uncomfortably in his seat. Alexander's body was practically shoved against his own on the small sofa. The room smelt damp.

'Have the Peelers found anything?'

'No, but we had thought we could—'

'How would you two be able to help?' she questioned, leaning forwards. Her eyes were a steady green, the colour of them having worn out over the years. 'I know you're not Peelers, or even remotely associated with them. Look at you two.'

Alexander looked down at himself, before looking back at Mrs Graham. She continued.

'I have gone to Scotland Yard every day this past week. Demanding justice. Demanding them to even acknowledge the atrocities that have taken place.' Her features had twisted into a scowl, her entire body rigid. 'And what have they done? Nothing. They wouldn't even look at me. They banished me from the premises in the end. Calling me a scorned, bitter old widow, gone mad at her husband's

unfortunate demise.' She shook her head, and then her tone softened. 'My Thomas was not an addict. He had only lost his way.'

'I am very sorry, Mrs Graham.'

She shot Alexander a dirty look. 'You two couldn't care less. Do not come into my house and lie to me.'

Gabriel raised his eyebrows. He was starting to like this woman.

Alexander blinked, surprised at the woman's sudden outburst. He opened and closed his mouth, failing to make any sound come out.

'You are right,' stated Gabriel. Alexander's eyes widened as he turned to look at Gabriel with a cautious expression. 'I cannot speak for him,' he jerked his head towards Alexander, 'but yes, I could not care less. I'm just here because he is paying me. However, that is not the point. The point is, we are working towards a common goal: solving your husband's murder. Now, if you wish to achieve that, which I think you do, tell us whatever you know.'

Alexander's face looked even more odd when he was angry, Gabriel thought. Colour had risen to his cheeks, his lips drawn thin. But to his surprise, the woman nodded, and through her eyes shone a sentiment close to respect.

Alexander's charm and politeness may have worked on most of the population, but not her. Gabriel had recognised something in the woman, a likeness, almost.

'He did not have any enemies,' she started. She looked back up at them, the fine creases around her eyes appearing even more deep set. She was most probably in

her late thirties, although she looked older. 'I assume that is the question you would ask first. Of course, he had a few drunken brawls from time to time, but nothing serious.' She paused, taking a deep breath before continuing. 'Lately, Thomas had been... struggling. He was a blacksmith, you see, and he adored his trade. He was always making things, intricate things. I told him he should have been an engineer, but we didn't have the money for that sort of training. It was his entire life. Then he injured his hand at work.' She sniffed, wiping her nose on the back of her soot-stained hand. 'He could still manage as a blacksmith, some way or another, but he couldn't craft things anymore. He had been working on a clockwork bird, and he couldn't finish it. It... it broke him. I saw the light slowly fade from his eyes as each day went by. That is when he succumbed to it. The Black Opium. My husband wasn't an addict, he was simply devasted, lost within himself, stripped of his identity.' She took a long pause. 'That is why he was out, you see. He was purchasing more of it.'

Gabriel's heart sped up in his chest, but he forced himself to sit still, keep his face expressionless.

'Purchasing it from where?' asked Alexander.

Mrs Graham shook her head. 'I'm not certain. Sometimes it was from opium dens, sometimes from various individuals.'

'Which individuals?'

'I have no idea. He never went into detail with it.'

Gabriel slowly let out a breath of relief.

'It changed him,' continued Mrs Graham, as if she couldn't stop the words of grief from flowing out of her.

'The Black Opium. He became... so different. It sucked all that was good out of him, leaving behind nothing but anger and despair.' She was now looking out the small window, onto the grey street outside. The candles upon the windowsill flickered, casting shadows upon her dry skin. Her stout features stood out more, like harsh lines upon a painting. 'He did not even want it. Someone offered it to him. In a pub. A bloody pub. After that, he couldn't help the addiction. It wasn't his fault.'

Alexander remained silent, his brows drawn together in sympathy.

'What type of man was your husband, Mrs Graham?' asked Gabriel.

Alexander looked at him with a sense of surprise in his eyes. He knew that Gabriel was aware it was not relevant to the investigation, and that he did not exactly care about the man enough to ask. He had done it for the woman.

Mrs Graham's lips curved up ever so slightly, as she continued staring out the window. But now, she wasn't looking outside, she was looking at the pictures within her mind. 'He was a loving man. Kind. Patient. We met when I was only seventeen. I was working in the Clerkenwell Workhouse.' She furrowed her brows. 'A horrible place. Just horrible. I worked there for years, under the administration of the most horrendous guardians that have ever walked this earth. One day, I was tasked with scrubbing the walls of the building. I wasn't going fast enough, and one of the overseers kicked me. He kicked me so hard it left me breathless. But instead of cowering, I got right back up and knocked a bucket against his head. It made the most

wonderful sound when it bashed against his skull. He was livid, of course. He drew a knife and charged at me. I knew he wanted to kill me, but I had nowhere else to run, until Thomas. A tall, broad man, with a disfigured nose which had been broken and did not quite heal right, appeared and punched the overseer unconscious.' Something danced in her eyes as she spoke. 'We ran away, scared the overseer would wake up, and spent the whole day together. He told me about his love for creating things, and I told him about my hatred of the world. I do not know what he saw in me, apart from the fiery anger that I could never contain and the bitterness that poured out of me like blood. He asked me to marry him by the end of it.' She wiped away a singular tear that had dropped upon her cheek. 'He gave me a better life. He gave me all I could have ever asked for and more.'

Gabriel pulled at his collar. The room had become too hot, and his vision blurred at the edges. A ringing sounded in his ears, getting louder and louder.

'Thank you, Mrs Graham. I believe that was all,' said Alexander. Gabriel could barely hear him.

'Florence. My name is Florence. Do not call me by his name, because he is no longer here.'

Alexander smiled sadly, nodding at Florence before rising from the sofa. Gabriel remained glued to his seat, oblivious to what was happening around him. He felt a pressure on his shoulder, and flinched before he, too, followed suit.

Alexander let out a long breath as they stepped out onto the street.

'God,' he muttered. 'That was rather inten—'

'Don't ever touch me again,' hissed Gabriel at Alexander, who stepped back in shock at the outburst. 'We are done for the day.'

CHAPTER XI

The Lamb and Flag

The stale aroma of beer wafted through the air as Gabriel pulled open the door of the pub. The Lamb and Flag was located in the rougher part of Covent Garden, established over a century ago. Gabriel enjoyed its raucousness, which enveloped him the second he stepped foot upon the creaky floorboards. The inside was packed, despite it only being five in the evening. He needed a distraction after the events of the morning, and the Lamb and Flag was the perfect place for it.

He took a seat at the bar, leaning his forearms upon the counter as he gestured at the barman. He was sat between two individuals. One of them was a large, sweaty man, who barely fit upon the stool, and the other a slim, well-dressed man who clutched his briefcase as if at any moment it would grow legs and run away. Gabriel assumed he was a lawyer or politician. Many different types of people visited

the Lamb and Flag, from writers like Charles Dickens and Samuel Butler to riotous brawlers coming for a beer.

'A pint as usual, Ashmore?' asked the barman, Robert. Robert was a stern man, large in size and limited in conversation. Gabriel had grown to like his silent demeanour, talking only when it was necessary. Gabriel had been coming to the Lamb and Flag ever since he was young, and so Robert always kept an eye out for him, even if he pretended like he didn't.

'Yes, Robert, thank you,' answered Gabriel. A thud sounded upstairs, followed by dust sprinkling down upon them. Shortly after, the sound of cheering reverberated through the ceiling. The large man beside him lifted his pint, letting out another cheer. The rest of the people followed suit. The Lamb and Flag hosted knuckle fights upstairs, earning itself the nickname Bucket of Blood.

Gabriel took a large gulp of his beer, and then kept on drinking and drinking until he had nearly finished all of it.

'What a coincidence.'

Gabriel closed his eyes as he heard the voice, pressing his lips into a thin line. He let out a deep sigh before he opened them again and turned himself to look at his brother. The politician had left, leaving Hugo to take his seat. Hugo took off his gloves, greeting Robert and then ordering a pint.

Gabriel and Hugo used to come to the Lamb and Flag together, sneaking out the house to watch the knuckle fights. They had their first drink here. Gabriel remembered how Hugo had drunk so much he vomited all over the street and had to be carried back home. They had frequented it ever since.

Robert set Hugo's pint down on the counter. His eyes passed over both Gabriel and Hugo, and Gabriel could tell he noted their changed dynamic, their cold demeanours. He was observant, and cleverer than he let on. Yet, as usual, he did not comment on it, just like he did not comment on anything, and simply moved to the next customers, keeping whatever he witnessed as a secret he never shared.

'Do you not have anything to say to me, brother?'

Gabriel's grip tightened on his glass. Hugo always had a way of drawing out anger, playing with his temper. He avoided looking at Hugo's eyes, focusing instead on the bottles lining the bar.

'Giving me the silent treatment now, are you?'

Gabriel's nostrils flared as he inhaled sharply. 'What do you want from me, Hugo?'

'Civil conversation would be a good start. But it appears you are not so good at that.'

'I wonder whose fault that is.'

Hugo sighed and turned towards Gabriel. 'I have no intention to relive yesterday's occurrences.' Another thud sounded from upstairs, this one louder than the last, followed by the shouts of the audience. Hugo looked up at the ceiling. 'Shall we watch the fight? It has been a long time since we last saw one.'

'No,' answered Gabriel.

Hugo's upper lip twitched. He took a sip of his beer to hide it. 'It shall only take half an hour.'

'I said no.'

'Gabriel, please.'

Gabriel was taken aback by his brother's tone. Hugo never pled, especially not to his own brother. Gabriel finished his beer, right as Robert brought over a new one. He grabbed the pint and, to his own surprise, headed towards the stairs.

The second he swung open the door, all of Gabriel's senses came alive. Excitement buzzed in the air, so potent he could almost taste it. Shouts and screams and chatter filled his ears. The humidity, caused by countless bodies packed in a small room, clung to his skin. The air smelt of blood and sweat and Eau de Cologne. Gabriel savoured the attack on his senses, allowing himself to become lost in the noise. Faces flashed before him, men whose features were twisted together in either pure joy or pure misery and anger. Some gulped down beers, some treating themselves to something stronger.

'It hasn't changed one bit,' stated Hugo from behind him, half-shouting to make himself heard over the ruckus.

They pushed through the crowd towards the centre of the room, until the ring came into view. It was nothing when you compared it to the way prize fighters like James Burke used to fight, but on its own, it was certainly something. One of the fighters, a fat, balding man, circled around the other. His opponent was on the slimmer side, but his look conveyed all that they needed to know. The big one started stepping closer.

'Come on, Danny!' someone from the audience shouted. More shouts and cheers followed.

'Beat him, William!'

William, the slimmer one, took a step towards Danny. Danny, grinning through the blood and grime that had gathered in his mouth, pulled his arm back, ready to deliver a harsh, powerful blow. But then, just as Danny's fist almost collided with William's face, William ducked, and simultaneously delivered him a blow from below.

Hugo grinned beside Gabriel. 'Dutch Sam's undercut.'

'And Tom Spring's Harlequin Step,' added Gabriel.

Being at the Lamb and Flag with his brother made Gabriel feel a sense of normality again. For a second, it seemed like only yesterday they had gulped down six beers each and shouted and hollered along with the crowd. How when they returned home, their mother always lectured them about visiting such places.

'I have come back for a work opportunity.'

Hugo's voice pulled Gabriel out of his own mind, and immediately he felt the warmth of the memories fade, and again they felt like they had occurred a million years ago.

'Pardon?'

'A work opportunity,' said Hugo, louder this time. Danny and William continued throwing punches. Gabriel could sense Danny was getting weaker. 'I contacted the leading merchants of London, and they allowed me to purchase part of their ships and sell some of their merchandise.'

'I had thought the London merchants wanted nothing more to do with the Ashmore name after Father's failure.'

'That was true, but I managed to convince them. You see, in Liverpool, I had an excellent track record for making sales. I imported tea from India and China and sold every

single batch to the dealers. I suppose I seemed to have a way of making people purchase things. Soon enough, fellow merchants paid me to sell and distribute whatever they couldn't themselves, such as leftover linen, cotton, wine. Alongside trading across the Atlantic, I made quite a bit of money selling items on the side. Some wealthy merchants even employed me to sell their entire merchandise for them, giving me a rather generous cut. I believe they wish for me to do the same for them here in London.'

Each word Hugo spoke was like a slap in Gabriel's face. Whilst his brother had left them, found himself a reputable profession and made a life for himself, Gabriel had been forced to deal with everything he left behind. He had been turned away from the London merchants, sacrificed his hopes and dreams, forced to make a living from immorality and delinquency.

The room erupted into a chorus of cheers as William delivered a final blow to Danny, whose eyes rolled back before he hit the floor. The sound engulfed Gabriel, until all he heard were mere vibrations and blood pumping in his ear. Hugo spoke to him, but his voice was drowned out, barely audible. He turned on his heel, so fast it knocked the pint out of Hugo's hand and marched towards the exit.

Gabriel made his way through the falling snow. He dipped in and out of the glow of the streetlights, unaware of his destination, with only the knowledge that he had to keep walking. After several seconds, he heard a voice behind him. He shut it out as he increased his pace. It sounded again, and again, until he felt a pull on his arm.

Gabriel span around, snatching his arm away as fast as he could. His eyes were wide with anger, his arm still burning at the touch.

'I apologise,' said Hugo, holding his hands up as he stepped back. 'I only wished to stop you; I apologise.'

'What is it?' Gabriel hissed from between clenched teeth.

'You rushed off, Gabriel, I only wished to see if—'

'Oh, save it, Hugo.'

'I only—'

'Do you wish to tell me more stories about your success? About how well you are doing? Well, unfortunately, I do not wish to hear any of it.'

Hugo's brows furrowed. 'I told you that I came back for you. For Father.'

Gabriel scoffed. 'It seems to me you just came back to fill your pockets with more money.' He turned around, continuing his way down the street, before Hugo's voice sounded behind him.

'Is it so wrong that I am making a life for myself?' His tone had turned vicious, cutting through the cold winter air like a glowing knife. Gabriel halted. 'Perhaps you are the problem, Gabriel. Perhaps you are too preoccupied wallowing in your own misery to realise that the world moves on.'

Gabriel chuckled coldly, turning to face his brother. 'Have you *moved on* then, brother? Have you, truly? I see the way you looked at that whisky on the rack, or the way you looked at that brothel we passed. You can fool yourself all you want, speak whatever lies you wish, but you cannot hide what so blatantly reveals itself in your eyes.'

Hugo's features had twisted into pure disdain, and yet Gabriel kept going.

'I wonder how good that whisky would taste right this second. How it would make everything fade until all you'd feel would be a blissful nothing.' Hugo's lips twitched, nostrils flaring. 'I believe you should go back and try it, for old time's sake, and leave me alone.'

CHAPTER XII

Scotland Yard

Gabriel reached Scotland Yard, or as they now called it, New Scotland Yard, at exactly ten in the morning. Alexander, who seemed to be early for everything, was leaning against a tree, smoking a pipe. His head was tipped back, his round glasses perching down the bridge of his nose. The Big Ben rose behind him, peeking out through the mist.

'Ah, there you are.'

Gabriel frowned. 'Why do you speak as if I am late?'

Alexander cupped his hand over his pipe, extinguishing it. 'If you are right on time, then you, my friend, are already late.'

Gabriel rolled his eyes. 'What an idiotic philosophy,' he muttered as he walked off to the police headquarters. It was newly constructed just that year, positioned right on Victoria Embankment. It was a grand building composed

of brown brick and grey stone. He felt his skin heat up and sweat gather on his palms as he neared it. He forced himself to calm down. Nobody knew of his involvement, certainly not the police. He had nothing to worry about, all they had to do was ask about the knife. If they succeeded with it, he could prove he had nothing to do with the murders, that it was someone else entirely.

Alexander caught up to him, placing his pipe in the pocket of his long coat. 'Did you know that during the construction of New Scotland Yard, they found the torso of a woman within a safe, stored in the cellar of the building?'

Gabriel turned to look at Alexander with a rather uncomfortable expression. 'What?'

'Horrid, right? They never even found the perpetrator.'

'Are you speaking of the Whitehall Mystery two years ago?'

'Yes, I am. I find it rather unacceptable that the killer just managed to get away with it. If that does not show the incompetency of the current police force, I do not know what does.' Alexander scoffed. 'It happened right under their noses, upon the very site of their headquarters.'

'Was it not linked with Jack the Ripper?'

Alexander shook his head. 'The *modus operandi* was totally different. Jack the Ripper's victims suffered progressive abdominal and genital area mutilation, whereas the Torso Murderer merely dismembered his victims.'

'I find it rather disturbing you know such details.'

'It would be rather surprising if I did not. It has been all over the news.'

Alexander pushed the door open, and so they entered Scotland Yard.

They stepped into a large reception area. The lights that lit up the room flickered dimly. There was a lack of natural light due to the small windows, and the gloominess of winter certainly did not help. Alexander took off his hat, as Gabriel's analysed their surroundings. There were a few police officers stood chatting in the corner of the room.

Alexander approached the secretary, who was sitting behind a long oak desk.

'I am looking for officer Bertram Carter.'

The secretary looked up with a stern expression upon his face. He had a thin frame and appeared relatively harmless, aside from his obvious annoyance at being bothered.

'Are you a police officer?' he asked with a monotonous voice, looking Alexander up and down.

'No,' answered Alexander. 'I am acquainted with Mr Carter; I just need to ask him a question.'

'I am afraid I cannot help you,' said the secretary dismissively, before going back to filing the papers upon his desk.

Alexander placed his hand upon the desk, and then, discreetly, slid it towards the secretary. Gabriel noticed he was holding an envelope. He was bribing the secretary.

'I believe that ought to change your mind.'

The secretary pursed his lips as he slowly placed his bony fingers upon the envelope and opened it. His eyebrows rose slightly, before he placed the envelope into the drawer of the desk.

'It appears as though I can help you after all,' he said. 'Your name?'

'Alexander Wakefield.'

The secretary rose from his chair and disappeared round the corner. Alexander turned to Gabriel and shot him a wink. Gabriel rolled his eyes and turned away.

After several seconds, an officer marched into the reception. His brows were furrowed together, his features conveying a strong irritation. He pulled Alexander to the side.

'I told you not to contact me again, Wakefield,' he hissed. Chester appeared to be in his early thirties. He was slightly shorter than Alexander, but with a strong and broad-shouldered build. He had short, dark hair.

'I just need to see the knife. The one that killed the last victim, Nicholas Ward.'

'Absolutely not. You need to leave—'

'Chester, we only need five minutes. That is all, and then I shall never bother you again.'

'I said *no*.'

'How much do you want? Double what I gave you last time? Triple?'

'Watch your mouth,' Chester hissed, pulling Alexander further away from the others as his eyes darted around the room. 'I cannot help you, Wakefield. I cannot risk anyone finding out about it.'

Alexander sighed defeatedly. But before he could say anything, Gabriel stepped in.

'You will take us to the knife right now.'

Chester scoffed. 'And who are—'

'If you do not, we shall tell everyone here that you accepted bribes from an upper-class citizen, leaking whatever classified information he wished to know, purely because of your own greed. Let's see how well that shall go down with your Peeler mates, eh?'

Chester's lips curled. 'How dare you threaten a police officer? I ought to have you locked up just for that alone.'

Gabriel smiled. 'Locked up for what? Last I checked, speaking the truth was not illegal. But bribery, on the other hand, is.'

Chester's eyes angrily darted from Gabriel to Alexander and then back again. His fists were clenched by his sides. 'I am not foolish enough to fall for such a blatantly false threat.'

Gabriel shrugged, stepping closer to the man. 'Believe what you like. I only wonder what Commissioner Sir Edward Bradford shall think, once we tell him what a lying bastard you have been. I doubt that he, with such an esteemed military background, with such deep-rooted values of honour and loyalty, shall be very pleased to hear that one of the lead investigators in the Criminal Investigations Department is not only disobeying his orders, but also breaking the law at the same time.'

Red blotches formed on Chester's face. His mouth opened and closed as if he were short on breath, his eyes bearing a deep resentment as he stared into Gabriel's own. Gabriel did not flinch, did not move a muscle as he stared back at Chester. He eventually pressed his lips together, exhaling loudly. 'You're a real bastard.'

'I know,' said Gabriel. 'Now, take us to the evidence room.'

They entered the Criminal Investigations Department, which was located on the same floor as the reception. Chester reluctantly led them down several hallways, down a flight of stairs, until they stood before a wooden door in the basement.

'I do hope you have not brought us down here to murder us, Chester,' muttered Alexander as he peered down the narrow hallway they were stood in.

'If only I could,' said Chester. The gaslight cast shadows upon his features, making his wide jaw appear even larger. Chester took out a collection of keys and unlocked the door. It creaked as it swung open, revealing a small, dark room. Chester stepped in and struck a match, lighting a lantern. It cast a faint orange glow, enough for Gabriel to realise the room was filled with various shelves and wooden boxes.

Alexander looked around with a quizzical expression upon his face. 'Is this dingy chamber where they store all evidence?'

'No,' said Chester as he led the way to the end of the room, setting down the lantern on the shelf. 'It is where they keep evidence that they wish to dispose of.'

'What?' exclaimed Alexander. 'Why would the police destroy evidence of a criminal case?'

'Watch your voice,' hissed Chester with a glare. 'That is all I have been told. Do not ask me anything else.' He took out a wooden box, placing it on a nearby table. He then pulled out the knife, kept in a straw pouch. 'Here it is. You have five minutes; not a second longer. I will be waiting outside.'

Alexander waited until Chester closed the door to turn to Gabriel.

'You are truly mad, are you aware of that?'

Gabriel looked at Alexander with an unbothered expression. 'It got us what we wanted, did it not?'

'Yes, but it also could have got us in deep trouble,' snapped Alexander. 'Let us hope Chester won't go and report us for breaking into the premises right this second.'

'Quit your unnecessary worrying and inspect the bloody knife. We do not have long.'

Alexander shook his head. 'I cannot believe they would just destroy evidence. What are they trying to achieve?'

'Are you truly that surprised?' asked Gabriel. 'Nobody can blame them for not being able to solve a case if it does not have any evidence.'

Alexander sighed before he picked up the knife. 'And if there is no evidence, the opposition cannot solve it either.' Most of the blood had been washed off it, save for a few flaking bits near the hilt. Alexander turned it over in his hands, and then frowned.

'What?' asked Gabriel, taking a step closer.

'This is a sheepsfoot blade.' Alexander held the knife closer to the flickering light. 'It has a straight back and curves towards the end. These blades were made to cut things. Well, originally, they were made to trim the hooves of sheep. But now, they are most frequently used to cut vegetables. It is rather strange our killer has not utilised a spear or needle-point blade, which would be much easier to stab someone with.'

'Perhaps it was a quick act, and he has simply grabbed whatever he could find at home?'

'Yes, that could explain it, I suppose. I do find it odd for our killer to be unprepared in such a way. He has clearly planned all these murders. He had the intention of committing them from the start, so why would he utilise such a knife?'

'Pleasure.'

'Excuse me?'

Gabriel looked at Alexander. 'Our killer wanted it to be difficult. He wanted to feel the knife rip apart the victim's skin. He did not want an easy stab, he wanted it to be cruel, bloody. Painful.'

Alexander turned back to the knife, inspecting its handle. It was plain, made of wood that had worn down. He sighed. 'I cannot see anything of note upon it.'

'Look for an engraving.'

Alexander turned to look at Gabriel. 'Great suggestion, I had totally not thought of that, Mr Holmes!'

Gabriel shot Alexander a look of annoyance, before taking the knife from him. He turned it upside down, so the butt was facing them. He moved the lantern closer. Two letters came into view. *W&S.*

Gabriel raised an eyebrow at Alexander. 'Pardon me, what was it that you were saying?'

Alexander shrugged dismissively. 'The lantern was too far away; I simply could not see.'

Gabriel scoffed. 'Of course.'

'Now, the real question we ought to be asking, is what does W&S stand for?' He scratched his chin. 'It does sound awfully familiar, yet I cannot figure out what it is. Perhaps they are initials, or—'

'It is a shop. A shop for household items, located in Oxford Street.'

Alexander raised an eyebrow. 'Yes, that makes sense. Although, how did you know that?'

Before Gabriel could answer, a loud banging sounded on the door.

'Chester,' said Alexander. 'Let us get out of here before he changes his mind about not murdering us.'

CHAPTER XIII

————— • ▪ • —————

The Knife on Oxford Street

Gabriel and Alexander pushed through the large crowds of Oxford Street. They walked past maids, workers and shop owners as they headed towards Williams & Sons.

A carriage speedily charged past them, resulting in the wheels splattering mud onto the walkway. Gabriel dodged it, and a second later heard someone curse behind him. He turned around and saw Alexander's trousers covered in dirt. His upper lip was drawn up in disgust as he looked down at the damage.

Gabriel chuckled. 'Have you ever been out of that big house of yours before?'

Alexander scoffed, stamping his foot on the ground in the hopes of getting rid of some of the dirt. 'Of course I have. I merely do not go out to buy my necessities myself. That is what maids are for.'

'I see. You do realise that being able to endure mud is, I would say, an important quality in a detective?'

'Oh, of course I can endure mud,' snapped Alexander. 'But *this* is not mud.'

'Ah,' said Gabriel in realisation.

They entered Williams & Sons. It was a simple shop selling basic household items such as pots and pans, gardening equipment and, most importantly, knives. They headed towards the till and rang the bell.

Alexander leaned against a shelf, crossing his arms over his chest. They had entered the first shop they could find in order to purchase new trousers, as the smell of the others had become unbearable and Alexander refused to wear them a second longer. Unfortunately, that shop had been rather eccentric, and the only trousers they had left in stock were coloured a bright yellow.

The shop owner appeared from the back and approached the till.

'How may I help you lads?' His gaze lingered on Alexander's trousers as he looked at them. He cleared his throat, before he quickly looked the other way. Alexander pressed his lips into a thin line.

'We wish to see your kitchen knives.'

'All right,' said the man. He leaned over the till, gesturing to a brown-skinned worker who was placing plates in a cupboard in the corner of the room. 'Sanjay, bring me the knife collection, will you?'

The man nodded, before opening up another cupboard and taking out a long wooden box. He placed it upon a

table before them and opened it to reveal its contents. He then went back to work.

'There,' said Alexander, pointing at a sheepsfoot knife.

Gabriel picked it up, inspecting the handle. 'I believe we have a match.' He turned to the worker behind the till. 'Do you have a record of all those who bought this exact knife?'

The worker frowned, wiping his hands on his apron. He scratched his jaw. 'Well, we don't keep a track of names.'

'Well, do you recall anything unusual? Regarding the people who purchased such knives?' asked Alexander.

The man chuckled. 'My memory ain't that good, boys.'

'Look, this is important, old man,' snapped Gabriel. He lowered his voice. 'We are investigating the death of a fellow citizen, Nicholas Ward. This knife could be the key to finding his murderer, so I suggest you try a bit harder.'

'Nicholas Ward?'

Gabriel and Alexander turned around, and found the dark-haired worker standing behind them, holding a polishing cloth and a pan.

'Yes,' said Gabriel. 'Did you know him?'

'Yes,' answered the man with a sigh. He tightened his grip on the pan. 'We were friends.'

'We are sorry for your loss,' said Alexander. 'What is your name?'

'Sanjay Mahajan,' said the man.

'Would you, by any chance, be able to recall those that purchased this knife? Any records you may have kept, or anyone that came in here and struck you as odd?' asked Gabriel.

'Oh, yes. Nicholas.'

Gabriel frowned. 'Pardon?'

'Nicholas purchased this knife. He came here a lot to buy household items. Mrs Ward is very ill; therefore he always came in her place.'

'And do you remember anyone else that has purchased this exact knife?'

'Nobody else has purchased this knife in the last two years.'

'What do you mean?' questioned Alexander.

'This collection hasn't been for sale for two years now. It is too old, you see. I sold it to Nicholas at a discounted price.' The old shop owner shot Sanjay a glare. 'Just doing a friend a harmless favour, Mr Clark.'

'So, nobody except for Mr Ward has purchased this knife in the last two years?'

'That is correct,' answered Sanjay. He hesitated before speaking again. 'What exactly happened to Nicholas? The police are not telling us anything.'

'He… well, he—' started Alexander, uncertain of how to phrase it.

'He was murdered,' said Gabriel. 'I do not know what the police have told you in regard to his death, but he was murdered.'

Sanjay's jaw clenched. 'I knew it. They all blamed that opium, but I knew there was something else.'

Mr Clark loudly cleared his throat from behind the till. Sanjay ignored him.

'Are you two with *them*?' Sanjay continued. 'The police?'

'God, no,' said Gabriel.

'We are trying to bring justice to these victims,' said Alexander.

'Well, do you have any suspects?' asked Sanjay keenly.

Alexander shook his head. 'No, we are only in the early stages of our investigation.'

'What will happen once you find the murderer?'

'Well, we hope to have him arrested.'

'Will the police believe—'

'Look, mate, we cannot give you any more information,' interjected Gabriel.

Sanjay apologised, taking a step back.

Alexander furrowed his brows at Gabriel. He then turned to Sanjay. 'We thank you greatly for this information. Rest assured that we shall do everything in our power to find who murdered Mr Ward.'

Alexander shook Sanjay's hand before they headed for the exit. Just as they had stepped foot outside, Alexander suddenly stopped in his tracks. He rushed back inside the shop.

'Would you know anything about the Erebus?' he asked Sanjay. 'The Black Opium. Mr Ward showed signs of its consumption.'

Gabriel clenched his fists as he remained standing in the doorway.

'Are you going to pay me for his wasted hours?' snapped Mr Clark from behind the till. Alexander scoffed at the shop owner, before digging out a pound from his pocket and tossing it to him. Mr Clark's eyes widened as he watched the coin land on the till. He snatched it away and put it into his pocket.

'Do you?' asked Alexander. 'Did Mr Ward speak about it to you?'

A dark look passed over Sanjay's face. 'He did not speak of it much, but I knew he used it. I told him to stop, but he did not listen to me.' He crossed his arms over his chest.

'Did he name any individuals in connection with the Erebus? Any enemies? People he had disagreements with?'

'No, he had no enemies. Nicholas was a good man.' Sanjay then frowned, staring at the floor as if he were recalling a memory. 'He mentioned a man. A man he obtained the Black Opium from. A supplier, of sorts.'

Gabriel's heart pounded in his chest.

'What man?' asked Alexander. 'Do you know his name?'

Sanjay shook his head. 'No. I do not think Nicholas spent much time in his presence. He only said he was quiet and unfriendly. That is all.'

'All right. Thank you for the information, Mr Mahajan. We are most grateful.' Alexander smiled at the man, before he headed back towards the exit.

'The Prospect of Whitby,' Sanjay called out from behind him.

Gabriel's entire body froze.

Alexander turned to face him. 'Pardon?'

'It is a pub that Nicholas always frequented. In the east. Perhaps you may find more information regarding the Black Opium there.'

Alexander nodded.

'Nicholas was not a bad man,' said Sanjay. 'The Black Opium,' he shook his head, his eyebrows pulled together

in sympathy, 'it was due to grief. The doctors only gave his wife, Mrs Ward, a few months to live, and he could not cope with the imminent loss. He did not deserve what happened to him.'

Gabriel swallowed away the lump in his throat. The victims, Gabriel's customers, weren't just mindless addicts. They had been suffering and were just trying to find a way to ease their pain. And the Erebus had profited off it, off their sorrow and grief. It had destroyed these men and had eventually led them to their demise.

As they stepped out onto the street, and the smell of coal and excrement and sewage hit them, Gabriel felt nauseous. Alexander spoke to him, but Gabriel could not hear anything, because all he was thinking about was what Sanjay had said before they left.

Four words. Four words that could destroy his life forever.

The Prospect of Whitby.

CHAPTER XIV

The Prospect of Whitby

Many believed the Prospect of Whitby to be haunted.

It was one of London's oldest pubs, established in 1520, during the reign of Henry VIII. Back then, it was called the Pelican. It was built right beside the river, making it a den of pirates and thieves. These criminals would gather in the pub after stealing items from the nearby ships, which led to it becoming known as the Devil's Tavern. Ironically, it was also close to the execution dock, which served to hang those condemned to death by the Admiralty Courts. There was still a scaffold and a hanging noose outside the tavern.

Fog shrouded the air when Gabriel and Alexander arrived, just like it always did around the Prospect of Whitby.

Gabriel had tried to dissuade Alexander from coming,

but he had been adamant. Gabriel had even thought of not coming himself, but then he would not be able to hear what Alexander would find out.

Obscured shapes moved in and out of the fog. Some claimed to have seen the ghost of the Scottish sea captain, Captain William Kidd, walking the streets around the pub. He had been a pirate hunter, and had then turned into a pirate himself, realising it to be much more profitable. He was hanged at the execution dock by the Prospect of Whitby in 1697, then his body was dipped in tar and hung by chains on the bank of the Thames.

Loud evening chatter drifted from the pub, but it turned into mere whispers by the time it reached them. Gabriel heard the faint sound of waves splashing against the embankment. There was an odd smell in the air, a mix of smoke and copper and rotting flesh. It would not surprise Gabriel if there were dead bodies in the water below them. After all, the Prospect of Whitby was notorious for being a centre of crime.

'I suppose this should not take very long,' muttered Alexander, shifting on his feet.

'No. It should not,' answered Gabriel distantly.

The second they stepped into the pub, Gabriel recognised the distinct smell of wet stone, the sound of jingling coins and raucous visitors, because the Prospect of Whitby was not new to him. He had been here before. And he had supplied them with the Erebus.

The Prospect of Whitby had been one of the main pubs that the Erebus was supplied to. The individuals

that frequented it could not get enough of it, and so it had become a place Gabriel visited almost every week.

The inside of the pub was dark, only lowly lit by hanging lanterns. Shadows pooled in every corner, so thick that those sitting in it were nearly invisible. It provided a perfect cover for those engaging in questionable acts, giving them enough privacy to conduct whatever they needed to. The counter of the bar was held up by a row of barrels. There was a row of paned windows at the end of the room. Hanging Judge George Jeffries had a special window built, overlooking the execution dock, so he could sit and watch those who he had condemned to die. Some claimed to still see Jeffries' face gazing out the window.

Alexander moved to the bar and proceeded to order a drink. Some patrons shot him odd glances, most probably wondering what on earth someone like him was doing in the Prospect of Whitby.

Gabriel faced away from the bar. He looked different than he did when he delivered the Erebus. He was now dressed in fine clothes, his hair brushed neatly, but they could still recognise him. The barmen had seen him many times, and it did not help that Gabriel had caused multiple fights during his visits. He let his gaze wander over the room, which was filled to the brim with mostly rough-looking men and a few women with eccentric-coloured dresses.

'Would you like a drink?' asked Alexander.

Gabriel quickly shook his head, avoiding eye contact. 'No.'

'Are you certain? I reckon—'

'I do not want a bloody drink.'

Alexander sighed, shooting Gabriel a quizzical glance, before he gestured to the barman. Gabriel's blood pounded in his ears as he tried to listen to whatever Alexander was asking. He mentioned the victim's name, Nicholas Ward, and then asked if he knew of him. Gabriel turned his head ever so slightly, his gaze landing upon the barman.

He let out a breath of relief.

Gabriel had never seen him before. He must have been new. He allowed himself to slightly relax, his eyes skimming over the room to make sure there wasn't anyone else that might recognise him.

The barman, a lanky young man who did not appear older than eighteen, shook his head. 'I've only just started 'ere. No clue.' He went back to pouring pints for waiting patrons.

'Well, can you tell me anything about the Erebus?' Alexander called out. His gaze fell upon the bar counter, upon which traces of the black powder had accumulated. 'Is it sold here?'

'Do you want some?'

'No, I wish to know more about it.'

The young man shrugged. 'There ain't much to know. We just sell it.'

'This is pointless; let us depart now,' said Gabriel with a low voice.

The patrons sitting by the bar shot Alexander a dirty look for holding up the barman, who had now gone back to serving drinks. Alexander let out a frustrated sigh.

'We could ask the people in here if Mr Ward frequented this place as much as Mr Mahajan said he did? Someone must have seen him.'

'Have you seen the type of people in here? Do you truly believe they shall help you?'

His gaze fell on the patrons, who were already eyeing him up like he was fresh bait. Alexander's jaw clenched in irritation at his failed lead. 'Fine,' muttered Alexander. He straightened his jacket and put on his hat.

They both turned away from the bar, and then Gabriel stopped dead in his tracks. His entire body froze.

'Ashmore?' asked the man who stood before him. And before Gabriel could stop him, he said: 'Is there a delivery scheduled today?'

Alexander's brows furrowed together in confusion as he turned to look at Gabriel.

'I do not know what you are speaking of,' said Gabriel quickly to the barman, trying his hardest to keep his features neutral, but his eyes gave him away.

Alexander's expression of confusion soon turned into that of questioning anger. 'What deliveries?'

'The Ere—'

'Shut your mouth,' hissed Gabriel, shoving the man into the wall. They crashed into a nearby table, the glasses upon it shattering on the floor. Shouts and cheers erupted in the pub. Some men had risen from their seats to take a closer look at the commotion. 'Shut your damn mouth.'

'The Erebus? What is going on?'

Gabriel could not bear to look at Alexander as he shoved the barman away. The exit was crowded with new people coming in, so Gabriel marched out through the back of the pub. He went down the stone stairs outside, landing on the bank of the Thames. He marched upon

the wet stones covered in moss. The tide was low, so the Thames had retreated. His breath misted in the air as he looked for an exit back to the street, his blood pounded in his ears. He had to get away.

Then, he heard footsteps and panting behind him.

'Stay right there!'

He turned to face Alexander, whose face had become red due to the exertion of running after him. He was breathing heavily, his tie skewed and his hair windswept.

'You are going to explain everything to me right this second.'

Gabriel looked out on the river. Moonlight bathed in the dark surface of the water. 'Just report me and be done with it,' he said. His eyes burned and his face felt too hot.

'No, first of all you need to tell me what you know.'

'There is no point.'

'Goddammit, Ashmore,' exclaimed Alexander unexpectedly. 'Tell me what you bloody know!'

'I deliver it,' hissed Gabriel. 'The Erebus. The Black Opium. I deliver it. Are you content now?'

'Is that why you were at the scene of the murder?'

'Yes. I delivered it to each of the victims before they died.'

'And did you kill them?'

Gabriel scoffed. 'Of course not.'

'I knew you had an involvement of sorts,' stated Alexander, folding his hands behind his back.

Gabriel looked up in surprise. 'What?'

'Oh, it was fairly obvious. You are not as good at hiding your panic as you think. I just had not known what sort of involvement.' He sighed. 'Why did you do it?'

Gabriel clenched his jaw. 'Out of necessity.' Gabriel knew he should have told him more. Told him how he had no choice, how he had to do something to provide for his family, how he lost so much, but he couldn't. The words got stuck in his throat like a jagged piece of glass.

'I see.'

'Are you not going to have me arrested?'

Alexander chuckled. 'What for?'

The execution noose swung between them, moving with the wind.

'I might as well have killed them.'

'But you did not.'

'Why do you trust my word?'

'I am not trusting your word. I am trusting your actions.' Alexander reached down and picked up a stone. 'You wish to solve these murders. I sensed a great deal of guilt in you, but not the guilt of a killer. Even if you cannot realise it yourself, you wish for justice to be served.' He threw the stone into the river. 'Now, you said you delivered the Erebus to each of the victims, before their time of death, correct?'

Gabriel nodded.

'And these victims were all regular Erebus users?'

'Yes.'

'And all of a sudden, they are found murdered, consecutively, all in different manners, with no connection between them other than the fact that they all utilised this drug. That means the Erebus is the only lead we have. Our killer must have something to do with it, perhaps he is linked to it in some form, or perhaps he simply has a deep

aversion to it.' Alexander crossed his arms over his chest. 'Tell me more about your deliveries. I believe learning more about it could reveal some sort of motive.'

Gabriel cleared his throat. Now that he had calmed down, he felt how cold the night air was against his skin, filling his lungs with ice. 'I have been doing them for almost two years now. I collect the product from the East End, in Whitechapel, from some sort of distribution point, along with a weekly list of recipients.' The mention of his deeds felt like poison in his mouth. 'I have not delivered anything in the past few days.'

A gust of wind swept through the air, making Alexander shiver. Something cold landed upon Gabriel's nose, and then his cheek. He looked up and saw that it had begun snowing.

'Perhaps we should continue this conversation tomorrow,' stated Alexander. 'It is rather late and cold.' He looked up at the noose hanging above them, and then back at the pub, where a few men had gathered around the windows, watching them. 'And I do not wish to be hanged.' He rubbed his hands together. 'Let us meet in the Natural History Museum, by the great mastodon in the south-east gallery. Ten o'clock sharp.'

CHAPTER XV

The Great Mastodon

As usual, Alexander already stood waiting as Gabriel approached him. He had spent quite a while locating the giant mammoth in the museum.

'You are late,' stated Alexander.

Gabriel scoffed. 'I am terribly sorry that I did not memorise where the great bloody mastodon was located.'

Alexander looked up at the skeleton of the mammoth, which towered over the both of them. Its long tusks curved upwards menacingly, and his feet were as thick as tree trunks. 'How foolish of you.'

'Why meet here?'

'To ensure my safety. You cannot kill me in public.' Alexander's lips curved into a slight grin. Gabriel shot him a glare. 'I am only kidding, of course. I enjoy it here. I used to visit it with my father as a boy, and this was my favourite animal.'

'So you thought it to be an appropriate place to discuss a murder investigation?'

'Precisely.'

A family walked past them, looking up at the mammoth in awe. Apart from them, they had the entire room to themselves; the museum was not as busy in the earlier hours. They moved on to the next sight, which was a sort of reptile kept in a vitrine.

'Now, I believe we ought to start with investigating the distribution point that you mentioned, in Whitechapel.'

Gabriel cracked his knuckles behind his back. 'Fine.'

'And who is the leader? The one giving you these orders?'

Gabriel hesitated. The person that got him involved was a man called Rufus. He wasn't a good man, but he had shown Gabriel kindness when no one else had. Gabriel had been unable to find any work, turned away from every shop he entered. And then he had seen Rufus, standing outside of the blacksmith Gabriel had just walked out of. He wore a frayed black coat which reached down to his feet, a peculiar hat, and he always had a cigar in his mouth. His teeth had been stained black from tobacco and he had a guttural voice. He started speaking to Gabriel, and then offered him the job. He was willing to pay him three times the amount he would make working normally, and Gabriel was too desperate to question it.

'Rufus,' he said finally. 'I do not know much about him.'

Despite Rufus being an immoral man, it was hard to believe he could be behind a sequence of murders. But then, how well did he really know him?

'Meet me at the house tomorrow, and from there we shall go to Whitechapel.'

'Are you certain you wish to come?'

'Of course,' said Alexander. 'Why would I not?'

'Have you ever even set foot in Whitechapel?'

'Well, no, I have not, but I hardly think that is relevant.'

'If you say so. Try and blend in,' said Gabriel, eyeing Alexander's shining white ascot tie and his matching vest. 'Unless you wish to be the target of thievery the second we step foot in there.'

CHAPTER XVI

Whitechapel

G abriel sighed as he watched Alexander step out of
his house.

'Thievery it is then...'

'Oh, what now?'

A day had passed, a day in which Gabriel braced himself
for venturing back to that place of oblivion. He had tried
his best to pull himself together, clear his head, focus. The
sky above them had swirled into a deep blue hue, casting
shadows on certain parts of the city and illuminating
others in a strange light, making it so that nothing seemed
quite real; only veiled, just hovering behind an invisible
surface.

'Change that tie. And vest. One can spot it from a
bloody mile away.'

Alexander had decided to dress himself as he usually
did, in a gleaming frock coat, a stiff Homburg hat, and,

most notably, a golden vest made of silk, finished with a painfully red ascot tie.

'And dress more like you? God help me.'

*

Gabriel watched the city roll past, listening to the wheels of the carriage, the hooves of the horses. Breathe. Frost had accumulated on the edges of the window. Gabriel focused on its crystalline shape. Alexander, sat opposite him, twirled his hat on his index finger before leaning forward.

'Do you believe we shall encounter Jack the Ripper?'

Gabriel frowned. 'What?'

'I was merely wondering if we should consider it to be a potential problem we may face.'

'Unless you are a woman and a prostitute, I believe you shall be perfectly safe. Moreover, Jack the Ripper has not struck this whole year, so he has either grown bored of killing people, or he is dead.'

The winter cold impaled Gabriel like a thousand knives the second he stepped out of the carriage, until it settled within his bones like ore in its rock.

'God,' muttered Alexander, pulling his coat closer to his body. 'If this weather continues, the Thames will soon freeze over.'

They both glanced around the street. In the distance, beggars lay twisting and turning by the pavement, attempting to ward out the unforgiving cold with thin, ripped blankets wrapped around them. Sharp angles

jutted out the fabric. Alexander's shoulders tensed, his lips thinning. Crooked, mossy buildings rose up around them like the teeth of an ancient sea monster. Smoke pumped out of the chimneys, colouring the heavens black.

As they neared the end of Hooper Street, Gabriel quickly looked back and forth along Back Church Lane. 'They are not out yet, but we must move quickly.'

'Who is *they*?' asked Alexander, the pitch of his voice slightly higher than usual.

'The gangs.' Gabriel marched further into the street, walking right into the heart of Whitechapel. The houses around them slowly rotting, the bricks chipping away. The smell of sewage hung in the air around them. Occasional pedestrians walked past them, scruffy men covered in soot and dirt, some shooting glances at Alexander.

'I beg your pardon?' exclaimed Alexander, his brows twisted together in protest as he stopped dead in his tracks.

'Be quiet,' snapped Gabriel. 'I doubt it is clever to alert every one of our presence.'

Alexander jogged towards Gabriel, who had walked further into the gnarling street. 'And when were you planning on indulging me in this knowledge?'

'I presumed it to be common knowledge.'

Alexander let out a sound of dismay as he followed Gabriel. A group of women stepped out of a brothel, flashing shades of ruby and emerald. Strands of their hair had become undone, falling around the nape of their necks. The aroma of violets swamped around them as they neared, shooting wide smiles adorned with slashes of scarlet. Alexander smiled back politely, inclining his head forward.

'They are prostitutes,' stated Gabriel as they walked past them.

'Yes, I am aware of that, Ashmore.'

There were fewer of them roaming the streets, still in fear of the Ripper. Instead, most kept themselves to the equally dangerous restraints of brothels.

'You seem to know this area rather well.'

Gabriel cleared his throat. 'Anybody in possession of a brain would be aware of these things.'

'Do you come here often?'

Gabriel turned to face Alexander. 'I did not come here to answer your trivial questions regarding my personal life.'

'I merely attempted to initiate conversation, not to extract your deepest, darkest secrets, dear friend.'

'It would be most optimal for you to keep that conversation to a bare minimum.'

Alexander remained silent for only a few moments as they continued down the street, nearing the corner.

'Are we going to be breaking in?'

'No, we shan't be breaking in. I will enter it, spin some sort of tale explaining my presence, and attempt to discover if anybody there may know more.'

'And what about me? Shall I be joining you as your handsome companion?'

Gabriel shot Alexander a sideways glance. 'No. You will remain outside, keeping a look out.'

They had arrived at a crossroads. A group of men staggered out of a dank, small pub, smashing their beer bottles to the ground. Alexander eyed them curiously. Gabriel came to

a halt, cautiously looking around the broad streets. The faint sound of laughter and shouts of men lingered in the distance, the occasional scream that everyone was now accustomed to. Gabriel wondered what it was this time, a stabbing or a robbery?

Alexander turned to Gabriel. 'Should we not help them?' he said in a huff of breath.

Gabriel raised his eyebrows. 'Help who?'

'Those screaming people, of course!'

'If you were to help each person that screamed in the East End, we would be here for an eternity.'

'What is the meaning of us doing all this when you refuse to help those in need?'

Gabriel sighed before taking a step closer to Alexander. His alien eyes stared back at him with narrowed lids. 'The meaning is that we shall be solving a murder investigation, not enacting charity work. Now, I implore you to *quit* wasting our time.' Gabriel made his way into a narrow street. 'There.'

Alexander halted behind him, looking up at a large townhouse adorned with dark shades of brick. The thick oak doors were shut, the blurred windows absent of light. Gabriel frowned as he neared the entrance, pulling at the handle. Locked. He attempted to look through the paned windows, but a thin curtain was drawn up from the inside, obscuring his view.

'This does not appear very promising.'

'Be quiet.' Gabriel looked down at the footpath, picking up a muddy cloth. He wrapped it around his knuckles before balling his hand into a fist, and then punched the

window. The glass shattered to the ground like falling snow.

'Yes, that works as well,' muttered Alexander.

Gabriel drew back the curtains. A shard of glass scratched against his hand, but he barely felt it. He cleared the rest of the glass with the cloth and peered inside the building.

He frowned.

The building was completely deserted. Shelves emptied; the cupboards of desks left open.

Alexander peeked in from behind Gabriel. 'Ashmore, is it supposed to look like this?'

Gabriel ignored him as he hoisted himself into the building, into a world of cracked stone and rot, a monument of antipathy. He stood as still as possible, listening. The wind whistled in through the window, bringing with it the smell of coal and dirt. The floorboards creaked beneath his weight, but apart from that, Gabriel heard nothing.

Then, glass crunched behind him. Gabriel jumped as he turned towards the sound. He was met with Alexander stepping in through the window.

'I apologise, I did not mean to alarm you.' He brushed off the dust from his coat and looked around the room. 'It appears this place is deserted. How is that possible?'

'I do not know. I was only here last week,' said Gabriel with furrowed brows. He stepped towards the desks upon which the clerks sat, opening up every cupboard and drawer he could get his hands on. He lit a lantern and moved it closer to a pile of documents he found. Alexander put on his glasses as he looked over Gabriel's shoulder.

They were nothing more than incoherent scribbles, most probably done by a bored worker. Gabriel passed them to Alexander, whose eyes skimmed the pages. He shook his head.

Gabriel headed to the back of the room, towards Rufus's office. Anything important would have been kept there. He reached for the doorknob, twisting it, and then it clicked. He sighed irritably. Locked. He took a step back and bashed his shoulder into the door. The wood had been worn down already, so it only took him a few tries to send it swinging open.

As he stepped into the room, Gabriel swore. Anger and frustration rose within him, hot and fast. He kicked a cupboard as hard as he could, barely even registering the flaring pain it sent through his leg. He ran his hands through his hair and attempted to steady his breathing. It was empty, with no sign it had ever been utilised. Gabriel shut the door behind him and slid onto the floor, his face in his hands.

Was he going mad? Was his sanity slipping between his fingers, just like it did his father's? His nights had been restless, filled with memories of the past and present sins, weaving together to form devilish hallucinations. Had his reality shifted somehow? Was he losing his grip on his memories?

As Gabriel sat there questioning his sanity, something caught his eye. Something small, a bright colour capturing the light of the streetlamp outside. It peeked out from beneath an empty shelf. Gabriel hoisted himself upright. As he neared it, he noticed it to be the edge of a piece of paper. He knelt down and pulled it out.

His heart skipped a beat as he read its contents. It was a list. A list of all his scheduled deliveries.

Alexander entered the room. 'God, you really destroyed this door, didn't you?' he said as he carefully moved the door to the side, which was only hanging from one hinge.

'I found something,' said Gabriel. His voice was hoarse.

'What is it?' Alexander moved closer to him, which made Gabriel take an instinctive step to the side.

'A record of deliveries I was instructed to make for this week and the next.' The paper had his name written at the top, followed by the days of the week, the number of deliveries, and the names of the clients.

It might not have been a substantial piece of evidence for Alexander, but to Gabriel it was a wicked relief.

'At least we have found something, however, I do not believe any of this information is new to us. You had said you receive such a list every two weeks; therefore are you not already in possession of this information?'

'No, you are thinking narrowly. This information being here could explain how the killer knew to target the exact people I had made deliveries to. He could have simply broken in here and taken it.'

Alexander's eyes widened. 'You are right.' He started pacing around the office, the floorboards creaking with every step he took. 'However, it still reveals nothing in regard to our killer's motive. Why that particular list? Why not simply pick Erebus users off the street? There are plenty of them.' He sighed. 'There is something that is missing. Something we are not seeing.'

They climbed out the window, stepping back into the grey-tinted streets of East London. The smoke and fog had accumulated in the air, crawling on the cobblestones like some sort of reptile.

'That was rather eventful,' stated Alexander, as they headed down the street. Faint chatter sounded in the nearby distance. 'Our carriage should be where we left it. I say we call it a day and reconvene—'

Gabriel held up his hand, silencing Alexander. He put his finger to his lips. A bottle shattered, followed by multiple shouts. Alexander's jaw clenched, his lips thinning. 'The Cutters. We need to depart. Now,' said Gabriel tightly. He started to head down the street, Alexander's footsteps loud behind him, before a figure stepped out of an alleyway. Gabriel halted, inhaling sharply.

'Well, well. Who do we have here?' said the man stood before him.

Eight more men, dressed in neat suits in shades of grey and black stepped out of the dank street, positioning themselves right behind their leader. Their hands were tucked in their blazers, presumably gripping on to pocketknives.

The Cutters.

'Andrew,' said Gabriel as a way of greeting. Alexander's brows formed into a faint frown. Andrew took off his cap, slicking his hair back.

Gabriel knew the Cutters. He had carried out a few jobs for them in the past when he desperately needed the money. They did not take it well when he told them he wanted out in the end.

He cocked his head sideways. 'What the bloody hell are you doing here, eh?' A strand of oily hair fell onto his forehead. His cold grey eyes drilled into Gabriel's own. 'We told you to never step foot in our territory again.' Alexander shifted on his feet, avoiding the glare of the men behind Andrew.

'I was merely visiting a friend,' Gabriel held up his hands. 'No harm in that.'

'Well, you chose the wrong night for that,' said one of the men. Gabriel shot him a dismissive gaze.

'I was not conversing with you.'

'What did you just say to me?' the man growled, charging forwards. Andrew put out his arm, stopping the man. He appeared young, composed of a slim frame with short hair the colour of sand. To Gabriel's surprise, Alexander had not moved even an inch from his side, and had actually neared closer.

'You don't do anything unless I tell you to,' hissed Andrew under his breath, shoving the boy back. 'Now,' he righted the collar of his blazer, 'hand us whatever you have.' His gaze fell on Alexander, looking him up and down. 'You especially.'

'Excuse me?' said Alexander. 'I do not think so.'

A muscle twitched in Andrew's jaw. The men behind him pulled out their pocketknives, the edge of the blade gleaming under the lamplight. 'I ain't asking again.'

Alexander's shoulders tensed, yet he stood his ground. 'I said no. Are you familiar with the word?'

Andrew stepped forward, ready to strike Alexander, before Gabriel blocked his path.

'*Enough.*'

The group of men stepped even closer. He lowered his voice, leaning in to only address Andrew. 'I think you have forgotten exactly what I've done for you.'

Andrew's gaze pierced Gabriel's, his nostrils flaring. Gabriel held his stare unrelentingly. Andrew cleared his throat, before forcing a grin. 'You are right, Ashmore. I owe you. And I am a man that keeps his word. But here is the thing, you see. I owe just *you*.' His gaze fell on Alexander. 'Nobody said anything about this one.'

'You won't be touching him,' said Gabriel.

The men behind Andrew chuckled. 'Is he your lover, Ashmore?' one of them said. 'You were always strange; it wouldn't surprise me.'

Gabriel did not even acknowledge the man, keeping his gaze on Andrew.

Andrew chuckled. 'You might be right, Price.' He stepped closer to Gabriel. 'After we rob your boy here, we might just see how much of a beating he can handle. I'm guessing he'll be dead after—'

Andrew staggered back before he fell to the ground, groaning as he held on to his nose. Blood squirted from between his fingers.

Gabriel had punched him. Hard.

For a few seconds, everyone seemed suspended in time, unmoving. Andrew's gang looked at Gabriel, wide-eyed with shock and surprise. Alexander's mouth hung slightly open. And then, all hell broke loose.

'What are you all waiting for? Kill the bloody bastard!' shouted Andrew, his teeth stained red and his

mouth puddling with blood. The men all pulled out their pocketknives.

'Run,' said Gabriel, grabbing onto Alexander's collar and breaking into a sprint.

Cold air cut through Gabriel's throat like a knife as he panted heavily. They ran as fast as their legs would carry them. The Cutters were close behind them, knives flashing, teeth bared. Gabriel dragged Alexander along, forcing him to increase his speed. Luckily, they were faster than the Cutters, who were most probably not accustomed to having to chase their prey.

Gabriel made a sharp turn into a narrow alleyway. He heard a crash behind them. One of the Cutters had tripped, causing several others to run into him. Two of them jumped over fallen ones, continuing their chase.

They came out onto a main street. Alexander breathed heavily next to Gabriel, appearing as though he might pass out from exertion.

'Almost there,' panted Gabriel. Sweat dripped from his neck down his back. 'Hold on.'

Gabriel led them through another alleyway, coming out onto a narrower road. The Cutters were still on the main street. Then, Gabriel saw it.

The curtains were drawn, but Gabriel recognised the terraced house.

Jinhai's Café.

He sprinted towards the hidden entrance, which was located on the building right beside it, dragging Alexander with him. They burst through the door, and immediately collapsed. They lay on the floor as they caught their breath.

Alexander coughed vehemently. Gabriel's own throat felt like it was on fire.

Gabriel steadied himself against the wall. The red wallpaper flashed before his eyes like splatters of blood, and then, when his breathing had steadied, the smell. It slowly circled his nose, until all he could smell was that ammonia-like scent.

'We should be hidden here,' managed Gabriel.

Jinhai's opium den was the only place Gabriel could think of that could hide them. It was made to be invisible, especially to gangs like the Cutters, so they would not coerce the owners into giving them a cut of their earnings.

'Dear God,' muttered Alexander. 'Did we just almost get killed?' He then started looking around. Alexander's features were half obscured by shadows. 'Are we in an opium den?'

Jinhai's den was sparsely decorated. A few sofas and mattresses were strewn on the ground and the candles lighting the room were minimal. It was a quiet night, with only a few men smoking away on the sofas, their heads lolling back in ecstasy. Gabriel had only visited the place a few times.

'Yes,' answered Gabriel in a strained voice. His skin had started to itch and his blood felt like it had turned to acid. He balled his hands into fists in order to hide their tremor. He forced himself to sit upright, attempting to listen for any sign of the Cutters. He peeked through the closed curtain and saw the men walk around the street. Fury shone from their eyes as they conversed with one another, and then retreated back to where they came from. Gabriel let out a sigh of relief, slumping against the wall.

'Are they gone?' asked Alexander.

Gabriel nodded, unable to articulate words. He had to leave, get away from the opium.

'Thank you. For what you did back there.'

Gabriel only nodded again before he forced himself upright. 'We must leave. Now.'

Alexander frowned. 'Are you certain? They could come back; perhaps we should stay put for a bit longer—'

'Now,' hissed Gabriel.

A sense of realisation flickered across Alexander's face, before he nodded, and they made their way out of the opium den.

CHAPTER XVII

Victoria

Gabriel had not slept well. His night had been marred with nightmares and whispers in the dark. He had arrived at Alexander's house in the early morning. A Christmas tree had been put up in the corner of the library, yet, somehow, it appeared out of place, as if it were an unsuccessful attempt to lift the spirits. Alexander's house was grand, a family home, yet it was always empty. Gabriel wondered where his family was or if Alexander simply lived alone, but it wasn't his place to ask.

Alexander was sat at the long table in the centre of the room, a large parchment spread out before him. He scribbled down all the clues they had found up until now, attempting to establish a connection. Beside him was a large pile of books, filling the room with the aroma of ink and musk. They had been conducting research into the murder patterns of other notorious killers, attempting to

establish a connection. Gabriel, sat opposite Alexander, skimmed through a book on murder tactics and what they could reveal about the killer. He scribbled relevant points down in a notebook.

Alexander suddenly sighed, leaning back in his chair. 'Why on earth would our killer target Erebus addicts?' The dull morning light cast a grey sheen upon his pale face.

Gabriel lifted the book he was reading. 'Williamson, a writer on the history of criminality, states that killers may not always have such clever patterns. Perhaps we are trying to find a link that is not there.'

Alexander rubbed his chin. 'Yes, perhaps we ought to look at things from a more practical perspective...' His eyes suddenly widened. 'You truly are a genius.'

Gabriel raised an eyebrow. 'To what do I owe such praise?'

'Ease of killing,' said Alexander. 'Yes, it is certainly a plausible explanation. Those addicted to drugs are significantly easier to kill than normal, healthy individuals. They would be weakened by the drug in their system.'

Gabriel frowned. 'Yes, but that still does not explain why the killer targeted the exact people I have made deliveries to. Even if he did have access to my schedule, how did he know what they looked like? How did he track them down?'

'The killer must have been following you.' He rose to his feet. 'It makes sense. There have been no more murders ever since you quit your deliveries.'

'But *why*?' hissed Gabriel, leaning forwards on the table. 'Why?' His voice broke. He cleared his throat, regaining his

composure. He leaned back on the chair, letting out a deep breath. The investigation was taking a bigger toll on him than he thought.

'I do not know, Ashmore,' said Alexander quietly. 'But we shall find out. I promise you.'

'If what you say is true, if the killer is truly following me,' said Gabriel, 'then I say we stage another delivery.'

'Yes, that is a brilliant idea. How foolish we did not think of it sooner.' Alexander then cautiously looked around the room. 'However, if our theory is correct, and the killer is indeed following you, would he not be aware that we are investigating him? We could be being watched this exact moment.'

'I doubt that,' said Gabriel. 'He would have intervened by now if that was the case.'

'What if you are wrong?'

Gabriel looked at Alexander with a grim expression. 'Then we'd be in grave danger.'

Alexander chuckled, although it came out rather nervously. 'Nothing we cannot handle. Sherlock and Watson have encountered countless dangers, have they not?'

Gabriel raised an eyebrow. 'Who am I? Watson?'

'Well, yes.'

'That is rather offensive.'

'Watson is a doctor, a highly skilled individual. I do not understand how that can be perceived as offensive.'

'Fine,' said Gabriel. 'Now, the delivery is set to occur beneath the Holborn Viaduct at Farringdon Street, at midnight. Wait for me there, and make sure to stay in the shadows.'

Gabriel arrived home in the early evening. As he stepped into the foyer, he noticed a coat and top hat had been hung on the wall. A faint glow shone onto the wooden floorboards, coming from the living room. He pushed the doors open. He was met with his brother.

Hugo was sat at the end of the table, appearing lost in thought before he looked up.

'Gabriel,' he said, rising from his chair. He sounded surprised, as if he hadn't heard his brother come in. Gabriel's eyes fell on the table. Hugo had set it for two.

'What is all this?'

'Dinner,' answered Hugo. 'I cooked chicken.'

Gabriel scoffed. 'Since when do you cook?'

Hugo shrugged. 'I became well acquainted with a cook on board a trade ship to France.'

'Well, enjoy,' said Gabriel dismissively before turning away.

'I would like you to join me,' Hugo called out.

Gabriel turned to look at him. 'I have no desire to do so.'

'Gabriel, I...' Hugo sighed, his eyebrows furrowed together in a sort of invisible battle. 'Being in this city again, it brings out all sorts of memories, memories I had thought were lost, and I... I just wish to have dinner together. That is all.'

Gabriel looked at his brother, someone he once knew better than himself, someone who was now a stranger, a cryptic imposter that bore his face. He saw the dark circles under his eyes, the creases in his eyelids. The way his gaze would shift and change, as if remembering something he had buried away.

Gabriel took a seat at the table, opposite his brother. Hugo's posture relaxed slightly. He then loaded chicken and potatoes onto Gabriel's plate. Gabriel thanked him, before he took off his blazer. As he hung it on his chair, something fell out, landing right in between Gabriel and Hugo. Before Gabriel registered the fallen item, Hugo leaned forwards and picked it up. His features fell, brows furrowing in a sense of confusion.

'Victoria?'

Gabriel looked up. His gaze fell upon the photograph Hugo was holding in his hands. 'Give that back,' he said.

'Have you seen her?'

'I said give it back,' hissed Gabriel.

Hugo's hand balled into a fist. 'Have you *seen* her, Gabriel?'

'No,' said Gabriel. 'I have not. Now give it back.'

Hugo slowly put the photograph down upon the table. Gabriel snatched it back, hiding it away in his pocket.

Hugo rose from his chair, his balance slightly off. He looked into the roaring fire, watching the flames. 'It has been so long,' he muttered.

Gabriel clenched his jaw. 'She left.'

Hugo turned to face Gabriel. 'What?'

Gabriel did not reply, avoiding his brother's gaze. Victoria had been the first girl Gabriel had ever loved, and coincidentally, she had also been Hugo's.

'Where did she go?'

'I do not wish to talk of Victoria to you.'

A part of Gabriel hated her. He hated her for loving both of them, for fooling him into believing her heart was

his alone. And yet, another part of him still loved her. A part of his heart still lay with her, dedicated to her and her alone.

Victoria had been clever beyond her years. She had filled him with new ideas, grander aspirations, a greater sense of curiosity towards the world. He had fallen in love with the sharpness of her mind, her clever tongue. With her ambition, which stopped for no one and nothing.

Hugo had fallen in love with her beauty. With the curve of her lips, the hypnotic darkness of her eyes. With the way her hair tumbled over her smooth shoulder and the sound of her laugh.

Victoria had loved Gabriel because he was stoic and devoted. She had loved Hugo because he made her laugh. He made the hardships of life disappear with a simple conversation, replacing fear and uncertainty with joy and bliss. She had loved him because Hugo had been everything he was not.

His love for her was another thing Gabriel could never forgive Hugo for.

Gabriel's appetite had left him. Now the aroma of roast chicken and garlic made him feel sick. He rose from his chair, holding on to the photograph in his pocket. Hugo had turned back to the fire, facing away from Gabriel. He did not say anything as Gabriel walked out of the room, and back onto the cold streets of London.

CHAPTER XVIII

————— • ·•————

The Fifth Death

The winter air bit at Gabriel's skin as he stepped out of the hansom cab. It froze his breath, creeping into the openings of his coat. Fragments of last winter danced in his mind, an endless composition of ice and fog. He still remembered the sleepless nights: the cold which crept even into the marrow of one's bones, the endless whistling of arctic wind, the shivers which seemed to never cease.

He had arrived at the Holborn Viaduct in Farringdon Street. Shadows pooled in the crevices of the tall Georgian houses surrounding him. The street was reasonably quiet, except for a few men retiring back into the tall building opposite him. The dome of St Paul's Cathedral hung in the distance, an ethereal backdrop against the darkness of the night.

Gabriel let his eyes glide over the street, searching for

any sign of the killer. If he was indeed following Gabriel as they had thought, he was doing a good job of staying hidden. Alexander was hidden somewhere close to the viaduct, having arrived before Gabriel in order to assess the area.

The Erebus was in the pocket of his coat. He could almost feel it burn through the fabric, into his skin, branding him forever. *Focus.* He took out his pocket watch and looked at the time. Midnight.

He stepped under the viaduct, shielded from view by the shadows residing beneath it. Gabriel waited for several minutes, his arms crossed over his chest, his limbs stiff. The street had emptied until all he was left with was the sound of his breathing and the blood pumping through his veins.

Then, he heard it. Footsteps. Crunching in the thick layer of snow as they neared him. Gabriel turned to face the customer. A thin-framed man stood before him.

'The Erebus, please?' he asked quickly. His voice shook slightly and his eyes were bloodshot. His skin was abnormally white, and his veins abnormally dark beneath his flesh.

Gabriel did not say anything as he took the Erebus out of his pocket. The man held out his hand containing a few pence.

Gabriel's shoulders stiffened. 'Keep your money,' he said as he handed the man the pouch.

A look of surprise passed over the man's features, before greedily shoving both the money and the pouch into his pocket. He nodded at Gabriel, before heading back down the street.

Gabriel let out a deep breath. He waited for several minutes, making sure the killer would not catch on to him. Alexander would already be tailing the potential victim. His hand went to the pocketknife he had put in the inside of his blazer. He had brought it along in case they had needed it, and now it was a comforting presence against the worries clouding his mind. Gabriel had never killed a man, but in this moment he would not think twice about it. He would be doing the city, the entire country, a service. He'd be eradicating a source of great pain once and for all, stopping him from claiming any more innocents.

He cracked his knuckles, before stepping out onto the street.

After ten minutes, Gabriel spotted the man. He made sure to stay hidden in the shadows as he trailed him. The man was walking, half-stumbling, across the street, and then turned into an alleyway. He halted, hastily pulled out a pipe from his pocket and started to load the Erebus in the chamber. Gabriel's eyes met Alexander's, who was hiding in a doorway. Alexander shot him a wink.

Gabriel remained where he was, pressed against the wall of the terraced house behind him. He was barely breathing as he examined the entire road, his eyes skimming every corner and crevasse for a sign of the killer.

The man took out a match and lit the pipe. He inhaled deeply, before blowing out black smoke. A sense of euphoria washed over his face as he leaned back onto the wall, his lips curving into a deep smile of contentment. And

then, he screamed. Those same features twisted into pure agony as he screamed and screamed.

Gabriel's eyes widened as he stood frozen, suspended in time.

The man started clawing at his head, and then bashed his head into the wall. Over and over, until he took out a gleaming object from his pocket, and before they could do anything else, slit his throat. His body slumped to the ground, the scarlet blood spreading rapidly onto the white snow.

Gabriel heard Alexander swear as he ran towards the man. He threw himself down onto the ground, pressing his hands down on the slit in the man's throat in an attempt to stop the bleeding.

Gabriel couldn't move. He could not do anything as he stared at the blood seeping into the snow.

After several seconds, his legs finally responded. He slowly made his way over to Alexander. He had ripped off the sleeve of his shirt, attempting to bandage the man's throat. The man's eyes were wide, his mouth opening and closing as he gasped. His veins had turned a deep black.

'Ashmore!' Alexander called out. 'Get help!'

Gabriel stood over the body, staring into the man's frantic eyes. Then, his eyes landed on the pipe. The Erebus. Images of the other victims flashed before his eyes. The veins and their injuries. Fallen out a window, a skull bashed in, strangled by a tie, stabbed in the side of the neck. The street remained empty, no killer in sight.

An overwhelming pain spread through his chest, burning his heart and lungs. He couldn't breathe. His hands trembled at his sides as he realised what he had done.

They hadn't been murdered. They had committed suicide.

'Ashmore, we are losing him!'

Suicide caused by the Erebus.

Gabriel staggered back, hitting the damp wall behind him. He turned away, heading out into the main street, and then heaved out the contents of his stomach. Sweat dripped from his forehead as he breathed rapidly. He spat out the sour taste in his mouth before wiping his lips.

'He is dead.'

Gabriel turned around to find Alexander stood behind him. His hands and ripped shirt were drenched in blood. It had spattered onto his glasses. His hands trembled slightly, but the rest of his body stood firm, unmoving. His stare was hard, and something had shifted in his eyes.

'I... I...' started Gabriel, but the words got caught in his throat.

'We could not have saved him in time,' said Alexander. 'His cut was too deep.'

'It was the Erebus,' managed Gabriel finally. 'It was the Erebus.'

'I know,' muttered Alexander. 'It explains everything. The missing link, the strange nature of the murders, the lack of connection.' He turned back to look at the alley. 'We must inform the police.'

'No,' said Gabriel, pulling himself together. 'We must leave.'

Alexander looked at Gabriel with an expression of outrage. 'And just leave him?'

'We do not have a choice here, Wakefield. If we inform the police, they shall question why we were at the scene of

the crime. They shall find out about our investigation, and they shall most definitely put a stop to it.' Gabriel glanced at the alleyway. 'The body will be discovered soon. Then, it—'

'No, I cannot do this,' exclaimed Alexander, shaking his head. 'I cannot just run away; I cannot leave him lying in a pile of his own blood and filth—'

'I do not wish to leave him either, but that is what we must do,' hissed Gabriel. 'If you wish to prevent this from happening a hundred times over, that is *exactly* what we must do.'

Alexander's face contorted into a regretful expression as he glanced back to the alleyway. He clenched and unclenched his fists, the muscles in his jaw feathering as he tried his hardest to make the right decision. He turned back towards Gabriel, a sense of mourning swimming within his eyes, and nodded.

CHAPTER XIX

Highgate

G abriel did not know what time it was. All he knew was the darkness before him, the cold of the snow upon his skin and the grass beneath his feet. He walked through the Egyptian Avenue, the obelisks and pillars twisting and turning around him. After they had left Whitechapel, Gabriel had immediately made his way to Highgate Cemetery. He had stepped through gravestones, through the fog and the thickness of dead souls, until he reached a single open patch of grass. It was located near an old stone chapel, right beside a thick oak tree. In the spring, it blossomed with pink flowers. In the winter, its thick branches were left bare like a skeleton's arm. He fell down onto his knees before it. The snow soaked through his trousers as he put his hands upon the grass. He bowed his head, letting the tears he had kept in spill out in a painful groan.

'It is all my fault, mama,' he whispered. He dug his nails into the earth. 'It is all my fault.' He could hear the wind whistle through the metal fences, and if he listened closely, whispers of the dead.

He had made it a ritual to visit the cemetery. Every week he would come here, sit in front of the exact same empty patch of grass and speak to his mother.

However, Gabriel did not actually know where she was buried.

Neither did Hugo. Their father had buried their mother without them. He never told them where. Gabriel and Hugo had begged him, shouted and screamed at him to tell them, but he never did. Gabriel still asked at times, but it only led to his father becoming completely silent for days afterwards. It had taken everything within Gabriel not to strike him, pin his frail body against the wall and threaten him until he told them where she was buried.

The cold penetrated his clothes, stinging his skin and filling his lungs with ice. His breath misted before him, mixing with the fog of the cemetery. Sometimes, Gabriel could swear he heard her speak to him, felt her hand on his shoulder, felt her caress his cheek. Hugo believed he had been closer to their mother, that somehow, he must have cared more for her. But Gabriel did not always show emotion the way Hugo did.

'I cannot forgive myself,' said Gabriel quietly, brows twisting together in misery. All of his sins weighed down on his chest, making it difficult to breathe. His heart ached, mourning the loss of a part of himself he could never get back.

*

Gabriel did not remember how he arrived home, but all of a sudden he was sat in front of the fire. Dawn crept up on him, soft rays of early light trying to break into the house. Upon the coffee table were a dozen opium pills. Gabriel breathed out slowly, already feeling the effects of another one that he took just half an hour ago. The room slightly swayed as he moved his head, his vision hazy. He had hidden them under the floorboards a while ago. He did not remember which one, so he had ripped out an entire section, leaving a gaping hole in the far end of the parlour.

He leaned forward, gathering all of the pills in his palm. He moved his hand up, so close he could see the grooves and dips in them, their varnish coat gleaming with the glow of the fire. If he took enough, he could fall asleep and never wake up. He moved his hand closer to his mouth. Then, a clatter sounded from upstairs. His father. Images of his face flashed before Gabriel's eyes: pictures of his father spinning him around as a child, smiling at him with pride. Then, he saw Hugo, the regretful look in his eyes that seemed to never quite disappear, his bright smile that used to make the entire world smile with him, his laugh as they ran through the streets together. He heaved himself up, around him, and threw the pills in the fire. He watched them hiss as they melted, shrivelling to nothing more than black waste.

He threw himself down upon an armchair, closing his eyes. His regrets and sins were now only mere shadows in the distance, fading away into absolute silence.

Just as Gabriel felt his eyelids become heavier with each

blink, on the edge of drifting away, he heard a knock on the door. His eyes opened gradually, the world around him spiralling.

Gabriel heaved himself up, each breath a tremendous effort as he slowly headed towards the door. Another knock. He steadied himself on the wall before pulling the door open. Gabriel winced as the morning light struck his eyes, shivering as the cold air penetrated his loose shirt. He rubbed his eyelids, before forcing them open. He blinked as he looked at the person stood before him.

'What the hell are you doing here?'

'Good morning to you too,' said Alexander, looking him up and down. 'I am here to further our investigation, of course. You left rather suddenly last night.'

'It was late,' said Gabriel slowly, attempting not to slur his words.

Alexander stared at Gabriel for a few seconds before speaking again. 'May I come in?'

It took Gabriel a while to answer. 'No.' He gripped strongly onto the doorknob, his knuckles white, his palm sweaty.

'Well, then I shall have to invite myself in,' stated Alexander as he pushed past Gabriel, who was too weak to resist him, and entered the foyer. He held a letter in his hand. 'I found it lying outside.' He looked back at Gabriel, who was still gripping onto the door. 'Are you all right?'

'Perfect,' muttered Gabriel, snatching the letter from Alexander's hand and stuffing it into his pocket. Alexander walked into the parlour. Usually, Gabriel would have been alarmed at Alexander intruding into his home. Now, it

only felt like a mere inconvenience, something Gabriel was too exhausted to address.

'God, what has happened here?' asked Alexander with a frown as he walked past the hole in the floor, before looking around the large room. 'It is awfully dark in this room. And rather cold.'

Gabriel did not say anything as he steadied himself upon the doorway.

'I am aware that our discovery last night may have been hard on you,' started Alexander, locking his gaze with Gabriel's. 'But this will not help.'

Gabriel let out a low chuckle. 'This?'

'You know what I am speaking of. It is rather obvious.'

Gabriel sighed, fighting the urge to let his eyes fall shut and retreat into a deep slumber. His whole body was heavy, pulling his weight to the ground. Alexander was right. Gabriel knew that. He just did not want to admit it. 'I do not see how it concerns you.'

Alexander scoffed. 'You are my partner. We are investigating a criminal case together. Your health certainly concerns me. I doubt anything shall get solved if you spend the entirety of your time taking liberties with opium.'

'Arrest me then if you so desperately wish to solve this case,' hissed Gabriel. 'It is my fault anyway. I gave the victims the Erebus; I gave them the very thing that killed them.'

'Do not speak such nonsense,' said Alexander, scoffing. 'You are the one person that can truly help me solve this case. Help me, so your name can be cleared, and you can be freed from such wicked dealings.'

Gabriel remained silent, dropping his gaze away from Alexander. He felt annoyance at Alexander's intrusion rise through the haze of the opium, yet he also felt something else, something strange. Something close to gratitude, close to a certain affection for the odd individual that had barged his way into his house.

'I did not set out to be a detective,' said Alexander suddenly, taking a few steps around the parlour. 'I always wished to be one, but it would never have been acceptable within my family. I studied History at Oxford. My father always thought I would end up following in his footsteps: manage the family land, end up owning a few ships, invest in banks. I soon realised all of that meant doing nothing, really.' He had reached the fireplace and ran his hand along the thick marble. 'I found that I never quite fit into that world. The world of mindless wealth and boredom, empty conversations and meaningless days. I told my father of my wishes, and he was appalled.' Alexander swallowed hard. 'I had never seen him so disappointed. Shortly after, he and my mother left for Paris. They claimed they needed a break from London, but I am pretty certain my father just could not bear to look at me any longer. They left me the house. At least it is something.' Alexander chuckled, but Gabriel heard the sadness in his voice. 'I wish to make my father proud by the time he gets back. I wish to solve this investigation and prove to him that I am capable, that I can make a real difference to the world we live in.'

Gabriel met Alexander's firm stare. His eyes were pleading with him, imploring him to not give up on the investigation. And in a part of it, in the deep depths of his

gaze, it asked Gabriel to not give up on him. To not give up on him as his father had done.

'I did it because I had to,' stated Gabriel. His voice came out hoarse. 'I did it for others.'

'I understand, Ashmore.'

Gabriel cleared his throat, brushing his hair back. 'Let's solve this case, then.'

CHAPTER XX

────── ▪ ▪ ──────

The Invitation

The next morning, the death of the man had already reached the papers. Gabriel read through the article in *The Times* with the headline: *THE DARK KILLER STRIKES AGAIN – WILL GASCOYNE-CECIL FINALLY ACT?* He read through the provocative piece, which branded the government and police force as shameful. Although in the last three years, London had fallen victim to an increasing rate of crime, these murders were different. They represented something strange, something ungodly. It made the public panic even more, fearing the unknown.

They were in Alexander's library, which they had transformed into a sort-of office. Alexander had pinned the map on one of the walls, alongside all articles he could find on the victims and the Erebus.

'They have discovered the body,' said Gabriel. 'His name was Arthur Brown.'

Alexander's body went stiff. 'What does the article say?'

'They blame the government and the police for their incompetency in finding the killer.'

Alexander nodded, slowly pacing around the room. 'The Erebus made them commit suicide,' he started, 'but why?'

'It must have driven them insane. Yet,' Gabriel frowned, 'the Erebus had never done that before.'

'The question is, how did this occur? Did someone orchestrate this? And if so, why?' Alexander came to a halt, tapping his foot on the floor. 'Perhaps something went wrong in the manufacturing of the drug. Yet, something tells me there is more to it.'

'Likewise,' said Gabriel. He shifted in his seat, and as he did, he felt something sharp press into his leg. He frowned as he reached into his pocket and pulled out a letter. For a few seconds, he started at it in confusion. Then, he remembered Alexander handing it to him yesterday. The Ashmore house received many letters, most of them from social clubs, some from politicians that used to be acquainted with his father, asking for political donations, and the rest from individuals advertising certain products. Some of them were merely delivered wrongly. He usually threw them out, but this one looked different. The envelope was thick and glossed, adorned with an intricate red stamp. He found a single card within it. He raised an eyebrow as he read the contents.

JOIN THE CONSERVATIVE JUSTICE PARTY BALL,
HOSTED BY PARTY LEADER LORD GRANVILLE.

*ATTEND THE CONSERVATIVE JUSTICE PARTY'S BALL
AND GAIN A PERSONAL INSIGHT INTO THE PARTY'S
MANIFESTO, WATCH LORD GRANVILLE'S LONG-
AWAITED SPEECH AND HELP SHAPE ENGLAND'S
FUTURE. THE POWER IS IN YOUR HANDS.*

'What is that?' asked Alexander.

Gabriel handed the card to Alexander. 'An invitation to a ball,' he answered.

Alexander read the card, before inspecting the envelope on the table. He frowned. 'I have seen this envelope today,' he said, rushing towards the end of the room. He opened a drawer filled with similar letters, rifling through them before pulling out the exact same one. He held it out for Gabriel to see. 'It arrived this morning. I have seen it lying on the neighbouring doorsteps as well.' He placed his copy of the invitation on the table. 'They must be spreading propaganda now that everyone is calling for a vote of no confidence.'

'I say we attend,' said Gabriel.

Alexander raised an eyebrow. 'Gabriel Ashmore, attending a ball? I had expected you to be too solemn for such things.'

Gabriel rolled his eyes. 'I do not wish to attend for my pleasure. I believe Granville is worth listening to. We might even encounter someone there willing to aid us with this investigation, since everyone there will have the same goals as us: eradicate crime.'

'Yes, you have a point,' said Alexander, rubbing his chin. 'The Conservative Justice Party would benefit greatly

by being able to solve a case that the government cannot. However, this would mean we are helping the party win. I am not so sure I would wish to see them in office.'

'Why not?'

'I am not quite so convinced in regard to their policies,' said Alexander. 'Their level of policing, their expansive military goals and, most importantly, their planned repeal of the Judgment of Death Act.'

Gabriel scoffed. 'Is that not everything that you are fighting for?'

'No, Ashmore, I do not desire the execution of all criminals,' said Alexander with a frown. 'I desire for them to go to prison. Spend their lives in confinement. I do not wish to take away their lives.'

'They do not wish to execute people blindly. They wish to add in a clause whereby the government must be consulted before a judge gives a criminal, intended for execution, a lighter sentence. Judges are being bribed every day, organised crime and gang members are getting away with all sorts of horrid crimes. This only serves to prevent this corruption from further infesting the rule of law.'

'Well, I believe in the separation of powers.'

'You can believe what you want, Wakefield, but that does not change the nature of our situation. The Conservative Justice Party would have the necessary influence to obtain more information for us. They could be a key part of our success.'

Alexander pushed his glasses up the bridge of his nose, sighing loudly. He knew Gabriel was right. They needed help.

'This entire investigation has become bigger than us,' continued Gabriel. 'We are looking into investigating a well-established, legally questionable drug organisation. We have not even skimmed the surface of this conspiracy, and we shall never be able to do so, unless we get real help.'

'Fine,' he said, finally relenting. 'When does this ball take place?'

'Tomorrow evening.'

'Well, then, I suggest you put on your best suit, Ashmore.'

CHAPTER XXI

The Ball

Gabriel looked out the window of the carriage. Before them stood a French-style, light-bricked mansion, bigger than most houses he had seen, with large paned windows covering the walls. Warm hues of gaslight shone through the curtains covering the windows, making visible the shadows of moving bodies. Numerous carriages, some much bigger than Alexander's, were stood in front of the mansion, with guests exiting them. There were various doormen, all dressed immaculately in shimmering suits, guiding the crowd of guests in. The ladies surrounding them wore extravagant dresses of rich colours, hues of red and green and blue, with thick fur shawls upon their shoulders. The men wore shining black suits, their ascot ties matching the dress of their companions.

The faint sound of the piano and violin wavered in the air around them like perfume as they neared the house.

The big double oak doors remained shut as the doormen checked everybody's invitations, exchanging warm smiles. Gabriel and Alexander queued with the others. Gabriel was dressed in a simple black suit and a silver ascot tie. He had to wear his father's tailcoat, as his own had become too small, and he had never bought a replacement. Alexander, on the other hand, instead of going along with a simple black vest, had opted for a deep scarlet one. Although it should have appeared odd, Alexander's confidence made it look strangely striking.

They both handed the doorman their invitations and stepped into the mansion.

They found themselves in the foyer. The walls were painted a deep golden colour, the ceilings incredibly high and the floor beneath them pure marble.

To their left was the entrance to the grand ballroom. Gabriel only saw a fraction of its enormous size as he peeked in. There were people standing around, speaking in a corner about business, or sitting on an ottoman, a thin glass of bubbling liquid in their hands.

A butler approached them, holding a tray of champagne glasses. Alexander gladly took one, whilst Gabriel shook his head.

The first thing Gabriel noticed was the gigantic crystal chandelier hanging above them, reflecting sparks onto the marble floor. A buffet was laid out at the side of the vast room: evening bites, fruits, dessert and delights of all sorts put on display. The musicians were placed at the far end of the room, on a slightly elevated stage; violins, cellos

and a grand piano, all gleamingly polished. There was an area designated for dancing, with a dozen guests moving in unison with their partners to the music. The rest of the people were stood around, drinks in hand, chatting busily with one another. Although Gabriel's had an aversion to festivities, he could not deny that there was something in the air, something that spoke of promises and new beginnings. Alexander led them to the buffet, plucking a grape from a tray and throwing it in his mouth. The sound of the violin drifted through the air, mixed with the aroma of Scotch and perfume.

'We ought to search the area,' stated Gabriel.

Alexander chuckled. 'And what are we exactly *searching* for?'

'An ally, of course. Someone with influence, knowledge.'

'Well, Ashmore, such things are not found by simply hunting for them. You ought to let it come to you. Engage in conversation, appear interesting and polite, make friends. Although I do realise that must be quite difficult for you.'

'Very comical, Wakefield.' Gabriel smoothed his blazer. 'Whilst you stand here, making idle chat, I shall be doing what we came here to do. Now, if you will excuse me.'

Gabriel pushed past Alexander, making his way to the musicians. He watched them closely, especially the pianist. He had to relax first, get used to his surroundings. Then, like an incoming tide, the dreaded feeling arose yet again in the pits of his stomach as he listened to the melody. His head still felt slightly fuzzy, the edges of his vision blurring only faintly when he turned his head too quick, but his reflexes and focus remained intact. He could feel his skin

burn as he looked around him. The ladies in bright dresses chatting heartily to one another, accompanied by groups of men doing the same. Gabriel caught bits of conversation regarding lands and titles. And then, he felt a light tug at his blazer. He immediately grabbed onto an arm, being all too familiar with the art of pickpocketing, and span around.

'Good tr...' he started, but then turned speechless as to who was standing before him.

It was a woman. She had raven dark hair and skin as white as snow. She was of Chinese descent, with dark, sleek eyes piercing into his own.

'My apologies, madam,' muttered Gabriel quickly, immediately dropping her thin arm. He noticed she wore a bracelet with a familiar Chinese symbol upon it, a symbol Gabriel had seen before in Chinatown. If he remembered correctly, it denoted luck. 'I thought you were a man.'

'Is stealing something only men can master?' she asked. Her voice was strong, unyielding, lined with a certain coldness. Strands of hair fell down her high cheekbones as she looked at Gabriel with something close to a glare.

'Well, you clearly have not mastered it if I managed to catch you,' responded Gabriel. She wore a dark blue dress the colour of the deepest ocean and gloves of the same colour, but what truly caught Gabriel's eyes was a dazzling necklace displaying a large yellow diamond. 'Who have you managed to steal that from?'

'Princess Beatrice.'

Gabriel's eyes widened slightly. 'The queen's daughter?'

The girl nodded.

Gabriel chuckled. 'That cannot be true.'

'Do not believe me, then. I do not much care for your recognition.'

Gabriel was taken aback by the girl's tone. She had a wild presence to her, as if the intricate dress, gloves and diamond she wore were a mere costume she had slipped on to play a part. He saw it in her eyes, dancing in there like wildfire. He wondered what her story was. 'What brings a thief like yourself to a ball like this, then?'

'I ought to ask you the same question.'

'I am not a thief,' stated Gabriel.

'You managed to catch me. That says enough.'

'I am not,' Gabriel repeated again, more forcefully this time. 'Your claims are ridiculous.'

One side of the girl's lip quirked up, shooting him something between a smirk and a grimace. 'Only fools do not know themselves.'

'Then I guess I am a fool,' muttered Gabriel, turning away.

'Why are you here?' asked the girl, stopping him in his tracks.

He turned towards her. 'To listen to Lord Granville.'

'No, you are here for something else.'

He looked her up and down, noting her nimble hands, her slender figure, her eyes that showed not a sliver of fear or uncertainty. 'How did you get in here?' he asked.

Her lips curved into that same unsettling shape. 'Through the window.'

'All windows here are locked.'

'The *third-floor* window.'

Gabriel took a step closer to her. 'And you managed break into Buckingham Palace?'

Her stare was unyielding. 'I can break into anywhere.'
'What is your name?'
'Xing Yang.'
'It was a pleasure meeting you, Miss Yang.'

Gabriel made his way back to the middle of the ballroom, watching the musicians on stage. He looked around the room for Alexander, but only saw the faces of strangers staring back at him. He sighed, clenching and unclenching his fists, the temptation to grab a glass of champagne getting stronger by the second, until the music suddenly stopped. The chatter around the room grew faint at the sudden sound of silverware against glass. All the guests had stopped dancing, standing still in anticipation.

The musicians cleared off the main stage. A man, dressed similarly to the doormen, moved onto the stage.

'Ladies and gentlemen, I present to you the leader of the Conservative Justice Party, Lord Benedict Granville,' he announced.

The room exploded in claps.

A tall man with a broad build appeared on the stage.

'Welcome,' he started. His hair was coloured a dark brown with large streaks of silver, matching the darkness of his eyes, a solid black, staring back at them. Gabriel guessed him to be in his late forties.

He had a confident look upon his face, the look of power, suggesting he knew everything and everyone, knew every working of the world as well as the palm of his hand. Yet, his features were also assuring, kind. He looked at the people as if each and every one of them was a life-long friend of his.

'I am delighted to have received you all in my home and I hope you will enjoy the refreshments and entertainment provided.' His voice resonated through the room, posh and articulate. 'On this night of unity and enjoyment, I wish to make a long-awaited announcement. However, before I do so, something critical needs addressing. Something none other than the state of our beloved city.' His eyes looked over the room. It made Gabriel straighten up, listen to whatever he was about to say with an even greater intensity. 'Crime has infested every inch of our city. It has endangered every citizen, torn families apart. Drugs, theft and, most recently, horrendous murder.' He remained silent for a few seconds, before continuing. 'These murders have shaken the city in unimaginable ways. Spread fear through all. It has made us doubt our own government. Our own police force. I say, no more!' Voices of agreement echoed through the room. 'We must eradicate this evil once and for all.

'During the last parliamentary meeting, I put forward a carefully selected list of measures to ensure your safety. Alas, the government did not listen.' He paused for a few seconds, sighing quietly before continuing. 'That is exactly why the Conservative Justice Party was formed. New legislation has already been drafted, plans on how we can best fortify our city have been designed and measures eradicating opium and all of its recent variations shall be implemented. All Chinese businesses associated with such drugs shall be destroyed and Chinatown shall be rebuilt into a police station overseeing the East. Our police force shall be expanded, carrying out daily patrols to ensure that the people of England remain safe.

'Therefore, I call upon your support, so we may finally attain true justice and end the root of criminality once and for all!' A few cheers sounded through the ballroom. Gabriel looked around him, faces of excitement and determination all stared up at Granville in awe, with several people clapping their hands. 'Times of fear and uncertainty must end,' continued Granville, his eyes staring into the crowd in an assertive yet trustworthy manner. 'And times of prosperity must begin.' The crowd gave another cheer, the sound of clapping growing louder. Granville was thriving off it, a look of complacency and satisfaction evident within every feature of his face. 'Together we shall make London, and then the whole of England, glorious again!'

The crowd of people clapped, followed by chatter to one another, appraisals and compliments. Gabriel noticed even Alexander joining in. Granville stepped off the stage, engaged in conversation with various men, accompanied by two guards Gabriel had not noticed before. The musicians stepped back onto the stage, filling the room with the soft sound of music again.

'There you are,' said Alexander, taking a large gulp of champagne. Gabriel blinked rapidly. He felt disorientated for several seconds. 'That was a rather hefty speech.'

'Yes, indeed it was,' muttered Gabriel.

'I believe we ought to approach Granville.'

'Pardon?'

Alexander stepped closer to Gabriel. 'I did not agree with many things he said, but I believe you may be right. He seems like he can help us. Solving this case would be a

great victory for the party, therefore, I believe he shall want our contribution.'

'Well, approaching him may pose some difficulties,' said Gabriel as he cocked his head towards the guards' direction.

Alexander eyed the guards, before glancing back at Gabriel and shooting him one of his famous winks. 'Leave it to me.'

Gabriel watched as Alexander approached the guards. He put a hand on one's shoulder, his posture relaxed, his mouth moving incoherently. The guard immediately spun around, holding out a hand blocking Alexander's path.

'Good start,' muttered Gabriel under his breath.

The guard's brows furrowed, followed by him pointing for Alexander to leave. Just as a chuckle was about to slip out of Gabriel's mouth, Granville's head turned towards Alexander, analysing him with his strangely dark eyes. He then whispered something to the guard, who nodded and stepped aside. Gabriel watched as Alexander, who looked rather relieved, spoke to Granville and then pointed at Gabriel. Gabriel stood unmoving as Granville's gaze fell upon him, a peculiar sort of gaze, strangely intimate yet detached, followed with a courteous nod. After several minutes, Alexander returned, a wide grin plastered upon his face.

'He has agreed to meet with us in a couple of days' time.'

Gabriel raised his eyebrows. 'You truly managed to convince him?'

'Did you not think I would succeed?' asked Alexander, scoffing dramatically.

'In all fairness, I did not think you even had a chance.'

CHAPTER XXII

Lord Granville

Two days had passed since the Conservative Justice Party's ball. The time had come to finally meet Lord Granville. Gabriel and Alexander walked up the drive lined with thick trees, until they reached the large front doors.

Alexander let out a deep breath, slicking his hair back and straightening his blazer. Gabriel looked at him out of the corner of his eye. 'For someone who dislikes the man, you certainly are making an effort.'

Alexander rolled his eyes. 'Just because I do not agree with certain party policies, does not mean I dislike him.'

Gabriel knocked loudly on the door. It swung open after several seconds, and to Gabriel's surprise, Granville greeted them. He had a kind smile on his face as he gestured for them to enter.

'Welcome, Mr Wakefield, Mr Ashmore. I trust you already know your way around,' he said. They stepped into the foyer they had visited only a few nights ago. 'Please, follow me.' He led them to a study to the right of the grand staircase.

'I must say, I was quite delighted when Mr Wakefield reached out to me.' Granville opened a pair of double doors. The first thing Gabriel noticed was the sheer volume of books that were contained within the room. Every inch of the walls was covered in bookcases, with various more piles stacked on the floor. A great fireplace made of white stone roared before them, yet the room remained cold. 'It is so very comforting to know that there are young people who care about the future of this city.'

'Of course,' answered Alexander. 'That is what's most important.'

'Please, take a seat.' Granville gestured to the leather sofas before the fire. 'Any refreshments? We have all sorts of things, many of which I do not know the name in all fairness. I usually only have coffee. Or whisky. Ah, Agnes.' He smiled at the maid entering the room. 'She shall have a better knowledge of the contents of the kitchen.'

'Please, Lord Granville, there is no need. My partner and I are perfectly well,' said Alexander.

'We wish to sincerely thank you for your time, Lord Granville,' said Gabriel. Granville's gaze landed on him. His eyes were sharp, shooting towards him as quick as lightning. 'I am a supporter of your ideals and your aims for this city, and I have the utmost confidence it shall create a better London for all.'

Granville smiled at them both. 'It warms my heart to hear that, gentlemen. This is exactly what I strive for. The opportunity to change the solidified, old way of thinking and completely reform the human mind in order to create an enhanced nation. A united nation. And most importantly, a safer nation.' Both Gabriel and Alexander nodded. 'However, I do not wish to be unreasonable in my aims. It is dangerous to ignore the irrational. One must see it, recognise it and battle against it with the same fervour of the culprits' malicious minds.' He paused before speaking again. 'The Romans valued order; it was their greatest strength, yet also their tragic flaw. In certain instances, order must be broken, then rebuilt again, because crime is not linear. It deviates heavily and we must accommodate those digressions.'

Gabriel felt a sense of grandeur as he listened to Granville. For the first time in his life, he felt like he was part of something important, something that truly mattered. Something that could make a difference.

'Now, you two have already been doing this great work yourselves. Tell me more about your investigation.'

Before Alexander could open his mouth, Gabriel interjected. 'At first, we had presumed there to be a traditional killer.' Granville's eyes watched him intensely, giving him his undivided attention. 'However, we then realised the victims killed themselves. We presume they were driven mad by the Black Opium.'

Alexander continued. 'Now, we are of the assumption that all of this is driven by whoever manufactured those new drugs. However, we are short on leads. Therefore, we

wish to ask you for your help, considering our interests are aligned.'

Granville paused for a moment before speaking. 'Yes, those murders have been a great grievance of mine lately,' he said with a grim expression. 'I wish I could do more *myself*, alas, it would be viewed as unconstitutional to meddle in such affairs of the state when I am not in a legitimate position to do so. However, there is nothing stopping me from helping *you two*. Therefore, I shall discreetly be able to provide whatever I can, on the condition you keep me informed on your findings, of course.'

Alexander looked as though he may kiss the man. 'Thank you, Lord Granville. We sincerely appreciate it.'

'However, I do have a question for you two,' started Granville, his gaze shifting between them. 'How did you find out about the involvement of the… Erebus, was it?'

Gabriel's heart rate increased, but he kept his face blank. Alexander shifted in his seat. 'We studied those who consumed it. They showed similar… attributes, such as the black veins. We made an educated guess.'

Granville smiled. 'How clever.' He stood up, buttoning his blazer before making his way to the drinks cabinet in the right corner of the room. He took out three thick crystal glasses, and proceeded to fill them with a measure of Macallan whisky. Gabriel's body stiffened as the smell reached him. Ever since his father turned to drink, he hadn't been able to stomach the smell. 'Have you considered the possibility of this distributor perhaps having made a manufacturing error? They would still be equally to blame for those unfortunate deaths, of course.'

They both glanced at each other as they considered Granville's suggestion, and Gabriel couldn't deny the fact it sounded more plausible than a drug distributor having some sort of malevolent master plan. Yet, something told Gabriel it wasn't as simple as that. Granville set the three glasses down on the coffee table. 'You must try this whisky; it is truly magnificent.'

'Thank you,' said Alexander, taking a sip of the dark liquid. 'Are you a lover of gin, Lord Granville?'

'Please, call me Granville. I hear that title enough every day as it is,' he said with a chuckle. 'And to answer your question, well, who isn't? What is your favourite, young man?'

'Gin Lane. London Dry Royal Strength.'

'Ah, a true classic. Created 1751, I believe. What botanicals were utilised again?'

Gabriel could tell Alexander was warming up to him. Gabriel was convinced Granville knew the exact answer to the question he had asked, but he asked it anyway for the sole purpose of making whoever he was talking to feel important; make them feel as though they were the ones teaching him something.

'Seville oranges, Sicilian lemon and juniper. Absolutely outstanding, such lovely undertones. The name itself, Gin Lane, pays homage to William Hogarth's print of the last century, depicting rather dissipated acts taking place by individuals having consumed too much gin. Although it was meant to deter people from the drink, I think it rather encouraged it,' said Alexander with a grin.

Granville laughed in such a way that he felt like an old friend. In many ways, his friendliness came across as

genuine. And in an odd manner, Granville's actions, the way he laughed and presented himself, the way his eyes met theirs with fascination and interest, seemed like a parallel between something Gabriel already knew, and yet something that was completely unknown. 'It is fascinating how art inspires everyday life, and vice versa. A perfect cycle.'

'Art is the foundation upon which society, as a collective, rests,' said Gabriel. Granville had a way of inviting conversation in such a manner it would be impossible not to join it. His eyes studied Gabriel again with their pleasant gaze, a glint of wonder, but not surprise, visible in his eyes. 'What are we without it?'

'We would be nothing,' said Granville in agreement. 'Art serves as a way of recording all human emotion. Love, joy, envy, wrath. It records our existence as a united species. It reminds us that no matter how much time has passed, human emotion never vicissitudes. There is a certain comfort in that continuity, I believe.'

An agreeing smile tugged on Gabriel's lips, to his own, and Alexander's, surprise. 'And it captures the impossible. Art completes what nature cannot bring to finish.'

'Aristotle,' stated Granville. Something shone within his eyes as he took a swig from his drink. 'Back to the matter at hand.' His gaze now turned to Alexander. 'I assume you are the lead detective on the case?'

Alexander straightened up, a faint flush visible on his cheeks at being called a detective. 'Well... Gabriel is also—'

'Yes,' answered Gabriel for him. 'He is.'

'How admirable,' said Granville. 'What made you undertake such a challenging task?'

Gabriel listened to Alexander as he explained his passion for police work. 'It has been fifty years since the establishment of the Peelers and another thirty-six years since the Police Act was implemented, however, they could not be any more ineffective. These last few years their numbers have just dwindled; especially the number of detectives within the Criminal Investigations Department.' Alexander spoke with great confidence, fully in his element. 'The harder things are getting, the keener they are to give up. That is what it seems like to me. I wish to change that, and I believe we could start by solving these murders.'

'Well, Alexander, I am very impressed. You have much ambition for a young man. I am convinced you would be an exemplary asset to the police force.'

Alexander flushed, yet again.

'If I may ask, Lord Granville,' interjected Gabriel, 'why is the government not properly acting on this matter, especially when it is a matter of life or death? Forgive my straightforwardness, but I had just thought you may have more insight on the matter, being a member of parliament.'

Granville's eyes shone with something Gabriel could not quite figure out as he looked at him. Was it pride? Relief at someone asking the right questions? 'I believe it would be unconstitutional for me to divulge private matters of the Lords.

'However, sometimes such things can be as simple as a government simply being too distracted, too preoccupied with other matters.' He leaned back on his armchair. 'You both know how well the Empire has been expanding in this century. It would be plausible to assume that Cecil is

simply too consumed with foreign policy: gaining further influence in India, encouraging further trade, trade which has already been most profitable, whilst also focusing great efforts on parts of Africa, Burmah, all the way to North America. This would require an enormous budget and a great dedication of time, leading to the unfortunate conclusion that domestic issues are left neglected. But this is just a theory, of course.'

'And the Liberals?' questioned Gabriel with a frown. 'Or the Unionist Party? Are they not challenging this? Or rather, would they not, hypothetically, challenge this?'

'Ah, you know how it works with opposing parties,' said Granville with a bitter chuckle. 'Deals can seem sweeter than sugar.'

Granville got to his feet, smoothing out his blazer. 'Although I do not wish to part from our conversation, gentlemen, I am afraid I have an appointment in the Commons.' Gabriel and Alexander followed suit. 'I shall contact some of my sources in Scotland Yard, request more information regarding these deaths and subsequently share my findings with you two. I have heard of some type of unrest within the police forces, which ought to make this process a whole lot simpler.' He held out his hand, first to Gabriel. Granville's grip was firm, yet also light; a beckoning touch promising the prospect of many more conversations to come. The smile he showed was warm, but sharp. Gabriel noted this paradox between his mannerism, but it only seemed to add to his charisma, which imposed an enticing breath of mystery into each word he spoke.

CHAPTER XXIII

———• •———

The Prudent Brother

For the first time in a while, Gabriel did not feel the need to plunge into oblivion when he arrived home. Their meeting with Granville had left him strangely energised, fuelled with an even greater desire to solve the mystery. He felt as if he were part of something significant, something that could create an entirely new society. The air in the foyer felt unusually warm against his chilly skin. A deep apricot glow flickered against the walls of the parlour as Gabriel walked further into the house. Cassius was seated on the leather sofa before the fireplace. Gabriel watched him reading a newspaper with great intensity, momentarily surprised at his father's unusual interest in daily affairs. Gabriel glanced around the room, until his eyes fell upon a glass of half-finished gin. His brother's drink. Gabriel sighed, loud enough for his father to jump, and almost frantically shut the pages of the newspaper he was reading.

He turned around to face Gabriel, smoothing the paper out on his lap with unsteady hands.

'You frightened me, boy.'

'Apologies, Father,' said Gabriel. Cassius's eyes were bloodshot, lined with dark circles. He only nodded at his son. 'Was Hugo here today?'

'Who?'

'Hugo. My brother.'

'Ah,' Cassius grumbled, his gaze falling away to stare at the wall behind Gabriel. He got to his feet, swaying slightly. Today he was wearing a thick jumper with a crinkled shirt underneath. His greying hair appeared to be windswept, as if he had recently been outside.

'Have you been outside, Father?'

The thought of his father wandering beyond the walls of the house procured an alarming fear within Gabriel.

'No,' he answered shortly.

The late afternoon sky was neither bright nor dark, but rather an intense grey which plunged the room into shadows. The fire created a glowing silhouette around Cassius, and in the dim light the fine lines on his face were even more prominent, prematurely carved into his skin. Gabriel waited, but his father did not answer, until eventually he started to walk to the foyer with slow but deliberate steps. Gabriel dug his nails into his palms, his teeth clenched as he listened to the sound of his father's slippers upon the wooden floor. He turned around in a swift motion, his eyes burning into the back of Cassius's head.

'Has this not grown tiresome?' Cassius came to a halt, without turning around. Gabriel took a step towards him.

'This *pathetic* charade of misery.' Cassius's shoulders slowly moved up, then down. Eventually, after what felt like a lifetime, he slowly turned his head in Gabriel's direction, so half his face was visible. 'The only thing you have ever cared for is yourself.'

'I still hear her,' Cassius said, his voice so faint Gabriel had thought he imagined it. 'Calling for me.'

'For God's sake, Mother is *dead*,' hissed Gabriel, in a tone so vehement it even shocked him. But Cassius stood there, unmoving, unfeeling. 'And so is Adelia, thanks to you.' He felt the familiar ache in his throat, but he continued. 'Did you even mourn her? My sister. *Your* daughter.' Gabriel let out a sour laugh. 'Of course you didn't. You were too busy wallowing in your own self-pity to even *think* of your children.'

Cassius only stared at Gabriel with those distant eyes. Gabriel never knew that silence could be so torturous, leaving him alone with his own careless words echoing through his mind. Gabriel watched as his father turned away from him, just like he had done a hundred times. He tried to swallow away the lump in his throat, but it remained stuck in place. He watched as his father ascended the stairs and disappeared into the darkness.

*

London transformed at night. The city shifted and changed, until it became a world composed purely of shadows and sins, forbidden desires and deadly lust. Gabriel had not been able to sleep, so he walked the icy streets of the city

towards Covent Garden. Shouts and hollers echoed around him, as if the wind carried them through the air, followed by the sound of breaking glass. After their meeting with Granville, he had resisted taking opium, despite his cravings for it. He never wished to touch or see it again. Therefore, he had to clear his head. The coldness of the night air helped distract him, even if it was for a mere few moments.

The faint sound of giggles rang in the air. He turned down Bedford Street and was met with a group of women. Bedford Street had become lined with brothels, providing a source of entertainment for the morally dubious. Men loitered across the street, following the girls into the houses one by one. The women wore tight dresses, and even in the cold of winter, put their breasts on display. They looked him up and down, before one, a blonde, curly-haired girl, approached him. Her skin appeared blotched under the harsh light of the streetlamps, and her lips were smeared with rouge, quirking up into a smirk.

'Hello there, sir; have you come to—'

Gabriel held up his hand. 'No.' He walked past them, further down the street. Just as he had almost reached the end, someone stumbled out before him. Gabriel halted, his body momentarily freezing with surprise.

'Hugo?'

Hugo had stumbled out of a brothel. His white shirt was half unbuttoned and untucked, his coat in his hands. He jumped as he saw his brother, swearing under his breath.

Gabriel's mouth went dry. 'What are you doing here?' he asked.

'I could ask you the same thing, brother.' Hugo's voice was thick and heavy. He had been drinking. Beads of sweat lined his forehead, his hair damp and dishevelled.

Gabriel's lips thinned. 'I see you are still caught up in your old ways after all.'

'Give me a break, Gabriel,' Hugo hissed. 'Do you not get tired of being so bloody conceited?'

'You have had enough for the night, go back home.'

Hugo chuckled bitterly, swaying on his feet. 'You have kicked me out of my home.'

'Go to wherever you have been residing.'

'Is it so difficult for you to show me a shred of kindness? Must you always look at me with hatred?'

Hot rage formed in the pit of Gabriel's stomach at his brother's hypocrisy. 'Kindness? I have shown you kindness, Hugo, over and over again, and each time you spit it back in my face.'

Hugo scoffed. 'Kindness? Do you call that kindness? You deserted me, Gabriel.'

Gabriel frowned. 'What on earth are you talking about?'

'Gabriel! Are you up there?' Hugo's voice echoed through the house.

Gabriel was deadly silent, his breath catching in his throat, unable to hear anything except the sound of his own blood pumping in his ears. The lump in his throat kept getting bigger until it felt like it was stabbing into his flesh. Every nerve in his body had frozen, turned to pure stone. He stared at what was in his arms blankly, as if it wasn't quite real.

Hugo walked into Adelia's room, his head heavy after long nights of drinking. His eyes fell on Gabriel, and then on Adelia in his arms.

'Gabriel,' breathed Hugo. He looked down at her, her face horrifyingly pale, her empty eyes staring at the ceiling. Her body appeared stiff, as if she had been in the exact same position for hours. 'Gabriel, what on earth is going on?'

Gabriel didn't answer. All he could do was stare at the wall, unable to look at his worst nightmare presented to him right in his arms. Hugo fell to his knees before him.

'Put her down on the bed, Gabriel,' Hugo managed to muster, every word like a knife stabbing into his lungs. Gabriel didn't move, his hands still tightly gripping on to his sister. Hugo stepped in, wrapping his arms around Adelia's body, lifting her up to put her on the bed. Gabriel remained silent, staring at the wall. Hugo turned to look at his brother, into his stare which had turned emotionless and cold, expecting him to comfort him, tell him lies, tell him she was in a better place, but none of that ever came. No matter how hard Hugo begged for it, Gabriel never gave it to him. It was at that moment, when Hugo looked into Gabriel's vacant eyes, he realised he had not just lost a sister, but also a brother.

'You were no longer yourself,' said Hugo. 'Days would pass where you would not even utter a single word to me.' His lips twitched. 'I would beg you to talk to me. To help me. I would bloody *beg* you, Gabriel.'

'You were barely even there, Hugo, do not speak such nonsense.'

'Oh, but I was. You just did not see me. Did not *want* to see me. You always say you lost me, but I lost you long before I left.'

'You are lying—'

'Who do you think took care of Adelia when you went to those filthy dens?'

'She was *asleep*,' hissed Gabriel. 'I only went at night—'

'Do you not think she woke up? Woke up and screamed for Mother and Father?'

Gabriel's jaw clenched, his entire body stiffening with hatred and fury. He felt it then, like a door closing, a curtain drawing. He felt himself withdraw, leaving himself behind. He stepped back, before marching down the street and disappearing into the darkness.

CHAPTER XXIV

The Dinner Party

The next morning, Gabriel found a letter by the door. He immediately recognised the glimmer of the envelope. He picked it up, the paper soft against his skin, and after seeing the red stamp, affirmed that it came from Granville. Gabriel opened it somewhat impatiently, curiosity prickling his fingertips. It was a personal invitation to a dinner party tonight, hosted by Granville himself. Gabriel wondered if Alexander had received one too, but something about the phrasing of the letter told Gabriel he hadn't.

*

Evening fell quickly upon the world. Gabriel stood in front of the mirror in his chambers, adjusting his tie, smoothing

his double-breasted waistcoat. He combed his hair neatly to fall to the side. The scar on his face was barely visible in the dim light, yet at that moment, he felt more deformed than ever.

He clenched and unclenched his fists in the hansom cab, watching the city drenched in warm hues of orange and cobalt roll past. He was nervous, wondering who else Granville had invited and considered how he should talk to them. It had been a long time since Gabriel had socialised in such a setting, and he feared he may have forgotten how to.

It had begun snowing when he reached Hyde Park Corner, steadily covering the streets in a thin layer of crystalline powder. Gabriel made his way up Granville's drive. Red winterberries he had not noticed before lined the entrance, peeking through the bare branches of the thick trees. Frost had accumulated atop them. He had thought of notifying Alexander he was attending the dinner, but then a part of him wished to keep it to himself.

The doors were opened by a butler, who bowed as he greeted Gabriel. He led him through the foyer and into a drawing room. A fire was roaring, casting an amber light upon the wood-panelled walls. Granville was seated in a leather armchair, a thick cigar in his hand. Upon the sofa beside him sat three men.

They all rose when Gabriel entered the room. Granville's lips formed into a smile as he shook Gabriel's hand.

'Welcome, Gabriel,' he said. 'I am delighted you could make it.' He stepped aside, allowing the men behind him to greet Gabriel. 'Allow me to introduce my companions.'

Granville put his hand on the shoulder of a dark-haired man. 'This is Sir Albert Beaufort, a great friend of mine.' He appeared to be in his sixties, with strong features and fine lines crowding his narrow blue eyes.

He turned to the next man, who appeared to be much younger than the other men. He had fair hair and a red-tinted face. 'Arthur Robinson, a well-accomplished lawyer.' He then introduced the last man. 'Percival Edgerton, an advisor of the queen.' Edgerton was a slim, narrow-faced man. He was wearing thin-framed glasses and sported an expression between cautiousness and neutrality. He shook Gabriel's hand, his lips pressing together in a form of greeting.

'This is Gabriel Ashmore,' said Granville, 'an intelligent young man currently investigating the murders that have been ravaging our city.'

'Ashmore,' said Beaufort, his eyes pensive. 'I know that name…' He drew a long puff from his cigar. 'Cassius Ashmore! Your father, I presume?'

Gabriel nodded stiffly.

'A rather successful merchant, I believe. Yes, I have heard much about him from my acquaintances in the shipping industry. It is lovely to meet you, Mr Ashmore.'

'Likewise, Sir Beaufort.'

'Now,' started Granville, putting down his cigar, 'let dinner commence.'

Granville's dining room was the grandest Gabriel had ever seen. A thick crystal chandelier hung from the high ceilings, submerging the room in warm candlelight. The long,

polished table was covered with various dishes: large plates of veal, filet of beef, roast turkey and an entire boiled leg of lamb. Alongside them, potatoes and vegetables, oysters and various different types of soups. Steam rose from the food, its fresh aroma wrapping itself around Gabriel's nose. Two servants stood in the corner of the room, ready to serve them whatever they desired.

'Please, take a seat,' said Granville. He seated himself at the head of the table. Gabriel sat on the chair to his right, opposite Edgerton and Beaufort, with Robinson beside him. The servants started filling all the guests' glasses with wine.

As the servants started filling their glasses with wine, Robinson started discussing tax policies with Beaufort. Edgerton remained stiff and quiet as he looked at the contents of the table. Granville spoke to one of the servants regarding the wine.

'Ah, Mr Ashmore,' said Robinson, turning to face Gabriel. 'How lovely to have made your acquaintance.' He looked Gabriel up and down. 'Do tell us more about yourself.'

The table went quiet, all men now ready to listen to whatever Gabriel had to say. He cleared his throat. 'I am afraid I am not quite so interesting, Mr Robinson.'

'Well, what do you do?' asked Robinson in a snide tone. 'Do you work? Study?'

'I wish to study.'

'Well, do tell us more, boy,' said Beaufort. 'What do you wish to study?'

'Jurisprudence. At Oxford.'

'Ah, Oxford is certainly the right choice. How fortunate for you that we are all Oxford alumni here. Well, Robinson here attended Cambridge, but we shall not hold it against him,' chuckled Beaufort.

Robinson laughed at Beaufort's joke, but his eyes remained sharp and cold.

'Well, what are you waiting for, then?' asked Beaufort. 'Should you not have finished the course by now?'

'I had... other matters to attend,' said Gabriel shortly. Robinson looked at him with a curious expression.

'When do you wish to start your studies, Gabriel?' asked Granville, taking a sip of his wine.

'I wish to do so after the investigation, Lord Granville.'

'I can certainly make a recommendation,' stated Granville. Gabriel perked up. 'Some of the professors do not look so favourably to latecomers, especially those teaching Jurisprudence. But with my support, it should not be a problem.'

Gabriel thanked Granville as the servants started serving the meats. His nerves buzzed with excitement, at an endless prospect of opportunities and new beginnings. Gabriel glanced out the window, noticing the falling flakes of silver and white as the thickening darkness of winter pressed against the glass. He watched Granville carefully cut up the veal upon his plate, his movements almost unnaturally precise.

'Now, tell us more about this investigation of yours,' stated Beaufort. 'Benedict mentioned how much you and your partner had already managed to discover, trumping even the detectives at Scotland Yard.'

Gabriel summarised the case for Beaufort, telling him only what was necessary. Edgerton, who had remained quiet, watched him intently. 'Now, we are trying to figure out who is responsible for the creation of the Erebus. It is proving a rather difficult task.'

Beaufort rubbed his chin. 'The Erebus,' he muttered.

'Many prominent opium distributors have been trying to do the very same thing,' stated Robinson, cutting up a piece of filet beef. 'Many come to our office seeking legal action against them for cutting their profits in half.'

'Have you tried investigating Harvey Blythe?' stated Beaufort suddenly.

Gabriel's eyes widened. 'Pardon?'

Harvey Blythe was the most notorious organised crime leader in London. He had managed to escape arrest ever since he rose to prominence. Gabriel was certain he bribed the whole of Scotland Yard. He owned a total of five extravagant gambling clubs in the very heart of London and had ties to prominent aristocrats, occasionally helping them take care of their rivals.

'A few years ago, we were making crime reports for the Conservative Justice Party ahead of its formation. Harvey Blythe was a main source of havoc. One of our investigators visited one of his gambling dens and reported a sighting of a strange substance. Black Opium. Now known as the Erebus,' explained Beaufort.

'The Erebus was first seen in one of Harvey Blythe's gambling clubs?' asked Gabriel.

Beaufort nodded. 'I believe it was the Silverton. However, I cannot be absolutely certain.'

'Harvey Blythe…' muttered Robinson, tapping his fork on his plate. 'Did you know he was an orphan from the East End? He watched his parents pass away of typhoid when he was younger, even lived in their house with their bodies for an entire week before the authorities discovered him.' He looked Gabriel right in the eyes as he continued. 'Some believe he ate them to stay alive.'

Gabriel stared back at Robinson unflinchingly. 'Thank you,' he said to Beaufort, shifting his gaze away from Robinson. His nerves felt like they had been electrified. He struggled sitting still.

'Albert helped me form the Conservative Justice Party,' explained Granville. 'He served as an external advisor to former Prime Minister Benjamin Disraeli, from 1874 until 1880.'

'Yes,' said Beaufort with a smile. 'And what a fine job we have done.'

'Before you commence with praise, I do hope you shall not neglect further improvements to your policies, Sir Beaufort,' said Edgerton, speaking for the first time since Gabriel had arrived. Everyone's eyes fell on him. Beaufort smiled, although his eyes spoke a different story.

'I believe our policies are rather well developed, Mr Edgerton,' said Beaufort dismissively.

'I do not think so. I believe the policies you wish to implement are not simply bordering radicality, but are in their very nature unacceptably radical.'

Beaufort opened his mouth, but then closed it again. Gabriel glanced at Granville, whose stare was pinned on Beaufort, yet his expression gave nothing away.

'Alienating ethnic communities and policing the people are not in the party's best interest. It is, in its very essence, immoral.'

'Thank you, Mr Edgerton. I believe you certainly have a point. Sir Beaufort and I shall work closely together to resolve these grievances.'

Edgerton did not appear convinced, yet he nodded, and retreated back into silence.

For the rest of the night, they ate and drank and laughed. Beaufort was a surprisingly pleasant man to be in company with and told them multiple stories of his wild youth at Oxford. Granville spoke about his adventures in the Mediterranean, where he often went sailing as a young man. Even Robinson joined in and became much more amiable after a few drinks. Edgerton left after dessert was served and the rest of them stayed behind to smoke cigars. Gabriel spoke to Granville about his thoughts on Plato's the *Republic*, and as the night got darker they spoke of ancient myths. Granville asked him questions, interesting questions, and truly listened to his answers.

When Robinson had also left, and it was just Beaufort and them, they spoke of religion. Granville turned to Gabriel, and asked:

'Do you believe in an afterlife, Gabriel?'

Gabriel hesitated before answering, slightly surprised at Granville's straightforwardness. 'To believe in an afterlife, one must be religious.'

'Yes, in some cases.'

'I have lost my faith,' said Gabriel unflinchingly. 'I have

lost it and it has not come back. Therefore, I presume my atonement is not God's will.'

'Too much faith inhibits man from thinking critically.' Granville took a long puff from his cigar. 'But I am wondering, what event could lead to a loss of something so ingrained within our society?'

Gabriel's body stiffened. 'Family.'

'Family,' repeated Granville. 'Many would call it one of the fiercest things in existence.'

'I would not. After all, what is family when compared to greed? Envy? Wrath? Kronos devoured his own children in the hopes his power would never be diminished.'

'Yet, there is also love. Affection and care. Was it not for love that Orpheus ventured into the underworld? For the affection he had for his beloved wife?'

'Was it not for pride that Achilles left hundreds of men to die?'

Granville's eyes shone under the light cast by the crystal chandelier. 'You believe greed trumps this?'

'I believe egotism trumps it.'

'Yet, I have a feeling you do not adhere to this notion yourself.'

Gabriel took a deep breath. 'No. I do not.'

'Interesting.'

'Our world has existed for millions of years. It saw the wrath of gods and heroes, witnessed ancient wars and battles, the downfall of kings and emperors. What remained unchanged, even to this day, are the rudimental emotions causing these events. Greed. Envy. Wrath. Therefore, how can one say that these do not come above love? Menelaus

did not start the Trojan war for his love of Helen, but instead did so as it undermined his power as a ruler. He did it due to his ego, wishing to impose his wrath upon the city.'

Granville smiled, not a demeaning smile, but rather one filled to the brim with an ancient omniscience. 'And yet, Menelaus's wrath and ego obtained him Troy. No man is ever free of sin, Gabriel. At times, he can even use it to his advantage. What matters above all is if the ends really do justify your means. Each person is only trying to do good in their own eyes.'

Eventually, when the clock struck midnight, it was time to go.

As Gabriel stepped into the night, a part of the weight he carried within him lifted. He felt as though for the first time, his life had direction. He had someone who cared about him. Someone who saw his potential.

He had found a purpose.

CHAPTER XXV

Harvey Blythe

'And I was not invited?' exclaimed Alexander.

Gabriel shifted in his chair. They had met in the London library, surrounded by the literature of the ancient world, of forgotten cultures and formidable lands. They were seated at a corner table, overlooking St James's Square.

'It appears you weren't,' said Gabriel uncomfortably.

'How discourteous,' muttered Alexander, crossing his arms over his chest.

'Well, forget about that. I believe I have discovered a new clue.'

'Do go on.'

'Harvey Blythe.'

Alexander frowned. 'Harvey Blythe? *The* crime lord, Harvey Blythe?'

'Yes,' stated Gabriel, leaning forward onto the table. 'Precisely.'

'Bloody hell,' muttered Alexander. 'Are you certain about that?'

'Yes. Well, that is what I have been told, but it makes *sense*. I cannot believe we had not thought of it before.'

'Probably because Blythe would skin us the second we even looked in his direction,' muttered Alexander.

'Blythe has the monopoly on gambling, he has gangs that work for him, and he is involved in the opium trade,' continued Gabriel. 'It is very plausible he might have something to do with this as well.'

Alexander's eyes widened as he turned to look at Gabriel. 'This could explain why the police are neglecting this investigation. Blythe could have simply bribed them all.' Alexander ran a hand through his hair. 'Christ…'

*

Gabriel and Alexander standing before the Silverton. It was London's most exclusive gambling club, and Alexander had spent all day trying to obtain an invitation. In the end, he had managed it, for the extortionate sum of £100 each for a single night.

Mayfair buzzed with excitement. Carriages lined the street, all heading for the same destination. Colourful gowns and gleaming suits flowed before them in waves, laughter filling the air like perfume.

Alexander scoffed. 'These are the very same people who detest brothels and pubs, yet they come here to do the very same thing.'

'In more extravagant surroundings, of course,' said Gabriel.

'And with incredibly expensive entry,' muttered Alexander as he handed the doorman their tickets.

The club was a palace filled with opulence and dim lights, crystals and silk, opportunity and loss. It hung in the air around them, clung to their tongues like copper. Lustful gazes between handsome pairings, passionate embraces of joy by friends. The suppression of distraught expressions, the celebration of winnings. The main hall was filled with round tables. To Gabriel's surprise, half of them were occupied by women.

Gabriel's eyes fell upon a woman sitting on the table nearest to them. Her thin, gloved hands held the cards elegantly, her wrist adorned with a thick diamond bracelet. Her dark hair was done up, just above the nape of her long neck. Alexander started walking forward, heading down the clearing of the room as his eyes scanned the tables. Gabriel swallowed hard. He wondered if his father had ever frequented a place such as this. Perhaps he had lost a portion of their money on one of these very tables, played alongside the men who now breathed the same air as Gabriel. He cleared his throat before following Alexander, letting his gaze wander over concentrated gentlemen, their colourful companions, blood-red curtains hanging down from an endlessly high ceiling. A smirk caught his gaze, a small turning up of pink lips, a glisten in a brown, hooded eye. The club smelt of perfume and whisky, wrapping itself around Gabriel's nostrils.

They had neared the bar at the end of the gambling area. Alexander ordered himself a drink.

'What now?' asked Gabriel.

'We watch people.' Alexander leaned back, shooting him a grin. 'And gamble.'

Alexander took a hold of his drink, which the bartender had just set down, and started to approach one of the tables. Gabriel grabbed him by the collar, yanking him back to the bar.

'Christ, Ashmore!' exclaimed Alexander. 'What on earth are you doing?'

'I do not believe now is the time for a game of poker,' Gabriel hissed.

'We must blend in,' stated Alexander. 'How else do you expect—'

'No,' said Gabriel, in a tone so cold it stopped Alexander's insistence.

*

After half an hour in the main hall, Gabriel and Alexander ventured into one of the private lounges of the club to re-think their strategy.

'I could not see a sign of the Erebus,' said Alexander as he inspected a Roman head statue. Upon the walls hung exquisite paintings held by golden frames. Various sets of cigars were readied on one of the coffee tables. Gabriel had picked up the Highclere Castle, smelling its tobacco.

'Those cigars shall ruin your teeth. I suggest you do not smoke them,' stated Alexander.

Before Gabriel could answer, the door opened, revealing a trio of gentlemen. The middle one, appearing

to be the youngest, sported a mournful expression, his red brows twisted together in frustration. His companions gave him a pat on the back.

'Good evening,' greeted one of them, a rather heavy man with a thick moustache. A sheen of sweat was visible on his forehead.

Gabriel nodded. Alexander smiled politely.

'Thompson here has just lost his house,' the moustached man announced with an amused grin, before seating himself next to Gabriel. Gabriel shot them a glance out of the corner of his eyes.

'Goodness,' muttered Alexander. 'Not quite your lucky day, eh?'

'Certainly not,' said the unfortunate young man, rubbing his eyes. He had pinkish skin, which appeared even more aggravated due to his current stress.

'It's quite all right, Thompson, it was only the Mrs's favourite one,' the moustached man joked.

Thompson cursed, throwing his head back on the back of the sofa. 'I really thought I was going to win. Bloody hell, I would have won a fortune. Damn that Hughes. He's gotten all of it; he does not even have possession of a wife, nothing to maintain! This is of the utmost absurdity; I reckon if I had not—'

'Yes, all right,' said the third man as he fumbled in his blazer pocket, pulling out two pouches. He tossed one towards Thompson, keeping the other to himself.

'This should cheer you right up.' He slicked his mousy brown hair back, licking his lips before carefully prying the pouch open with his slim fingers. 'I have obtained the Black

Opium that everyone has been speaking of lately.'

Gabriel's head cocked towards them. Alexander's eyes came to a rest on the pouch.

The man poured the black powder out onto the table. Gabriel felt his stomach rattle at the sight of it.

'Where did you obtain this?' asked Alexander, taking a step forward.

The third man looked up at him with uninterested eyes, irritated at the interruption. 'I cannot remember.'

'Did you obtain it here?'

The man contemplated his question. 'I must have done so. I had quite a few drinks, you see? My memory can get hazy at times. Now, if you would excuse me.'

Gabriel rose to his feet. 'Do not consume that. It shall lead to your death.'

The moustached man chuckled at Gabriel's words. 'Are you two not joining in today?' he asked, grinning. 'Or perhaps you're just observing. I would be more than happy to share our tricks with you. If you start counting—'

'In all fairness, I do not wish to hear your useless tricks, especially since you just managed to lose tremendously,' said Gabriel, rising from the sofa. As he left for the exit, he snatched up the Erebus from the table. The moustached man blinked, mouth half-open in shock.

'Do not consume this,' stated Gabriel. 'Unless you wish to die a horrible death.'

'That was rather rude,' muttered Alexander as they entered the main hall of the club again. 'They seemed relatively harmless.'

'They were relatively idiotic, and we do not have time for chitchat. The Erebus distributor is here. Look out for him.'

CHAPTER XXVI

A Judge Before a Father

Gabriel's head pounded. He stood in the entryway, away from the tumult and music, the crowds and cards. He had failed to find any sign of whoever was distributing the Erebus. Perhaps Beaufort's findings were outdated. Perhaps Blythe no longer distributed the Erebus.

He saw his reflection in an antique mirror. A reflection of black smears and scratches upon the material, his own alien face staring back at him. Dark circles, a scar, dry lips and sharp bones. That is what he narrowed himself down to and that was what he was. At that very moment, he was nothing else.

Sharp laughter reverberated in the air around him. Gabriel looked around, but the foyer was empty. It sounded again, an orchestra of them this time. Gabriel's gaze fell on a set of wooden doors, right beside him. It was left ajar, spilling a warm, intense light onto the

marbled floor. He heard chatter as he neared it. It must just be another lounge, thought Gabriel, and turned his back, ready to enter the main hall, before a clear voice cut through the air like a blade. It was a voice unlike any he had heard before; a euphonious yet brittle sound, laced with a sense of great authority. Gabriel stepped closer, holding his breath as he peered into the room. A group of five gentlemen were sitting by a round, oak table. A grand fire roared behind them. The room was hazy, filled with the smoke of pipes and cigars. And, at the very top of the table, sat Harvey Blythe.

Harvey Blythe held a black pipe in one hand, the other laid flat upon the armrest of his chair. He had a narrow face, alongside a thin strip of a black moustache. His black hair was slicked back, not even one strand out of place. Black pits of eyes stared ahead, devoid of any emotion whatsoever. A grey-haired man from beside him leaned forwards, his lips moving incoherently, to which Blythe turned his head; and that was the exact moment Gabriel saw the mask slip upon his face.

Blythe's eyes filled with pride and joy as he listened to the man beside him. He smiled in agreement, a smile which even reached those despondent eyes. He wore a blood-red tie. His suit was coloured a dark grey, decorated with thin, grey lines; its material gleaming under the chandelier above them. Yet, the grey-haired man's expression remained stern, his eyes flickering to an individual across the table. Blythe took a long puff from his pipe, exhaling the smoke out into the air. Through it, Gabriel only saw those narrow

eyes before it cleared. Blythe rose from his chair, buttoning his blazer. The chatter of the men around him fell silent. The shadows of the room made his face appear skull-like, carved out like an ancient trunk of a tree.

'*God is merciful to all, as he has been to you; he is first a father, then a judge.*' Blythe smiled, a smile of elation yet also sharpness. 'Can anybody tell me which passage this proverb is from?'

The group of men all remained silent, looking at each other from the corner of their eyes.

Blythe raised an eyebrow. 'Anyone?'

'Matthew?' guessed a thin man, sat near the end of the table.

Blythe's features twisted into amusement. 'Close. Alexandre Dumas. *The Count of Monte Cristo.*' He tutted. 'You are all terrible Christians.' He took a glass of wine from the table. 'I thank you all for joining me here.' His voice vibrated in the air, wrapping itself around Gabriel's eardrums. He raised his glass. 'First and foremost, a toast to our dear Douglas. Congratulations on the safe arrival of your ship. I hear you went to Calcutta yourself to oversee the opium production?'

'Yes, sir,' a man, sat on his right side, said.

'Tell us, how did you find India?'

'It was an adventure, to say the least.'

Several of the men chuckled.

'Now, I wish I could say we all share Douglas's success.' His eyes skimmed the room, predatory in their movement as they passed each of the men. 'Alas, I am afraid some of us, have rather suffered a great deal.'

The entire room descended into an even deeper silence, a silence so profound Gabriel thought the men must have stopped breathing. He himself, had stopped breathing.

Blythe's eyes were cold and hard; a different mask present upon them now. His jawline, so tense, as if it would snap out of place at any minute. He put a step forward, his movements like clockwork. He brushed his hand on the back of the wooden chairs as he made his way around the table. The veins in his hands protruded from his skin, the way it would in the elderly, although Blythe looked no older than thirty-five. He came to a halt behind a fair-haired, young man, both his hands clenching the chair. Colour rose to the man's cheeks, large blotches of red. His hands, placed upon the table, shook. His breathing was fragmented, his chest shaking as it rose up and down. His blue irises were muddled with redness forming in the corner of his eyes.

'Please, Mr Blythe, I did not mean to...' he sputtered, his voice breaking.

Blythe nodded, a strange calmness presiding over his features. 'Of course, Daniel.' He placed his hands upon his shoulders, resting them lightly. Daniel flinched. 'Of course you did not mean to. You only tried to steal what is mine.' He looked up at the table of men, sitting so still they appeared like statues. A coldness spread across Blythe's face, before he placed his hands upon the back of Daniel's head and slammed it into the table. Gabriel flinched at the sudden sound echoing throughout the room. The men at the table remained silent and unmoving, their lips pressed together in a fine line. Blood gushed from Daniel's nose,

broken at an odd angle. He let out a loud groan, attempting to heave himself up, but instead Blythe intertwined his fingers in his hair and slammed his head down again, and again, and again, until Gabriel had lost count and Daniel's face was nothing more than a deformed red lump. Blythe sighed as he let Daniel's head go, his body slumping to the ground. Gabriel swallowed away the bile that had formed in his throat, attempting to block out the sound of blood pumping in his ears.

Blythe produced a handkerchief from his breast pocket and carefully wiped away the blood that had spattered onto his face. He looked down at his sleeve, upon which multiple blood stains had imprinted themselves.

'Pity,' he muttered as he wiped his hands on the handkerchief, before dropping it onto Daniel's body. Then, his eyes met Gabriel's. 'I hope you enjoyed the show.'

Gabriel inhaled sharply, taking a step back. Before he could distance himself further, the door swung open, revealing Blythe before him. His eyes appeared even darker up close, an empty, black pit, now filled with an odd curiosity. Gabriel stared back at him, watching his eyelids narrow.

'Do introduce yourself,' said Blythe.

Gabriel hesitated, letting his eyes rush over the men sat around the table, all staring at him with expressions of shock, curiosity and, for some, indifference. 'Richard Morgan,' he said finally.

Blythe's eyebrows rose, ever so slightly. A flicker of something passed over his face, something which could have meant anything within that assortment of emotions,

carefully selected to best suit the situation. 'Who are you, Richard Morgan?'

'Nobody.'

Blythe chuckled sharply. 'Nobody?' He took a step closer, his head moving to the side like that of a reptile as he analysed Gabriel. 'What a creative answer. What are you looking for?'

'Nothing.'

'He was spying on us, Harvey!' an old man gargled from the table. Gabriel's eyes fell on him. The first thing he noticed was the man's fat around his neck, spilling over the collar of his blazer. His skin was coloured a light pink, already reddening as he looked at Gabriel with anger lining his gaze. Gabriel shot him a glare.

'Were you indeed spying on us, Mr Morgan?' asked Blythe.

Gabriel sighed, looking Blythe straight in the eyes as he relaxed his posture, rolling his shoulders back. 'Yes, I was.'

And there it was. The flicker of surprise within Blythe's eyes, the crack in the façade.

'I wish to find out more about the Erebus,' Gabriel continued.

Blythe stared at him blankly for a few seconds, before chuckling loudly. A few seconds later, the men behind him joined in, until the room was filled with the chorus of seeming amusement.

Gabriel pressed his lips together until they formed a thin line, his shoulders tense. Blythe turned to face the men behind him, amusement dancing within his eyes.

'Did you hear that, gentlemen?' he said, before turning back. Something else danced within his eyes now, something close to a warning. 'Do you believe I would associate myself with such lowly business?' He chuckled again before Gabriel could answer, lifting his arms up. 'Look at this place. Filled to the brim with politicians and men of the law. Rich men and women coming from hundreds of years' worth of wealth. And you insinuate my involvement with a petty new drug distribution?' He laughed sharply. 'A drug that does not even *work*?'

Before Gabriel could answer, Blythe's eyes landed on something behind him. Gabriel could see the turn of the cog, the exchange of anger for curiosity.

'And who may this be?'

Gabriel turned around. His posture stiffened. Alexander stepped towards them, eyes slightly widened as he took in Blythe and the body upon the floor. Gabriel wanted to curse, kick him, for joining them. He shot Alexander a glare, who came to a halt beside him.

'Oscar Wright,' he answered, his voice surprisingly steady. He held out his hand, which Blythe, after a second of contemplation, shook. 'It is a real delight to be able to meet you in person, Mr Blythe. We thank you for welcoming us to your club, its extravagance is unrivalled.'

Blythe eyed Alexander with precision, raising his chin slightly.

'We work for an opium trader,' continued Alexander, articulating every word confidently. 'And were sent to find out more about the new drug that has been gaining popularity. We had thought we could perhaps strike a deal;

we only came here to see if you may know more, Mr Blythe, as you know everything that goes on in the city.'

Gabriel had imagined Blythe to be flattered at the lies rolling off Alexander's tongue, instead, his eyes narrowed. 'An opium trader you say,' he started. He cracked his knuckles. 'My apologies, gentlemen, but that simply does not make any sense. All opium traders of any importance are sat behind me.'

Alexander's eyes fell on the chorus of men sitting behind the table, carefully watching them. And just as Gabriel thought he might give in, make a mistake, he smiled. 'Yes, of course. We work for Mr Zhāng. He has just recently moved to London from Shanghai. Therefore, he is yet to build his presence here in England.'

Blythe didn't shift his gaze from Alexander's for even a second, shooting a certain mercilessness, yet also, strangely, that same amusement from before; a puzzle which Gabriel could not solve. 'And what would this deal include?'

Alexander hesitated only for a second, a second so short Gabriel doubted even Blythe had registered it. 'An agreement. Mr Zhāng distributes the Erebus in China, where he has significant influence in the opium market, with the promise that whoever controls the Erebus distributes Mr Zhāng's opium here in London.'

Blythe stepped closer to them. Then, he grabbed Alexander's face, his nails digging into his skin. Gabriel instinctively stepped forward, but then stopped himself. Alexander's eyes were wide, his hands trembling by his side. Blythe leaned into his ear, his voice cold and venomous as he spoke.

'Tell *Mr Zhāng* that I am not the orchestrator behind all of this folly. I do not busy myself with foolish investments.' He released Alexander's face, who stumbled back.

'Very well, Mr Blythe,' said Gabriel, stepping in before Blythe. 'We are sorry to have wasted your—'

'Get out of my club.' His eyes flickered from Alexander to Gabriel, his jaw tense. 'Now.'

✳

Alexander was still shaken as they walked on Raphael Street. 'That went rather well,' he said as an attempt at humour, but his tone suggested the opposite.

Gabriel clenched his fists behind his back. 'Harvey Blythe is a bastard.'

'Careful, he might hear you.'

'Do you now understand why I believe the Conservative Justice Party shall be good for England? They aim to eliminate criminals such as Harvey Blythe; you saw what he did to that man.'

'Yes,' muttered Alexander. 'At least we did not end up like him…'

'He is lying to us,' stated Gabriel.

'I know.'

Gabriel adjusted his top hat. 'He was angry. Angry in regard to the Erebus. At our assumption. Why?'

'Perhaps he does not wish to be associated with it? He might believe it would harm his self-image.' Alexander's face fell in and out of illumination as they passed the lamps lining the street.

'Yes, but then why orchestrate it all? And why did he just let us go? Why not get us arrested for trespassing? Or worse? We must go back.' Gabriel's green eyes shone with vivacity.

'Excuse me?

Gabriel halted, his eyes latched on to Alexander's. 'We must go back to investigate. He must have an office of some sort in his club.'

Alexander raised his eyebrows. 'You wish to *break into* Harvey Blythe's club?'

Gabriel's lips quirked up. 'Yes.'

CHAPTER XXVII

Xing Yang

'Are we truly planning on breaking into the Silverton Club?'

Gabriel took a sip of coffee. 'Indeed.'

Gabriel had been unable to sleep, so he had made his way to the Wakefield mansion in the early morning, to find Alexander suffering from the same dilemma. Rays of the morning sun started creeping into the study, a strange and beautiful light, a lost period between the past and present. Gabriel took a bite of one of the breakfast pastries Alexander's maids had prepared, filling the room with the rich aroma of butter and sugar.

'And how on earth do you plan to do that, Ashmore?'

Gabriel picked up a copy of *The Times*. The headline '*MURDERS REMAIN UNSOLVED, MURDERER REMAINS ON THE LOOSE AS BODIES PILE UP*' decorated the front page, alongside a caricature of the prime

minister, Gascoyne-Cecil, running away from the Houses of Parliament. Gabriel swore as he read the article. 'Five more people have died.' He passed the newspaper to Alexander. 'This is why we must act, no matter how dangerous it is.'

Alexander read further down the newspaper. 'The MPs are going to call in a vote of no confidence.'

'Thank God,' muttered Gabriel.

'There are rumours that even the queen is deeply unsatisfied,' stated Alexander.

'Yes, well, the queen, in this case, is pretty much useless.'

'How sacrilegious!'

'Oh please,' said Gabriel, rolling his eyes, 'I am certain you think the exact same thing.'

'Not exactly. I quite like Queen Victoria.'

Gabriel chuckled. 'And why, may I ask?'

'She seems deeply loyal. I believe it makes her quite likeable.'

'Loyal?' questioned Gabriel. 'How so?'

'Well, it is quite evident in her dedication to her former husband, Prince Albert. When he passed away, it devasted her so much that she only wears black now. My father met him a few times, he said he was a great fellow.'

'Ah,' muttered Gabriel. 'I always wondered why she dressed so drearily.'

'Did you not know that?'

'No.'

Alexander grinned.

Gabriel narrowed his eyes at him. 'What?'

'Nothing. It is just very rewarding to know something you do not. You tend to be such a know-it-all.'

Gabriel scoffed. 'Inconsequential matters, such as the love life of a monarch who does not even reign, do not interest me.'

'Are you calling the queen inconsequential?'

'Yes, that is exactly what I am doing. She has barely even been involved in public life.'

Alexander raised an eyebrow, sporting a bemused expression. 'I believe the monarchy is of great importance. History has always been inanimate. A wall of a crumbled castle. A parchment. A painting. But a monarch is a living piece of history. Their lineage goes back to all those great leaders of the past.'

'Well, it is great that you think so,' said Gabriel, 'and although I would be delighted to further discuss the monarchy with you, I am afraid we must solve a series of murders first.'

＊

Gabriel and Alexander headed back to Mayfair. Careful not to be seen, they inspected the building of the Silverton Club, looking for any entrances they could utilise. During the day, it served as a private gentlemen's lounge, and therefore it was less busy. The front entrance was impossible as it was manned twenty-four hours a day and equipped with the strongest lock on the market. They checked the windows, which were all crafted of thick glass, with no way of opening them. Their only option would be to break it, which would notify the guards and lead to their most definite demise. Their best bet was to climb to either the top or the upper

floors of the building, whose windows appeared less sturdy, and find a way in through there.

'This task appears to be impossible,' muttered Alexander.

Gabriel stared at the tall building, following it all the way to the top. Then, an image came to his mind. The image of a woman with sharp eyes and raven hair.

'You are wrong, Wakefield.' He turned to Alexander, eyes shining. 'I believe I know how to get in.'

*

Gabriel pushed through the crowds of Chinatown in Limehouse. He was looking for Xing Yang. He had made a wild guess as to her whereabouts, remembering the symbol on the bracelet she wore. He remembered seeing the exact same ornament, the same colouring and shape, hanging on the door of a Chinese restaurant he passed by each time to get to Sing's opium den. He knew he was being wishful; however, he was desperate.

He passed by various gambling dens, which were already operating in the early afternoon. Residents were out on the streets, washing their clothes and bedsheets. They looked at him strangely. He was an outsider to them. Gabriel refused to let his eyes fall upon the opium dens he passed. He kept his gaze steady, focused on the road ahead, until he had finally reached it. Qianfan's Restaurant. Gabriel looked up at the symbol hanging before him, bordered in azure ceramic. He took in a deep breath, hoping he would find what he was looking for, and entered the restaurant.

It was mostly empty, save for a group of men huddled at a corner table. Gabriel walked further into the restaurant. The men eyed him curiously. He reached the counter, leaning in to look into the kitchens.

'Hello?' he called out. After several seconds, a thin woman with short, black hair appeared.

'Yes?' she asked. 'How may I help?'

'I am looking for someone,' said Gabriel. 'Xing Yang.'

The woman's features went sour. 'No. No Yang Xing.' She turned away from him.

Before she could disappear back into the kitchen, Gabriel called out after her. 'I do not wish her any harm. I am here to offer her work.'

The woman halted, slowly turning back around. 'Who are you?'

'I am Gabriel Ashmore, madam,' said Gabriel, taking off his hat and bowing slightly. 'I wish to offer Miss Yang work, in exchange for a large compensation.'

The woman's eyes narrowed as she stared at him. A minute passed, before she finally nodded. 'Yang Xing is there,' she said, pointing at the street.

'In the house opposite?' asked Gabriel.

The woman nodded. Gabriel thanked her before heading back out onto the street. He approached the low-built terraced house. It was falling apart. The windows were cracked, the bricks coming loose. Gabriel knocked on the door, which rattled on its hinges. He stepped back, waiting.

The door opened, and before him stood Xing Yang. Her hair was loose, thick dark strands tumbling down her

shoulders. She was only wearing trousers and a bodice. Gabriel looked away.

'You,' she said, leaning against the doorway. She crossed her arms over her chest. 'How did you find me?'

'An educated guess.'

'How?'

'Your bracelet.'

'You do not need to look away. I am hardly a lady,' said Xing.

Gabriel met her eyes. 'Lady or not, a woman is entitled to privacy.'

Xing chuckled. 'Says the man that came all the way to my doorstep. I assume you need my help?'

Gabriel nodded. 'I need you to break into the Silverton.'

She raised her eyebrows. 'Harvey Blythe's gambling club?'

'Yes.'

'Are you aware of the difficulty? Guards patrolling the entire building every few minutes, all windows and doors reinforced with steel and the best locks money can buy, an underground safe set within a labyrinth, so nobody will even be able to reach it to try and crack the code?'

Gabriel's eyes narrowed. 'It seems as though you have tried it before.'

Xing shook her head. 'No. I have only studied it.'

'Is there any way in?'

'Yes.'

'How?'

Xing's lips curved into a smirk. 'Mr Ashmore, do you truly believe me that foolish?'

Gabriel ground his teeth. 'Will you help us or not?'

'Yes. On one condition.'

'We shall pay you however much money you wish.'

Her eyes narrowed. 'I do not want money.'

Gabriel frowned. 'What is it that you want, then?'

'I want safe passage to China. To Guangzhou.' Her eyes shone brightly as she spoke, stepping closer to Gabriel. 'Can you guarantee me that?'

Gabriel thought about her request. He did not know any sailors that could bring her across safely, but he knew one person. Hugo. He had told him he frequently traded with China, so he must be able to offer transport on one of his ships. Gabriel held out his hand. 'Only if you can guarantee you can break into the Silverton.'

Xing's eyes gleamed boldly as she shook his hand.

*

'Excuse me?' exclaimed Alexander with wide eyes. 'What were you thinking?'

'We have no other option, Wakefield.'

Gabriel had returned to the Wakefield residence to notify Alexander of Xing Yang's participation.

'And therefore you employed a Chinese *criminal* to help us? Someone who has broken into *Buckingham Palace* and stolen from the *queen*?'

'Well, technically, she stole from Princess Beatrice. I am certain that old hag has enough diamonds to—'

'That is not the point, Ashmore,' snapped Alexander. 'We are going against everything we stand for—'

'What we stand for does not matter if people keep dying,' hissed Gabriel. 'What do we become if we are not willing to do what is necessary? We would be the same as the police force, useless and afraid. This is what sets us apart; we are willing to do whatever it takes. *Whatever it takes*, Wakefield.'

Alexander sighed, running his hands through his hair. 'How much money does she want?'

'She does not want any money. She wants safe passage to Guangzhou.'

'How are we—'

'I will arrange it.'

'How?'

'My brother. He is a merchant.'

Alexander paced across his library. 'Well, I suppose we have no other choice.'

'Are you two done arguing now?' said Xing Yang, strolling into the library.

Alexander's eyes widened, a mortified expression plastered upon his face. He turned to Gabriel.

'You had her present this entire time?'

Gabriel pressed his lips together. 'Well, I did not think you would have such an aversion to the idea.'

Alexander shot Gabriel a look of annoyance. 'I am truly sorry, madam. I was not aware—'

'Oh, save it,' said Xing. 'When is the soonest you can get me on that ship?'

'Next week,' answered Gabriel.

'All right. Let us get started on this right away, then.' She marched towards the table, picking up a large sheet

of parchment and sketching large lines upon it. She wore a jumper and a hooded black robe on top of it, with the same trousers Gabriel had seen her in earlier. She had long boots on, which reached to her knees. People seeing her on the street must have assumed her to be a man, which Gabriel believed was exactly her intention. Her sleek hair was pinned at the nape of her neck.

Gabriel and Alexander neared her, peering over her shoulder to see what she was drawing. They noticed she had sketched the Silverton Club, with all of its windows and exits.

She pointed at the front doors. 'Two guards are stationed here. Another guard patrols around the building.' She pointed to the roof of the building. 'I believe there may be an entrance here that I can gain access to.'

'That is six floors up,' stated Alexander.

'Yes, I am aware,' said Xing. 'With the guard patrolling around the building, I would only have a total of ten seconds to climb the wall, which is impossible. Therefore, I shall need you two to distract the guard for a total of sixty seconds. That is all I need. After you have done that, I can make my own way out. I shall meet you two back at this house.'

Alexander raised an eyebrow, clearly impressed. Gabriel shot him a glance, stating 'I told you so'.

'If I do not arrive back at this house an hour after my entry, then you must assume I am dead.'

Alexander looked at Gabriel with a slightly horrified expression.

Xing leaned back in her chair. 'Now, tell me what I am exactly looking for in the Silverton Club.'

'Well, that is a great question. An excellent question, really,' said Alexander. 'We would be—'

'We do not know,' stated Gabriel simply.

Xing raised an eyebrow.

'We are looking for something in relation to the Erebus – the Black Opium on the market. Anything that links Blythe to it, or any other clue in relation to the substance. I am assuming you have a certain skillset in locating items?' Gabriel thought back to the yellow diamond necklace.

Xing nodded.

'Well, that could come in useful for this task. Is everything clear?'

'Most certainly,' stated Xing. 'When do we start?'

CHAPTER XXVIII

The Silverton Club

Their carriage halted a street away from the Silverton Club. They had arrived at four in the morning. An hour after closing time. Gabriel, Alexander and Xing stepped out of the carriage, all dressed in black. Xing had a hooded cloak on, concealing her face.

Gabriel inhaled the cold air, letting it prickle his lungs. The three of them remained in the shadows as they made their way to the club. The Mayfair streets were engulfed in a deep silence: a city drowned in deep slumber, yet to awake.

As they rounded the corner of South Audley Street into Deanery Street, the Silverton Club appeared in the distance. They saw the faint outline of two guards before the entrance.

Gabriel took out his pocket watch, before turning to face them. 'Xing, make sure to be where you need to be at exactly ten past four. Alexander and I shall cause a

commotion in nine minutes. I estimate the guards shall take around a minute to investigate this, which gives you the opportunity to strike.'

'Shall we decide on an emergency call?' asked Alexander.

Both Gabriel and Xing turned to look at him. 'What?' questioned Gabriel.

'A specific sound we produce if we are in distress. Like a mating call, but for the opposite purposes.'

'If we are in that much distress, then we're already dead,' stated Xing.

'All right,' muttered Alexander.

'Alexander and I shall break the windows of the house beside the Silverton. That ought to distract the guards long enough for you, Xing.'

'What if it does not? What is your back-up plan?'

Alexander scratched his head, looking at Gabriel for guidance. Gabriel blinked.

'Well, that is pretty much the only plan we have got,' answered Alexander.

Xing sighed. 'You better make it work because I am not dying in this godforsaken country.'

'Why do you reside here if you detest it so?' questioned Gabriel.

Xing's jaw tightened. 'I am not here out of choice, Mr Ashmore.'

'Then why are you here?'

Alexander shot him a frown, dismayed at Gabriel's blunt inquisitiveness.

'I was taken from my family in Guangzhou,' Xing said. 'I was only four years old. I have been here ever since.'

Gabriel's mouth went dry. That is why she wished for passage to China. 'Oh, I am sorry.'

'That must have been very difficult,' said Alexander sympathetically.

'Yes. It was,' said Xing. She did not say another word as she pointed at her watch, and then disappeared into the shadows.

Gabriel sighed as they started to head towards the club. He watched Xing head to the east wing of the building, her agile body flowing and morphing with the shadows around her. They stayed hidden in the doorway of a large mansion, peeking at the guards. They leant on the door, their faces sporting bored expressions.

Gabriel checked the time on his pocket watch. Eight past four.

'Something tells me this plan shall go horribly wrong,' muttered Alexander, taking out a handful of rocks from his pocket.

'It certainly shall,' stated Gabriel. He looked at his watch. Eight past nine. 'Ready?'

'As ready as I shall ever be.'

They stepped out onto the pavement. They pulled their shoulders back, gaining traction, and then slung two large rocks into the shop beside the Silverton. The glass shattered like ice, creating an ear-deafening sound as it rained upon the street. Gabriel and Alexander disappeared around the corner, just as the guards' heads whipped towards them. They listened from behind the wall, the voices of the guards coming closer and closer. They stepped further down the street in an attempt to remain hidden, before suddenly halting.

The third guard stood behind them. He must have taken a shortcut, through the back of the houses. He grimaced at them, baring his crooked teeth as he stepped closer. He was intimidatingly tall and broad, towering over the two of them.

'Causing unrest now, are we?' he growled.

Gabriel swore as they both stepped back.

'Well, you two are coming with me.'

Just as he reached forward to grab them, Gabriel saw something whizz before him. The guard fell back, groaning in pain as he clutched his forehead.

Gabriel frowned, turning to look at Alexander. He had thrown a rock at the guard's face. Voices, then footsteps, sounded behind them.

Alexander looked at him, with panic yet also excitement shining from his eyes. 'Run.'

And so, they broke into a sprint. They ran down the street they had come from. The guards followed behind them. They weren't as fast as Gabriel and Alexander, but they had stamina. After several minutes, they found themselves back in South Audley Street. The carriage stood in the distance. Gabriel panted, his lungs burning as he forced his legs to go faster.

They had finally reached the carriage. Gabriel glanced at Alexander, his face red and blotched, and then looked back at the horses. 'Are you thinking what I am thinking?'

Alexander coughed, nodding his head. 'Let's do it, Ashmore.'

As the guards finally reached them, Gabriel and Alexander had climbed atop the horses. The guards looked at them

with wide eyes as they began to gallop down the street. They jumped out of the way as the two horses charged past. Gabriel held on to the black horse's long mane as he headed back towards Deanery Street, Alexander following closely behind on the white one. The cold wind blew through his hair and shirt, lighting his nerves on fire. The guards ran after them. They came to a halt before the Silverton. Gabriel looked up at the building. Xing was nowhere to be seen, which meant she had succeeded. She had broken into the Silverton Club.

The edge of Gabriel's lips quirked into a smile. Alexander came to a halt beside him, a grin plastered upon his face.

'We did it, Ashmore,' he chuckled. 'We did it.'

Several moments later, the voices of the guards rang through the street again. Gabriel and Alexander repositioned themselves on the horses, shooting one last glance at the club, before galloping away.

CHAPTER XXIX

The Letter

Thirty minutes passed before Xing arrived. Gabriel and Alexander were waiting in the Wakefield library. Alexander paced continuously, and Gabriel impatiently bit his nails as he looked out the window for any sign of her.

'Thank God,' exclaimed Alexander, as she strolled into the library as if she had merely gone out for a walk. Her long hair had become loose, falling down her shoulders. Her cheeks had a red tint to them. She had a letter in her hand, which she threw upon the table.

'How did you escape?' asked Gabriel.

'The guards are idiots,' she stated, cracking her knuckles. Gabriel noticed that her hands were covered in cuts and bruises, her fingernails split and broken. 'They did not even notice me come down until I hit the ground. After

that, it was easy. I just ran. They could not keep up with me, so they gave up eventually.'

'We are glad you are all right,' said Alexander. Gabriel could tell he meant it.

Xing only nodded awkwardly.

Gabriel grabbed a hold of the letter. It appeared old, slightly crumbling at the edges and discoloured due to sun exposure.

'It is written by a doctor named Heinrich Wagner.'

Alexander took the letter from Gabriel, his eyes moving back and forth as he read its contents.

Dear Mr Blythe,

I hope this letter finds you well. The delivery of the trial product has been scheduled for Monday. It ought to arrive in a wooden crate, no later than the afternoon. Please let me know how the product fares and if any complications present themselves.

Yours sincerely,
Dr Heinrich Wagner.

His eyes lit up. He looked back at Xing.

'Thank you for your services,' said Alexander.

'Where did you find this?' asked Gabriel.

'In a safe.'

Gabriel raised his eyebrows. 'You managed to crack into a safe?'

'Yes.'

'How? Harvey Blythe uses the most advanced safes—'

'There was a locksmith near the orphanage I grew up

210

in. I helped him out in his shop and in return he taught me a few tricks.' She smiled slightly. 'I still occasionally visit him.'

Alexander poured them all a glass of gin. He brought the glasses back to them, handing one to Xing and then to Gabriel. He raised his glass. 'This calls for a celebration.'

Gabriel shook his head.

'Oh, come on, Ashmore. We have progressed massively in our case. We deserve a drink.'

Gabriel looked back at Xing, who had already drunk the entirety of her gin. She looked at them blankly.

'You two were taking too long.'

Alexander sighed. 'Right, come on.' He held up his glass, raising his eyebrows at Gabriel. 'Just this once.'

Gabriel rolled his eyes, before clinking his glass with Alexander's and swallowing the burning liquid.

Alexander scrunched up his nose, smacking his lips together. 'God, I always forgot how strong that gin is.'

Gabriel picked up the letter, re-reading it. 'We must go back to the library tomorrow and find out whatever we can about this Dr Wagner.'

'Certainly,' said Alexander, sinking into an armchair. 'Do you wish to join us, Miss Yang?'

She shook her head. 'I must prepare for my departure.'

Gabriel took out a note from his pocket and handed it to Xing. 'This is my brother's name. Meet us at the given location. The time and date are on there, too. Keep in mind that the journey takes around six months or more, dependent on weather conditions, so prepare accordingly.'

Gabriel had not asked Hugo about it yet, but he knew his brother would agree to it.

Xing nodded. 'Thank you, Mr Ashmore.'

'Good luck,' said Gabriel. 'I hope you make it to your family.'

Xing smiled. It was not a half-smile, nor was it a smirk, but it was a genuine smile which transformed her features into something wonderful.

CHAPTER XXX

―――•・•―――

The Doctor

'Here,' said Gabriel, pulling out a large leather-bound book from the shelf.

They were back at the London Library at St James's Square, occupying a corner table filled with gaslight and the burning smell of candles. Gabriel seated himself beside Alexander, placing the book upon the table.

The Principles of Dissection, written and researched by Heinrich Wagner.

Alexander raised his brows, glancing at Gabriel. 'Ah, he seems like a lovely individual.'

Gabriel leaned forward, letting his eyes skim the text. 'Apart from creating deadly opium variants, our doctor also appears to have a great passion for dissections.' He pointed to the third paragraph on the page. 'Here he even makes the argument that the medical sector ought to increase the number of human dissections they perform.'

Alexander pushed his glasses up the bridge of his nose. He raised a quizzical eyebrow. 'And it appears he is also an advocate of human experiments. God. Let us be careful not to end up on a surgical table.'

'Indeed. Have you found an address within it?'

Alexander leaned back on his chair. The candlelight cast shadows upon half of his face, whilst accentuating the sharp angles of the other. He sighed. 'No.'

Gabriel rose from his chair, heading back towards the bookshelf. He brushed his fingers over the spines, before finding another book with Dr Wagner's name upon it.

'These concern surgery,' stated Gabriel as he passed the book towards Alexander.

'Ah, so he is a surgeon as well. What a talented individual we have here.' He flicked through the pages of the book.

'Yes, a man of many talents…' muttered Gabriel, rolling his sleeves up as he looked over Alexander's shoulder.

After several minutes of flicking through each page, Alexander slammed the book shut. Dust particles rose up in the air, right where a sliver of daylight shone in. 'No address.'

'There must be some sort of indication of where he is based within the text itself.'

'Yes, and that would require we read about 1,800 pages in total. Since he appears to also be an active surgeon, I say we go directly to St George's Hospital and enquire about him there, someone must know of him.'

Gabriel furrowed his brows. 'You want to visit St George's?' He chuckled. 'You must have a death wish.'

Alexander waved his hand dismissively. 'Oh, come on, it cannot be that bad.'

Gabriel scoffed. 'It most certainly is. Have you ever set foot in there?'

'Well, no, but—'

'The smell alone is unbearable. It makes your eyes water the second you step foot in the building. Then, let us not forget the actual diseases roaming every inch of the place like rats. Moreover, be prepared to carry the lingering smell of rotten flesh with you for several days.'

Gabriel still remembered the horrors he had witnessed when he was desperate to find Adelia medicine. She had become unwell during the night, and so it was the only place he could obtain something to soothe her pain.

Alexander's face had gone slightly white. He nervously chuckled. 'Oh, please. Perhaps seventy years ago, yes, but surely it has improved by now.'

'You can go in alone. Inform me of the findings later.'

Alexander scoffed. 'You cannot tell me that the tough Gabriel Ashmore is afraid of visiting a hospital.'

Gabriel could not care less about visiting the hospital. He was not scared of blood or pus or the smell of rotten flesh, it was the things he felt the last time that he was there that scared him. 'I do not believe it makes a difference if I accompany you or not.'

'It certainly does; you are my partner.'

'I do not think your plans of becoming a detective include me constantly at your side.'

'I know you are not exactly a benevolent person, but to send me to a house of death all alone would be unforgivably

cruel. Oh, and I shall increase your weekly wage.'

Gabriel let out a deep breath. He knew he had to face his fear sooner or later, and a part of him, a strange, unfamiliar part, did not wish for Alexander to go in alone.

'Fine,' he said eventually. 'It better be a good increase.'

CHAPTER XXXI

St George's Hospital

Thick fog hung over London the next morning, impenetrable waves engulfing the pedestrians with each step they took. Gabriel looked out his bedroom window. The corners of it had crystallised and snow had built up on the windowsill. He moved towards the mirror, righting his tie. He avoided looking at himself, but he still caught his reflection out of the corner of his eye. Exhaustion was evident in every inch of his face. He seemed thinner, making the angles of his face appear even sharper. He brushed his hair back, an attempt to make himself look more presentable, and left his room.

Gabriel's head pounded as he headed down the stairs. He still had that pesky tremor in his hands, caused by opium withdrawal. His body craved it, begged for it, each waking second. At night, as he lay awake, sweat dripping down his neck, when the memories came back to haunt him in the

solitude of the darkness, he would wish for nothing else but the blissful escape, those hours of numbness.

Gabriel halted. 'Father.'

Cassius stood in the foyer, dressed in his scarlet gown. His feet were bare. He looked up at Gabriel with that same despondency that lingered within his eyes ever since her death.

'I have forgotten why I am here,' he said blankly, looking around the foyer.

Gabriel carefully stepped down the staircase, as if approaching a wild animal. 'Were you about to get something to eat, perhaps?'

Cassius shook his head.

Gabriel still remembered how his father detested waking up earlier than he had to. Yet, he still did it, every morning, because his mother did. He wished to wake up before her, so he could prepare her breakfast and talk to her before he had to leave for work. He followed this routine like a ritual. Cassius's white-streaked brows were furrowed, deep in thought.

'Everything gets muddled these days; so very difficult to keep track of the thoughts.'

'Perhaps you should go lie down, Father. I can prepare you something.'

'No, no,' he muttered, turning away from Gabriel, shoulders hunched over, as he continued his train of thought. 'Ah!'

Gabriel watched as his father's eyes lit up and he made his way down the hall, disappearing into the kitchen. Gabriel clenched his jaw, pressing his lips together firmly

as he tried his hardest to suppress any emotion from breaking through the surface. He knew what his father had gone to do, and he knew that as he made his way upstairs, into her room, the realisation of his loss would sink in all over again, and he would break, all over again.

St George's Hospital loomed over the fading mist, an impressive and imposing structure with vast pillars. It was positioned in the beauty of Hyde Park Corner, yet it dulled the street with impending death. The ghosts of screams and cries brushed against them, caressing them, as if telling them: *Look what happened to us.*

'Ah,' said Alexander contently, clapping his gloved hands together. 'It does not appear all that bad now, does it?'

Gabriel watched as crowds of people entered and exited the building, bringing in the dirt and grime of the street, and bringing out the blood and pus of the hospital. 'If you say so.'

The entry was grand, with a large staircase leading to the upper floors. It was filled with flocks of men who busily chatted away, nurses in their black and white uniforms rushing from one wing to the other. There were buckets in the corner of the hall, filled with either urine or bloody water, waiting to be thrown out. They made their way to the centre of the space. Gabriel's chest tightened.

'Well, this is certainly not as horrendous as you made it out to be, Ashmore.' Alexander's eyes skimmed the room. 'Now, we just have to ask for directions.' He stopped a nurse that was making her way across the room. 'Hello

Miss, I apologise for the interruption, but where would we find the surgery wing?'

'The third floor, sir.'

'Thank you,' said Alexander with a smile.

'But I warn you, it is not pleasant.'

Gabriel glanced at Alexander, raising an eyebrow.

Alexander forced a smile. 'That shall not be a problem; I am tougher than I look.'

Gabriel snorted at the statement. Alexander shot him a glare. He thanked the nurse again, before they started their way up the stairs.

The first floor was filled with resting beds. The number of patients had increased greatly ever since the Erebus had made an appearance. Gabriel tried to look away from the patients, but for some reason, he couldn't help himself, as if they had some gravitational pull on him. He wished he could say that most of them were recovering, but he knew that most of them were dying. What was it about death that drew people in? Should it not be the other way around, whereby people would be confronted by anything *but* death? Perhaps it was the attraction of the unknown. There were several people with darkened veins, shaking feverishly, some screaming out. His eyes fell and lingered on an old man, shivering under his thin and dirty sheets. He did not appear to be wounded or have undergone surgery of any kind. He was just old, consumed by the withering of his body. He had come here to die.

'Gabriel? Gabriel?'

Gabriel blinked. He saw Alexander's face, his glasses slightly askew. He did not realise he had stopped walking.

'Are you all right?'

Gabriel cleared his throat. 'Yes, yes.' His voice was hoarse. 'Let's continue.'

He glanced back at the man. A nurse was holding a damp cloth to his forehead, smiling down at him as if everything would be all right, as if they could cure him of his malady that was old age. That's when Gabriel realised why the man had come here.

They ignored the cries and screams of the second floor, piercing through the air like bullets. Alexander's shoulders stiffened as he worked hard to focus his gaze. Some begged to be freed from their misery, some spoke to God, asking Him why he had failed them, and some chanted the names of loved ones like a spell.

When they reached the third floor, they had to cover their noses. The scent of blood and rotten flesh wafted through the air like the Great Stink. Alexander held back a gag. They stood at the beginning of a long, wide corridor, which was filled with crowds of men. More buckets stood by the doors leading to the surgery rooms. This time, Gabriel did not look to see their contents.

'God...' Alexander muttered in a muffled voice. There were groups of men huddled around the surgery rooms. 'What are all these people doing here?'

'They have come to watch the surgeries.'

Alexander scoffed. 'Are you serious?'

'Yes. I suppose it is interesting to some, like going to the theatre.'

'No wonder mortality rates are so high...'

They peered into one of the rooms. A crowd was

gathered around the operating table. The surgeon's blood-covered gown flashed through the people. The table remained obscured from view, and all they heard was the terrible sound of sawing. Then, one of the onlookers moved away, and Gabriel's eyes widened. Alexander gasped, before he retched the contents of his stomach out into a bucket. The surgeon had amputated the leg of a patient. A stump of rugged flesh and bone stared back at them. The spectators cheered as the surgeon put the leg aside. Gabriel clenched his teeth together, resisting following in Alexander's footsteps. He turned away, leaning his back against the wall of the hallway. He looked at Alexander, who had turned a sickly shade of green. He kept a hand on his stomach, eyes fixated on the floor.

'I told—'

'Do not say another word.' Alexander hissed, stepping away from the bucket. He steadied himself on the wall. 'Jesus Christ.'

'Do you wish to go in and ask the surgeon about Dr Wagner, then?' suggested Gabriel, holding a handkerchief to his nose. 'He can give you some spatters of disease-filled blood to take with you as a parting gift.'

Alexander glared at him, just as a dark-haired man walked out of the operating room. He struck a match and lit a cigarette. He inhaled deeply, exhaling a long puff of smoke before sighing. He noticed Gabriel and Alexander and chuckled.

'First time, eh?'

Gabriel nodded. Alexander only groaned as an answer. The man took the cigarette out of his mouth. He glanced

back into the room. 'They cut his leg off to see if they could stop the spread of the Black Opium.'

Gabriel immediately stiffened. He felt Alexander take a step closer. Gabriel's heart pounded in his chest, his stomach churning. '*What*?'

'The Black Opium seems to...' he waved his cigarette as he searched for the right word, 'poison the limbs. It starts off with a darkening of the veins. With this unfortunate individual, it started on his leg.'

'The surgeons believe they can stop its spread by simply amputating limbs?' questioned Alexander, steadying himself on the wall.

The man shrugged. 'Apparently.' He flicked his cigarette into one of the buckets and headed back into the room.

Gabriel remained silent. His head spun; his mouth felt dry. His throat felt like sandpaper each time he tried to swallow, and sweat had started accumulating on his temples. But above all, what he felt more than anything was that desperate craving to make it all disappear. He considered rushing out of the hospital, making up some sort of excuse and heading straight towards Chinatown, but he couldn't. No, he couldn't do that to Alexander, to the investigation.

Alexander let out a deep breath. 'Well, that was certainly an experience,' he started, attempting to humour their way out of the deep anguish that had started tormenting them. 'May we, perhaps, find a surgeon who is not... preoccupied?'

'Yes.'

Gabriel rolled his shoulders back, exhaling as he calmed

his nerves, pushing away those deadly feelings to a remote corner, the haunted graveyard of his mind. They walked further along the long hallway, peering into each chamber, and then immediately averting their gaze. They did not speak of what they had been told.

Gabriel's eyes landed on a room, an office of some sorts. Luckily, there was no sign of an operation going on. Within it sat a broad-faced surgeon. He still had his gown on, which was covered in dried blood, and he scribbled something in what appeared to be a journal. 'There.' He cocked his head towards the entrance.

Alexander's eyes lit up with relief as he also registered the absence of a live operation. He knocked on the open door. The surgeon's head shot up, assessing them with beady eyes.

'Yes?'

'Hello, we apologise for the interruption,' started Alexander, stepping into the room. 'We were wondering if you knew a surgeon we are seeking?'

The surgeon went back to scribbling within his journal as he stiffly nodded his head. 'Yes, go on, I do not have all day. What is his name?'

'Heinrich Wagner.'

The surgeon stopped scribbling at the sound of the name. He looked up at them, eyes more focused than before. 'Heinrich Wagner?'

Alexander and Gabriel nodded simultaneously.

The surgeon cleared his throat, his shoulders stiffening. 'Heinrich Wagner has not been a surgeon for some time.'

'Did he ever work in this hospital?' asked Gabriel.

The surgeon seemed reluctant to speak on the subject.

'Yes, he did. A long time ago.'

'What happened?'

The surgeon hesitated before answering. 'Wagner was… different. He was excellent at what he did, but he was also radical in his ideas.'

'What ideas?' asked Alexander.

'Let's just say his ideas were rejected,' answered the surgeon firmly.

'Would you be able to tell us where he is based now?'

'What business could you possibly seek with Heinrich Wagner?'

'Important business,' interjected Gabriel, before Alexander could answer.

'Please,' added Alexander. 'We shall be gone in a heartbeat. All we require is an address.'

The surgeon sighed. He grabbed a piece of parchment, scribbled a street name upon it and folded it. Alexander reached out for it, but he withheld the paper. 'Be careful.' A shadow cast over his eyes as he spoke. 'Heinrich Wagner is not normal. He is not like you or me, or anyone you've ever met. His mind… works differently.' He handed the parchment to Alexander. 'Good luck.'

'Bennet Mews, Stamford Street.'

Alexander read out the street name about a hundred times as they walked down the hospital stairs, waving the parchment before Gabriel's face, all whilst telling Gabriel: 'I told you so.'

Gabriel snatched the parchment away, crumpling it

and tossing it into one of the buckets. Alexander's mouth fell open in shock.

'Oh, save it,' Gabriel snapped, 'we have both memorised it by now, thanks to you.'

CHAPTER XXXII

Dr Heinrich Wagner

The scent of beer and cigarettes drifted through the cold air, as if it were seeping out of the very woodwork of the buildings around them. They were at the edge of South Bank, walking along the cramped Bennet Street by Blackfriars Bridge. Gabriel cursed as he stepped into a puddle of mud, which squelched uncomfortably under his shoes.

'Not very pleasant, now, is it?' remarked Alexander, pointing towards the mud, which Gabriel feared may have been something else.

Gabriel rolled his eyes as they continued down the road. He came to a halt, pointing at a building on their left. 'This should be it.'

'Goodness,' muttered Alexander as they halted before Bennet Mews: an old, crumbling building right by the river. Thick fog hovered above the water, making it impossible to see across to the other side. 'I say this is the ideal location

to manufacture something bringing chaos down upon the earth. Would you not say?'

'Certainly.'

And so, they entered the building. They were met with a nearing darkness, thick and heavy, descending upon them as the door fell shut. Alexander cursed under his breath, fumbling in his trouser pockets for matches. Gabriel pulled his own out, swiftly lighting one. Alexander glanced at him from the corner of his eye, the grey of his eyes a dark muddle in the glow of the fire. They moved further down the corridor, the wood creaking beneath their feet. Some parts felt soft, having grown mould from the inside. A thin silence enveloped them. Gabriel could see dust particles, illuminated by the fire, floating in the air. Then, slashing through that peculiar silence, was a clatter. Alexander's head cocked to the side, listening for the source of the sound. It sounded again, coming from the end of the corridor. Alexander gestured for them to move forwards. They took slow steps, until they found themselves before a paned wooden door, slightly cracked open. Bleak daylight spilled out. Gabriel and Alexander exchanged a glance, before Alexander leaned in, peeking into the room. Gabriel moved behind him, steadying himself upon Alexander's back, peering in. As his eyes landed on the occurrence within the room, he stepped back in shock. As he did so, he accidentally shoved Alexander with his hands. The last thing Gabriel heard was a curse, before Alexander crashed into the room. Dr Wagner jumped as the door swung wide open, dropping the scalpel that had been in his hand. He was a tall man of older age, with white hair slicked to the

side, small, round glasses perched on the bridge of his nose. His facial features were abnormally sharp, skull-like in the harsh gaslight, yet the thing that struck Gabriel the most was the fact that he was entirely covered in blood, standing over a dissected dog. His sharp gaze fell on them, a look of unsettling calmness.

'Who are you?' he asked, continuing to pierce his gaze into them. He had a heavy German accent and a strange pitch to his voice that prickled at one's skin.

Alexander heaved himself off the floor, rubbing his elbow as he took a slow step back. His eyes lingered on the dissection table, upon the dog tied up by its legs, upon the blood pooling on the surface of the table. The metal stench bit at Gabriel's nose. Alexander swallowed hard, before countering the doctor with:

'The real question ought to be who *you* are.'

The man narrowed his crinkled eyes. 'You two have broken into my facilities and are now questioning *my* identity? Get out.'

Gabriel's eyes darted around the room. He had been expecting something along the lines of a laboratory, with boiling flasks and smoking substances, not a cut-open dog. Several scalpels, of minuscule up to gigantic sizes, hung on the left wall.

'No,' said Alexander. 'I do not think we shall be doing that.' Gabriel could see he was desperately trying to find a way through the precarious situation. In the end, he pointed at the dog and then at Dr Wagner's blood-covered robe. 'What is all this?'

Gabriel closed his eyes, whispering: 'Idiot.'

Dr Wagner raised an eyebrow. 'Nothing you boys should concern yourself with.' He tightened his hold on the scalpel in his hand. 'Now, depart.'

Gabriel further inspected the room, searching for any sign of the Erebus production. Instead, he only spotted a side table littered with medical instruments, syringes filled with strange liquids, a crate, buckets of blood in the corner and a desk upon which multiple books were sprawled open. Gabriel's eyes landed upon the dog again. He looked at its tied legs, which the rope had bitten into, thinking why an animal that was being dissected had to be restrained to such an extent, before finally realising what Dr Wagner truly had been doing.

Gabriel's brows furrowed into a frown. 'You had been performing a vivisection.'

'A vivisection?' questioned Alexander.

Gabriel's lips thinned. 'He was operating on the dog whilst it was still alive.'

Dr Wagner's bony features showed no emotion other than distaste and annoyance.

'The surgeon at St George's was right,' muttered Alexander.

Gabriel's eyes fell upon the surgical table again. He forced himself to look at the cut-open dog. Its intestines had been moved around, with some hanging out the side. Blood dripped onto the table, and as Gabriel watched it drip, he felt his mouth dry at the realisation. He tried to swallow but failed. The table was far too large for animals. His eyes darted towards the wall, falling on the scalpels and knives, which also were far too large.

The table was not for animals. It was made to fit humans.

Dr Wagner carefully stepped forward with predator-like precision.

'How do you believe Galen shaped the understanding of anatomy? How do you think he proved that the brain's nerves are used to control the muscles involved in speech?'

'What do you know about the Erebus?' said Alexander, ignoring Dr Wagner's crazed ramblings. 'Who is behind it?' But Gabriel already knew what Dr Wagner's answer would be. A sense of dread prickled at his nerves, a dread different to anything he had ever felt before. He took a casual step back, grabbing Alexander's sleeve and attempting to pull him back, but Alexander wouldn't budge.

'The Erebus?' asked Dr Wagner, raising a thin eyebrow. 'The Black Opium?'

'Yes.'

Dr Wagner chuckled, a harsh, guttural sound. 'Whoever it is, I know that he has a mind greater than any of ours. A mind capable of death and destruction, of great things. Of something this world has never seen before.'

'Who is it?' hissed Alexander. 'Who is behind this?' His brows were furrowed in abhorrence at the man before him. Gabriel could tell his patience was wearing thin. He nudged his back, attempting to convey to him what he just realised, but Alexander ignored him. His grey eyes were fixated on Dr Wagner's pale blue ones.

'Do you really think I know?' said Dr Wagner, a harsh laugh escaping his lips. 'I wish I did.'

'If you do not tell us all you know, we shall spread the word of what you are doing in here,' said Alexander.

'I am pretty certain Scotland Yard shall be interested to hear about a doctor conducting human experiments. They might even blame you for the recent murders. It would be an easy victory.'

Dr Wagner's features turned sour. 'You boys are foolish,' he hissed. 'You would not dare.'

'Oh, yes, we would. Therefore, I suggest you tell us whatever we wish to know.'

Dr Wagner's nostrils flared. 'How dare you threaten the course of science? Do you know how far you shall set humanity back?'

'I do not care,' stated Alexander. 'Tell us what you know.'

Dr Wagner took a step towards the operating table, his movements serpent-like. He ran his fingers along the edge, until he reached the end of it. He put down the scalpel in his hand and picked up another one that was lying on the table. It was bigger and sharper, its edge gleaming as it moved.

'We ought to *go*,' Gabriel urgently whispered to Alexander. '*Now*.'

'*No*,' snapped Alexander. 'He must know something, he—'

'It is rude to whisper about someone when they are in the room,' said Dr Wagner, a strange sort of calmness having settled over him. 'I have always found that the English have no manners.' He pointed towards the dog. 'It is of absolute importance for a scientist to study organs before decomposition. Therefore, it must be carried out on a subject that is still alive.' He poked the dog's paw with the scalpel. 'This one has bled out. It is of no use to me now.'

Alexander's features displayed nothing but disgust. 'Everyone is familiar with basic anatomy. I doubt you are conducting ground-breaking work by torturing a helpless dog.'

Dr Wagner shook his head. 'Oh, no. It is not merely studying the anatomy. I watch how diseases manifest themselves, which organs are affected, how sick the subject becomes.'

'You infect them?' questioned Gabriel.

Dr Wagner stared at him as if he had asked the most foolish question on earth. 'Oh, yes. Of course. How else do you suppose one can actually *discover* anything?'

Gabriel turned to look at Alexander, urging them to leave, but he was no longer there. He had moved across the hallway, standing before an open door to a room. The light from Dr Wagner's laboratory had illuminated the space. Gabriel narrowed his eyes as he looked closer, and realised it wasn't just any door or any room. It was a cell door, and the room was a prison. Alexander slowly turned around, and Gabriel knew he had realised it too as his gaze conveyed pure horror and revulsion.

'We need to go...' started Gabriel, until Alexander's brows furrowed together, his lips moving incoherently as he pointed at something behind Gabriel. Before Gabriel could finish his sentence, he felt his body collapse. His head hit the ground, and his vision swayed, turning everything into a whirlwind of dark colours. He heard a voice shouting, but he did not recognise it. He winced as he steadied himself upon his elbows, attempting to heave himself up. He blinked and saw the shape of Dr Wagner

advance past him. He frowned, muttering: 'Did that bastard just hit me?'

'Yes, he certainly did, and now he is charging at me, so get up!' exclaimed Alexander.

Gabriel groaned as he forced himself to his feet. His head pounded awfully, and he wondered what on earth Dr Wagner had hit him with, but he did not have the time to contemplate it. His eyes focused on Alexander, who was cornered in the cell. Dr Wagner neared him with careful steps. Gabriel looked closer, and realised he was holding a pipe in one hand and a large scalpel in the other.

'This is the most difficult part of my profession,' muttered Dr Wagner, taking another step towards Alexander. 'I cannot kill my subjects, you see. Death is my biggest adversary.'

Gabriel's gut wrenched as he realised what Dr Wagner intended. His eyes frantically searched the hallway for anything he could use as a weapon, but he found nothing. His eyes fell on Alexander again. His friend's face had gone a sickly white, his body rigid as he desperately tried to look for a way out of the cell.

'Bloody hell,' muttered Gabriel, before taking in a deep breath, and charging at the doctor. His body collided with Dr Wagner's before they both hit the ground. The clatter of the pipe reverberated through the air as it fell from Dr Wagner's grasp. Gabriel attempted to restrain the doctor's arms, but instead was met with a blow to the face. Dr Wagner let out something close to a growl as he rolled free from Gabriel's grasp. His face had turned a deep shade of red, his eyes nearly bulging out of their sockets.

'Jesus Christ, how strong is this man?' exclaimed Alexander from behind Gabriel. Dr Wagner ran towards the hallway, entering his laboratory. Gabriel sprinted after him, lunging across the hallway and latching his hands onto Dr Wagner's ankles. He stumbled, before hitting the ground. Gabriel crawled towards Dr Wagner, and then a silver object slashed the air in front of Gabriel, mere inches from his face. The scalpel. Dr Wagner still had the scalpel. Gabriel grabbed at the doctor's wrist, but his fingers were clamped so tightly around the handle Gabriel could not pry it from his grasp.

'You *fools*,' Dr Wagner spat. They had both managed to get to their feet, still fighting for the scalpel. Dr Wagner kneed Gabriel in the stomach. 'I fought in the German army; do you really think you can best me?'

Gabriel gasped for breath, but he did not loosen his grasp. Instead, using all his weight, he hit his shoulder into Dr Wagner's chest. They both went flying backwards, crashing into the cabinet behind them. Glass beakers and flasks rained down upon them, shattering on the ground. One hit Gabriel's head, but he barely felt it as they continued to struggle for the scalpel. Gabriel's back hit the operating table. He winced at the impact. Dr Wagner bared his yellowing teeth as he forced the scalpel closer to Gabriel. He landed a punch to Dr Wagner's bony face. Dr Wagner swore in German but maintained his grasp. Gabriel clamped his other hand around Dr Wagner's wrist and started to twist it, and then his vision went black. A searing pain throbbed at his forehead before speckles of vision started to reappear. He saw Dr Wagner's face before his

and felt a weight pressed against his chest. The bastard had headbutted him. Dr Wagner was now holding the scalpel against his throat. He let it bite into Gabriel's skin, drawing warm blood. He smiled as he looked down at Gabriel. His teeth had turned red.

'I told you, you cannot best me.' He pushed the scalpel deeper into Gabriel's skin. Gabriel refused to acknowledge the searing pain of it. 'It is a shame you had to probe into matters that were none of your concern.' He sighed. 'You could have been so much more useful to me. You remind me of the injured men in the army, the way they used to put up such a fight—'

Gabriel saw something swing in the air, and then Dr Wagner's eyes went white, before he dropped to the floor. The scalpel fell from his grasp, clattering onto the table. Alexander now stood before him, holding a pipe. He had hit Dr Wagner on the head.

'God, he talks a lot,' stated Alexander in a shaking voice.

Gabriel let out a sigh of relief, slumping forwards. Alexander's hands shook as he gripped the pipe, his knuckles white.

'You really took your time, didn't you?' remarked Gabriel, steadying himself upon the table. 'One more second and I would have been dead.'

'Yes, well, it was rather difficult trying to hit a specific someone on the head when you two were constantly rolling around. I also tripped when I ran in here.' Alexander looked down at Dr Wagner's body.

Gabriel sniffed, wiping his nose as his gaze followed Alexander's. 'I do hope he is unconscious and not *dead*.'

He poked Dr Wagner's shoulder with his foot.

'It would serve him right, though,' muttered Alexander under his breath.

'Well, what now?'

Alexander put his hands on his sides, exhaling loudly. His eyes travelled from Dr Wagner to the destroyed laboratory to the hallway, until they came to a halt upon the cell. Gabriel raised his eyebrows, immediately knowing what Alexander was intending.

'Are you serious?'

Alexander grinned; despite the fact they had almost been killed by a crazed scientist. 'I am most serious.'

Gabriel narrowed his eyes. 'And then what? What is your plan beyond locking the doctor up in a bloody *cell*? Did you even think past that part?'

'I really do not appreciate your terrible negativity.'

Gabriel scoffed. 'My terrible negativity? You—'

Dr Wagner suddenly stirred, causing Alexander to jump back. He grabbed the pipe, keeping it at the ready as they watched the doctor. Dr Wagner did not move again. Alexander let out a deep breath.

'Thank heavens, I would have hated to hit an old man on the head twice.'

'Yes, well, let us execute your foolish plan before he awakes.' Gabriel bent down and grabbed Dr Wagner's arms. He looked up at Alexander. 'Come on, then.'

Alexander moved around the body and grabbed a hold of Dr Wagner's feet. 'Ah, wait.' He released the doctor's legs, causing them to fall to the floor with a heavy thud, before picking up the pipe. Alexander shrugged in reaction

to Gabriel rolling his eyes. 'You never know. He might wake up.'

'Yes, well, the cell is only a short distance away. So short, in fact, we could have already been there by now.'

'Yes, yes.' Alexander grabbed Dr Wagner's feet.

They lifted the doctor and started their journey towards the hallway. Alexander attempted to dodge the broken glass on the floor, which led to Dr Wagner being swayed in the air. Dr Wagner's nose twitched. They halted. Alexander's eyes met Gabriel's.

'Do try not to bloody wake him,' snapped Gabriel in a low tone.

'It wasn't my intention, was it now?' Alexander snapped back.

They increased their speed, both wishing to be rid of the doctor as soon as possible. Gabriel looked down as he stepped over a glass flask, and then a loud thud reverberated through the room. Gabriel cursed.

'Did you just hit Dr Wagner's head on a cabinet?'

'Be quiet,' muttered Gabriel as they stepped into the hallway. 'It was an accident.'

Alexander raised his eyebrows. 'Well, if the man wasn't dead before, he certainly almost is now.'

'And it was not a cabinet. It was a crate, if you must know.' Gabriel looked back at the obstacle, an old crate, with a number painted on its side. Beside it stood a skeleton model, hidden from view just behind the door. Gabriel quickly turned his gaze away from it, not desiring to wonder where on earth Dr Wagner had obtained it from. 'Moreover, I can feel his pulse, he is not dead.'

They laid Dr Wagner down in the centre of the cell. Alexander sniffed the air, screwing up his nose. 'God, it smells horrible in here.'

'Did you not notice it the first time you ventured in here?'

'Well, no, I was too busy being horrified at what I had just discovered.'

'It is most probably rotten blood. Or mould. Or a mixture of both.'

'Lovely,' muttered Alexander. His gaze fell back on Dr Wagner. He slowly poked him with his foot. He did not stir. 'What do we do now?'

Gabriel looked at Alexander with furrowed brows. 'This was your bloody plan! Figure it out.'

Alexander scratched his head, pressing his lips together. 'Well, I believe the most sensible thing to do is lock him up in the cell.'

Gabriel scoffed. 'Lock him up? And leave him to die?'

'Well, no. We could—'

Dr Wagner stirred again, his legs twitching.

'Jesus Christ,' muttered Alexander.

'You better make a decision soon before he wakes up and attempts to kill us again.'

'He did not attempt to kill *me*. That was directed at you.'

'Ah, yes, he was sparing you to experiment on. A much better fate.'

'Right, how about we keep him in here whilst we search this place? Lock him up, *momentarily*, so he does not come up from behind you and hit you with a pipe again.'

Gabriel looked down upon Dr Wagner. His nostrils

moved, as if also appalled by the smell of the cell. 'Fine.'

They stepped out of the murky cell and shut the heavy iron door behind them. Alexander peeked through the barred window with distaste. They headed back towards the half-destroyed laboratory.

'There must be something here. What could Dr Wagner have been testing for Harvey Blythe?'

'Clearly not the Erebus,' muttered Gabriel, letting out a deep sigh.

'Quit your pessimism and get to work,' said Alexander. He started to open all the cabinet doors he could get his hands on.

Gabriel scoffed. 'Watch your tone, will you?'

Alexander shot him a glare. 'I have just potentially murdered a man for you. Perhaps a little more gratitude would be better suited.'

'Barely!' exclaimed Gabriel. 'You almost murdered *me* with your horrendously slow pace.'

Alexander put a hand on his chest. 'Your appreciation is so very moving. What would I do without your undying support?'

Gabriel narrowed his eyes. 'Do you not have clues to be looking for?'

'So do you, Ashmore, so please, get to work.' He pointed at the cupboards lining the walls.

Gabriel stepped forward, passing the operating table. He screwed up his nose. 'This dog is starting to smell.'

'No,' snapped Alexander. 'Do not even mention it, because nothing on this earth will persuade me to touch that dog.'

CHAPTER XXXIII

————•·•————

Seven

Gabriel did not know exactly how he had passed the time, but when he arrived home darkness had settled over the city. An obscurity only ever seen in the heavy depths of winter, sucking out every source of light from the sky, making even the stars invisible. Gabriel stepped over the threshold which separated the large, stone steps that were frosted over and his dim foyer. His fingers itched yet again, his bones uncomfortable against his skin, and although the house was freezing, Gabriel was getting hot, too hot. He walked towards the parlour, determined in his desperation to find a certain liquid that could ease his unrest for a few moments, before he halted. His body turned stiff as he processed the sight of his father slumped back in his chair, a near-empty bottle of whisky on the floor. Before him, upon the coffee table, a map was sprawled open. Gabriel frowned as he took a step

closer, his heart racing faster and faster in his chest. He saw black lines drawn upon streets, arrows and scribbles. He had circled Charles Street. On the side, he had made a list entitled 'Seven Routes'.

'What is this?' asked Gabriel hoarsely.

His father did not look up at him. He merely rested his chin upon his folded hands, his gaze faraway and absent, his eyes frozen over with despaired intoxication. Gabriel leaned over, reading the location. He inhaled sharply.

'What is this?' he demanded yet again, although a pit had already started forming within his chest.

'Alternative routes,' muttered Cassius, reaching for his quill. 'Alternative routes I could have taken that night.'

Anger formed within Gabriel like a rising flame. His neck stiffened as he clenched and unclenched his fists. 'Why do you do this?'

Cassius did not answer as he pushed his reading glasses further up the bridge of his nose. Gabriel's nostrils flared before he stepped forwards and snatched the quill from his father's hand. His father looked up at him, faint surprise looming behind his eyes, obscured by intoxication.

'Just quit it,' hissed Gabriel, throwing the pen across the room. 'Do you not care about anything else? Must you always insist on bringing up hauntings of the past?'

'There is no need for such anger, Gabriel.'

Gabriel scoffed, his chest rising up and down, unable to contain the anger pooling around his heart. 'What about Adelia, Father? Ought you not draft up a list of medicines she should have got? A list of symptoms of the illness we did not detect soon enough?'

'Adelia shall return.'

Gabriel's nails dug into his palms. 'Adelia is *dead*. She is dead. And Hugo is gone. Mother is gone, everyone is gone.' Gabriel's voice broke. He exhaled shakily, taking a step back from his father. Cassius's red-rimmed eyes stared back at him blankly before he reached down to the floor and picked up his crystal glass. Gabriel stared back at him with disgust. 'It should have been you that died.'

Something flickered behind his father's glazed eyes, something so faint Gabriel thought he could have imagined it. But he had nothing left within him to think about it, and so he left his father staring after him as he disappeared back into the darkness of the house.

Images of the dead dog flashed before Gabriel's eyes. Buckets of blood, dim gaslight, a scalpel slashing through the air. Dr Wagner's sharp gaze, his lack of remorse and morality, his ardour and dedication. Gabriel was sat on the roof, watching the city that stretched out before him. Deep shadows and faint lights, a dark sky with no constellations. The silhouette of the Houses of Parliament seemed to waver before him like a hallucination. He closed his eyes. The ache in his head pounded against his skull. He savoured the icy wind upon his skin, feeling the minuscule snowflakes drifting through the air melt upon his face. When he opened his eyes again, he saw the river: the edges frozen over, the centre gleaming with the rays of the moon; he saw Charles Street in St James's and his father's seven routes. Then, all of a sudden, he realised. He knew what the next clue was.

*

The next morning, thick fog descended upon the city. Gabriel had, with a certain degree of difficulty, made his way to the Wakefield mansion. He knocked incessantly upon the door, before stepping back and crossing his arms over his chest as he waited. He looked around the street, yet he could barely see across the road. The sky was between light and dark, the cobalt glow of the early morning. After several seconds, he continued to knock yet again, before the door finally swung open. Alexander stood before the entryway, sporting an expression of great irritation. He was dressed in pyjamas and a long robe, barefooted, with dishevelled hair and narrowed, creased eyes.

'I knew it would be you,' he sighed. 'Now, *why* on earth have you awoken me at this unholy hour?'

'There was a clue. At Dr Wagner's laboratory.'

Alexander's eyes widened, his previous irritation slowly fading away. 'What was it?'

'The crate.'

Alexander's brows furrowed. 'The crate?'

'Do you remember when I hit Dr Wagner's head?'

Alexander chuckled. 'Yes, I do.'

'I hit it on a crate. It had the number seven painted upon it. I did not think much of it at the time, but thinking back on it I believe whatever we are searching for may be on the docks. I have only seen such crates being utilised in the merchant trade, so that must be it.'

'Yes, yes,' muttered Alexander, his previously fatigued eyes lighting up. 'And the number could be indicative of

warehouse storage. I have seen them before, and they were indeed numbered.' He ran a hand through his dishevelled hair. 'Now, the question remains, which one?'

Gabriel shook his head. 'Of that, I have no idea.'

'Then we shall have to try all of them. Let us start with the West India Docks.'

CHAPTER XXXIV

The Docks

A tangle of skeleton-like ships stood before them, most of their sails still half-concealed by the fog that had only slowly started to lift. Shouts and bellows of sailors reverberated all around them, mixed with the incessant chatter of merchants and the creaking of carriage wheels upon cobbled stone. As they walked further into the docks, the aroma of spices filled Gabriel's nostrils. He looked around, noticing a broken crate from which a colourful array of spices spilled out of. The smell transported him to faraway lands, across the oceans and into new territory. He inhaled deeply, before continuing on his way. He dodged a worker who rushed past, various papers in hand, flapping in the icy wind. Gabriel looked out on the ships: vast masts and wide sails, polished and frayed hulls, intricate carvings on railings. These images brought with them a great sense of melancholia within Gabriel, a

sense of abandoned dreams, of a lost future.

Gabriel lit a cigarette, deeply inhaling the bitter smoke, letting it fill his lungs as they pushed past a bustle of merchants. After several moments, when the fog started to clear, a long row of individual wooden buildings came into view.

'There,' said Alexander, pointing ahead. Gabriel squinted his eyes as he attempted to read the numbers upon them. 'We need to get closer.'

They headed towards the warehouses, walking along them as they searched for their number. Gabriel counted each one, and just as he found the number seven, two figures came into view. They paused right before it, their backs turned. Gabriel frowned as he stared at the man on the right, his instinct realising it long before his mind did, because at one point in time, he knew who stood before him better than he knew himself. He recognised his posture, the shape of his shoulders, the curve of his head. And then he turned around, and Gabriel's mind finally realised what his heart already knew.

Hugo.

His brother stood before them, staring out at the river in contemplation as he listened to the man beside him. The air felt thick and hot within Gabriel's own throat, suffocating him from the inside. Only yesterday he had spoken to his brother to arrange transport for Xing. He felt a weight upon his arm. He looked down. It was Alexander's hand. He tried to shake away his touch, but he remained frozen. He shifted his gaze towards Alexander, whose mouth was moving yet Gabriel could not hear whatever came out of it.

'That is my brother,' managed Gabriel, speaking over Alexander. 'He is a merchant. He must be here on business. He cannot...' Gabriel's voice faded out as he watched his brother unlock the warehouse.

'I had no idea you had a twin,' said Alexander, brows furrowing as he watched Hugo. 'He is entering the warehouse, Ashmore—'

'Just be quiet,' hissed Gabriel. He stepped back behind a brick wall, obscuring himself from his brother's gaze. He let out a deep breath, leaning his head back. 'We must wait until they are gone.'

*

And so, they waited until all crates had been loaded into the warehouse, until Hugo had long left and Gabriel's chest felt numb. They approached the warehouse, making sure there was no sign of the other merchant accompanying Hugo. Alexander grabbed onto the door and pulled. It did not budge.

He swore. 'They have locked it already.'

'Yes, that was to be expected,' muttered Gabriel as he started to walk down the length of the warehouse. Alexander's footsteps sounded behind him as he headed towards the back of the building. The scent of washed-down beer wafted in the air, interlaced with the aroma of mud and dampness. A narrow door stood before him, built of only a few wooden planks nailed together. Gabriel stepped back, before hitting the makeshift door with his shoulder. He barely felt the collision as the door swung

wide open at the impact, revealing a wide space lined with countless crates, all stacked up atop each other in the far-right corner. Alexander stepped in, letting his eyes roam the space. Daylight streamed in from the cracks of the wooden walls, like something mystical descending from the sky. Gabriel swallowed as he neared the crates. Alexander took one of them, setting it upon a wooden table. He looked up at Gabriel. Gabriel nodded. Alexander grabbed a crowbar, shoving it into the edge of the lid and popping it off. Gabriel's heart pounded in his chest, his fingers fluttering by his sides. Silence filled the room like thick smoke, heavy upon them.

Alexander frowned.

'What?'

'Have a look,' said Alexander with a sigh, stepping back from the crate.

Gabriel leaned forwards, and in that very moment, he did not know if he should rejoice or wallow in disappointment. 'Tea,' he said blankly. 'It is tea.'

Before Alexander could reply, a creaking sound filled the air around them, and the main door swung open. Gabriel and Alexander both turned to face the sound. Before them stood the merchant that they had seen earlier with Hugo. The man was of reasonable height, with a slim figure, dull brown hair and tanned skin. He frowned.

'I thought you had left, Hugo.'

Gabriel blinked, before his common sense returned to him. 'Apologies, I seemed to have forgotten my pocket watch.'

'Ah, the curse of forgetfulness. It happens to the best of us.' The man spoke in a peculiar manner, as if he had

lived for many years yet he did not appear a day older than thirty-five. He pointed at the crates. 'We are very lucky they arrived safely from Guangzhou. I was informed there were quite a few storms on the Indian Ocean.' His eyes landed on Alexander, who was conveniently obscuring the crate they had pried open from the merchant's view. 'Oh, my apologies, I have failed to introduce myself.' He held out a hand. 'My name is Charles Anderson. Merchant and explorer.'

Alexander smiled as he shook the man's hand. Anderson shifted his gaze back to Gabriel. 'Like I said last evening, you must accompany me across the Indian Ocean. One sees the most beautiful scenery upon the journey. At times, my crew and I stay a night on one of the islands. I cannot put into words how magnificent the experience is.'

Gabriel tried his best to convey his brother's smile, the smile that never quite reached his eyes. 'Yes, I would be positively delighted.'

Anderson raised his eyebrows. 'Well, I have finally managed to convince the man.' He leaned over towards Alexander. 'Months I have been trying to convince him to undertake something joyful. You must be in a rather brilliant mood.'

Gabriel refrained from cursing. Of course, his brother would not be keen on such a prospect.

'Yes, I had thought it would be wise to undertake something... engaging.'

Anderson smiled, whilst Alexander looked at him with hints of mocking amusement. 'Good to hear.'

'Did you say these crates arrived from Guangzhou?' asked Gabriel, hoping to extract more information from Anderson.

Anderson chuckled. 'Well, yes. You oversaw them yourself, Ashmore. Are you feeling quite all right? You look slightly ill if you do not mind me saying.'

Alexander snorted, before quickly covering it with a cough.

'A stomach flu, unfortunately. I caught it recently.' He looked back at the crates. 'Are there any other shipments scheduled to come in this week?'

'Not that I know of,' said Anderson. 'But an unusually large shipment is set to come in from Guangzhou soon, although I am not exactly sure what it is.'

'Does anyone know? And when is it set to come in?'

Anderson's gaze lingered upon Gabriel's face for slightly longer than usual. 'I do not know much of it, it falls outside of our area of trade,' said Anderson. His eyes narrowed slightly.

'Ah, well, thank you, Anderson. I am afraid I must depart now,' said Gabriel quickly, before they both headed out of the warehouse.

*

Alexander threw back a glass of gin, scrunching up his nose as he swallowed the liquid. He set the glass back down, clinking it hard on the counter of the bar. The sky had started to set, the last of the daylight weakly flickering through the paned window of the pub. Something gnawed

at Gabriel. Something as little as a tickle in one's throat, a tickle that would soon develop into an incessant cough. The tickle was his brother. As they had returned from the docks, sitting in the carriage in complete silence, Gabriel had been thinking. Thinking about his brother's sudden return, right at the start of the murders. His absence, his abrupt presence. The depth in the words he spoke, hidden shadows behind each letter.

CHAPTER XXXV

The Silver Tie

Gabriel exhaled steadily as he poured freshly brewed tea into a china cup. The steam rose into the air, lingering above his father's desk before disappearing. Gabriel's mind was clouded with the events of the previous day, haunting his every waking thought. Cassius looked up at Gabriel through the fogginess behind his eyes. His robe was wrapped tightly around him, a silk scarf tied around his neck.

'Without milk, as usual?' asked Gabriel.

Cassius looked away, gazing out the fogged-up windows. Drops of rain trickled down. Gabriel's lips thinned as he set the teapot upon the desk. The edges of the wood were stained with faint yellow paint. He remained standing before his father, looking at the side of his face: the premature wrinkling of his skin, creased like thin paper in certain corners, the slight shadow of the veins

protruding from his neck, the colour of ice streaked within his dark hair. Gabriel's eyes fell upon his desk, the scattered papers, the spillage of ink, scribbles upon ancient-looking parchment like it came straight from the writings of Plato.

'I cannot seem to locate my tie,' said Cassius suddenly, a stern expression upon his face.

Gabriel's head cocked up. 'Which one?'

'The grey one. With those…' he waved his hand around, 'patterns. Made of silk.'

Gabriel drew a breath before answering. 'You got rid of that one, Father.'

Cassius finally met his eyes, furrowed brows and squinted lids piercing into Gabriel, his gaze filled with nothing but vehemence.

'No, I certainly did not, boy! Tell me, where have you put it?'

'I have not put it anywhere. You threw it out a few months ago.'

'No, I did not!' he repeated, slamming his fist on the desk. Gabriel didn't move an inch. 'Your mother gifted me it; whyever would I throw away her present? She shall certainly be very cross with me now due to your incompetence. Now, *where* have you put it?'

Gabriel did not say anything, *couldn't* say anything, as he stared at his father, his arms stiff by his sides.

Cassius rose from his chair in one harsh movement, knocking over a bottle of ink which shattered on the floor.

'You are trying to sabotage me, are you not, boy? Why do you taunt me? Why be so cruel?' Cassius shot Gabriel a look of the greatest disdain, a look conveying hatred

immeasurable in words, an abhorrence running deeper than the valleys of Tibet.

Gabriel's eyes furrowed. He tried to speak, but no sound came out of his mouth.

'I am not…' he managed, his breath heavy. 'I am not taunting you, Father. Nor am I sabotaging you, what nonsense are you speaking?'

'*Get out*,' Cassius hissed, steadying himself on the table as he stumbled forwards in his rage.

Gabriel took a step back, staring at his father, before leaving and slamming the door behind him.

London's skies were grey. The cobblestones beneath Gabriel's shoes were newly wet with rain, evaporating a damp, cold smell into the air. He walked out of Belgravia, passing through Wellington Arch and then along the edge of Green Park. He noticed a crowd of people in the distance. He narrowed his eyes, attempting to obtain a better look. He noticed they were carrying red and white banners, the colours of the Conservative Justice Party. As they neared him, Gabriel could hear chanting.

'*Cecil out, Granville in! Cecil out, Granville in!*' they shouted. Several onlookers on the street joined them, until their initial crowd had doubled in size. Gabriel could not blame them.

He walked away from them, turning left onto Old Bond Street. After several more minutes of walking, he entered Savile Row. He stopped before Henry Poole & Co, sighing. He remembered exactly where his mother had bought his father the grey tie, because he had come with her. He

remembered he insisted on trying on one of the blazers. He had been engulfed by the size of it. His mother's laugh still echoed within his mind. He remembered it as a perfect day.

He pushed open the door. A bell rang above him. An assistant headed towards him from the back of the shop.

'Good morning, sir; how may I be of assistance?'

'I am looking for a tie,' said Gabriel, letting his eyes glide over the interior of the shop.

'Certainly,' said the man, heading towards the till. He pulled out a book. 'Your name, sir?'

'Ashmore.'

The man flicked through the logbook. 'Ah, Mr Ashmore, how lovely to have you back. It has been a while, has it not?'

'Yes,' said Gabriel shortly.

'Is there anything you are looking for in particular?'

'I believe I have already stated what I am looking for. A tie. Silver. Made of silk. It is imperative that I find that exact one.'

'I see, do you remember what range it was from?'

'Pardon me?'

'The collection. We have yearly and seasonal—'

'No,' interrupted Gabriel. 'I do not. It is simply a grey silk tie with… patterns on it.'

'Certainly. I shall have a look at our inventory.' The thin man walked towards a shining mahogany drawer. The top part was made of glass, making an assortment of ties visible. He rolled out a drawer with ties neatly lined upon it. The man turned towards Gabriel.

'I am afraid we do not have any in stock, Mr Ashmore.'

Gabriel sighed with frustration, taking a step towards the drawer. He frowned, pointing his finger. 'I can see a grey tie right there.'

The man blinked. 'Ah, yes, that is the showpiece. The actual stock has not arrived yet.'

'Well, just give me the showpiece, then.'

'I am afraid we cannot do that, sir.'

'Why not?'

'It is the showpiece. Otherwise, our customers would not be able to see all of our available—'

'I need it today,' stated Gabriel coldly.

'We shall have it in stock in the coming weeks, I—'

'How about you just give me that damn tie?' snapped Gabriel.

The man raised his brows, folding his arms behind him as he took a step back. 'Perhaps I can make an exception,' he said sourly, lips pursed. 'Just this once; but it shall cost more.'

Gabriel let out a heavy sigh as the door fell shut behind him. He had spent too much money. He threw off his coat, carrying the box in which the tie was packaged with him. He peeked into the parlour. Empty.

'Father?' he shouted, heading back into the hallway. He must still be in his office. Just as Gabriel climbed the set of steps to the first floor, he heard an answer downstairs. He headed down the corridor, going into the dining room. Gabriel halted.

'Hugo.' His voice held no emotion. It held none of

the spite, the rage or coldness it had in previous days, but instead twisted into something far worse.

The fireplace flickered behind him, crackling as the logs burned. Upon the long oak table stood three plates. His father was sitting at the top of the table, his hand shaking slightly as he held a fork.

'Ah, Gabriel, at last,' said Hugo, ignoring his brother's hostile demeanour, just as he always did. 'We were waiting for you.'

'What is this?'

Hugo looked down at the plates of mutton and potatoes. 'Lunch.'

Gabriel put down the box in which the tie was stored, remaining silent.

'Well, do sit down,' insisted Hugo.

'Why? Why are you here?'

Hugo sighed. 'I wished to see my father and brother. This is the hundredth time you have asked me that question.'

Gabriel's eyes fell on his father, who was staring into the fire with the same absent expression, watching as the orange flames engulfed the logs.

'Father?'

Cassius turned at Gabriel's voice. 'We are having lunch.'

Gabriel looked at his father with a hint of surprise at the clearness of his speech. Hugo eyed Gabriel, nodding towards the chair across him. Gabriel kept his teeth clenched together tightly in the hope it would prevent something unwanted from slipping out of his mouth, something he would never be able to take back. Reluctantly, Gabriel pulled out the chair, scraping it on the wooden floor before

sitting down. He looked down at the plate, before looking back up at his brother.

'Gravy?' asked Hugo, lifting a porcelain saucière.

'No.'

'You always have gravy.'

'I said I do not want it.'

Hugo poured the gravy onto his father's plate, drizzling it over the potatoes and mutton, before starting on his own. Gabriel took a hold of the silver cutlery, the same cutlery which he had sold half to provide them with money. Gabriel started cutting the mutton, the knife scraping against the plate. He wasn't hungry. Hugo's eyes were on him, analysing him. What was he thinking? Gabriel stared back at him, jaw clenched, knuckles white as he gripped his fork. Hugo's gaze turned back to his father, who was slowly cutting up his potatoes in small pieces. Outside, it started hailing.

Gabriel cleared his throat. The tickle had become heavier, too heavy for him to keep in. 'How was work, brother?'

Hugo did not hesitate with his answer. 'It was fine. Busy. We handled a large shipment of tea from China.' He swallowed the piece of mutton he was chewing on. 'A few crates got lost at sea due to a storm.'

'Awful, that is,' muttered Cassius suddenly. Both Gabriel and Hugo's heads turned towards their father, whose eyebrows were furrowed as he looked down at his plate, moving his potatoes around. Gabriel's eyes fell on his shoulders, how sharp they were as they poked out of his dressing gown. He looked back at Hugo, who already knew exactly what he was thinking.

'Did that befall you frequently too, Father?' asked Hugo, moving his eyes away from Gabriel. He reached towards the bowl of boiled potatoes, placing more onto his father's plate. Cassius held up his hand, shaking his head.

'I am satisfied, thank you.'

'You have not eaten anything, Father,' said Gabriel.

Cassius looked at his plate. 'Yes, I have.'

Gabriel pressed his lips together before speaking. 'No, you have not.'

Cassius had only been cutting up his food into smaller pieces, without ever actually consuming one of those pieces. Cassius started frowning, shaking his head.

'Just eat, Father, we have spoken about this before—'

'I have eaten before your brother came—'

Gabriel frowned. 'No, you have not; why are you lying?'

'Gabriel, that is enough.'

Gabriel shot Hugo a glare. 'What?'

'I said that is enough. You are distressing him.'

'*Distressing* him? I am trying to ensure he does not starve.'

Cassius let out a grunt of frustration, moving around in his seat. 'I must return to—'

'Oh, just stay still, for God's sake!'

'*Gabriel*,' hissed Hugo.

'Shut your mouth, Hugo,' snapped Gabriel, pointing a finger at his brother.

'Always starting trouble, you...' muttered Cassius, glaring at Gabriel from beneath his brows.

Gabriel let out a chuckle. 'Oh, really?'

Hugo sighed. 'Let us just continue lunch—'

'Ah *yes*, Hugo here believes years of his incompetence can be fixed with a pathetic little lunch—'

'Your mother would be disappointed.'

Gabriel went silent, slowly letting his gaze fall upon his father. His eyes narrowed, his shoulders stiffening. 'Excuse me?'

Hugo's eyes had widened slightly, looking back and forth between his brother and father, caught in a peculiar, frozen moment of time, the calm before the storm.

Cassius remained silent, stubbornly staring at the wall in front of him.

Hugo cleared his throat. 'Gabriel—'

'Do not speak to me of my mother,' said Gabriel in a low tone, 'ever again.' And with that, he rose from the table. His chair fell back, crashing against the floor. He charged towards the exit, before coming to a sharp halt. The words had accumulated in his throat, desperate to be released. 'Perhaps I would not have been such a disappointment if you had not been such a failure of a father.' He reached for the box he had placed on the end of the table. 'I bought this for you,' he said coldly, waving the box. 'It is the tie you lost, the one you were incessantly complaining about.' Gabriel put it down, sliding it across the table. Hugo caught it before it hit the plate of mutton. 'Enjoy your meal.'

'You look so silly,' laughed Gabriel, dipping his hand in more of the red paint.

Cassius raised his eyebrows. 'Do I?'

'Yes!'

'I do believe you are not being very artistic, my dear boy. I had thought artists painted with multiple colours?'

Gabriel dipped his hand in another pot, before smearing it on his father's other cheek. He was grinning, displaying all his little teeth. 'Now you have red and blue on you!'

Cassius rose from the floor, looking at himself in the mirror in his study. 'Will you look at that? Magnificent.' He turned to face Gabriel again. 'Do you think Mother shall like it?'

Gabriel shook his head fervently 'No, she will say we have made a mess.'

Cassius grinned. 'Care to find out?' Before Gabriel could answer, he called for Eliza. Gabriel giggled, covering his mouth with his hand, and thereby accidentally smearing the paint all over himself too. Footsteps sounded down the hall.

'What have you two been up to?' said a soft voice, a perfect equilibrium between calmness and authority, melodic in nature. And then she appeared in the doorway. Her dark hair fell down her shoulders, not yet put up for the day. Her skin gleamed as the sun shone in through the windows. Her eyes, reminiscent of warm caramel and honey, fell on Gabriel first, and then Cassius.

'Goodness,' she said. A laugh escaped her lips as Cassius grinned at her. 'You two have made quite a mess.'

'Unfortunately so, my dear, but we are having tremendous fun. Perhaps you should join us.' Cassius took a step towards Eliza, making her take a step back. She held out her hand.

'Oh, no, no,' she laughed. 'I must prepare for the day, and—'

Before Eliza could say anything else, Cassius had pulled her down with him. She let out a yelp as he planted a kiss on her cheek, smearing the paint upon her face. Gabriel laughed as he dipped his hand in a pot of yellow paint and pressed it on his mother's white dress.

She gasped. 'Gabriel, you did not!'

Gabriel mimicked her gasp. His mother narrowed her eyes, and instead of storming off to wash her dress, she dipped her entire hand in the pot paint and, before Gabriel could jump out of the way, smeared it across his face. Cassius tipped his head back, revelling in laughter. Gabriel's mouth hung open in surprise as he stood frozen. Before he knew it, all three of them had grabbed a pot each, and started attacking each other with paint. Colours splashed everywhere, creating a whirlwind pool around them.

Gabriel gasped as he woke. His mother's warm laughter still reverberated in his head, a painful contrast against the darkness and solitude of his room. He heaved himself out of bed, resting his forearms on his thighs. Instead of setting into motion his usual distractions, he put his head in his hands and sobbed.

CHAPTER XXXVI

Journey Upon the Styx

Alexander sighed as he threw the newspaper down on the table. Gabriel, in the process of sipping his tea, put his porcelain cup down and picked up the paper. His eyes widened. A vote of no confidence had finally been passed, and a general election was set to take place within the week. This was followed by an article announcing more deaths. *TEN MORE MURDERS.* Beneath the headline were countless columns condemning Gascoyne-Cecil and his ministers, the House of Lords and even Queen Victoria herself.

'Have you seen this?' asked Gabriel, showing Alexander the newspaper. Alexander grabbed the paper.

'Well, it was about time.' He read further down the article. 'The Conservative Justice Party has the most support. I believe your dreams of their victory shall come true in the end.'

The door to the breakfast room opened, followed by two maids rolling in a tray filled with pastries. Gabriel put his head in his hand, closing his eyes for several seconds.

'We have a slightly different assortment today, Mr Wakefield,' started the one with short, brown hair. 'Madeira tartlets with—'

'Yes, that is fine, Emma, just leave them.'

The maid did as instructed, gesturing for the other one to hurry up. After several seconds, they swiftly closed the door behind them as they exited the room. It was a cold morning. The branches, visible through the long, towering windows at the end of the room, were covered in frost. The city was plunged in an icy shimmer, as if one was looking at the world through a sheet of ice.

'I do not quite know what to say,' said Alexander.

Gabriel remained silent, listening to the crackling of the fire, watching the gardens outside in their perfect stillness. He breathed in deeply, laying his palms flat on the table. 'I know what you are thinking.'

'Pardon?'

'My brother.'

Alexander opened his mouth, before closing it again. He pressed his lips together as he looked at Gabriel with sympathy. 'I suppose that is our only clue.'

'Perhaps we should re-focus our attention, rather than chasing the same clue. It is leading us nowhere. We are not digging deep enough. We are merely skimming the surface.'

'Dr Wagner and the warehouse are amongst the most solid clues we have, Gabriel.'

'Then why is it leading us nowhere?'

'It has led us somewhere.'

'To whom? Hugo?' Gabriel scoffed. 'Do you truly believe my brother could have had any part in this?'

Alexander remained silent as he looked at Gabriel. 'I know this is difficult to accept, Ashmore, but—'

'What on earth are you speaking of?' exclaimed Gabriel, his brows furrowed. 'We did not find anything to actually link Hugo with the Erebus. Why are you so insistent?'

'I am not insistent; I am merely following the clues we have—'

'No, you are just desperate to solve this hellish case and prove yourself to people who do not care about you.'

Alexander scoffed. 'Oh, really? What are you then, Ashmore? Desperate to cling on to your brother's innocence rather than actually solve a crime that is killing multiple people a day, which *you* helped spread in the first place?' Alexander let out a shaky breath. He sat back on his chair, not realising he had been leaning over the table. 'I apologise, I did not mean to—'

'Forget it.'

'Ashmore, I—'

Alexander's voice was cut off by Gabriel slamming the door. The sound echoed through the halls as he charged down the foyer, his footsteps reverberating against the walls, yet all he could hear within his head was deadly silence.

His breath formed clouds around him as Gabriel walked home. He felt the sharpness of winter even more harshly now, creeping through his wool jumper, nearly penetrating

his skin. An old woman sat at the corner of Belgrave Square. She had withdrawn into herself, attempting to preserve whatever warmth she had left in her body. Her silver hair was dull and matted at the back, the thin coat on her back full of holes. People passed her by, oblivious to her existence. Gabriel looked away and crossed the street. He took long strides as he headed for Upper Belgrave Street. He halted. He then turned around, heading back towards the woman. He came to a stop before her; she did not even notice his presence. He took his coat off, and carefully put it over her shoulders. She jumped at the touch.

'I apologise, I did not mean to scare you,' said Gabriel. Her eyes opened, a crystal blue like that of ice, staring up at him behind squinted and sagging lids. She did not say anything as she held her gaze. 'The coat is made of pure wool. It ought to keep you warm.' The woman retained her silent demeanour, and so Gabriel continued on his way. He only looked back once, when he was far enough that the woman wouldn't notice him, and saw her dried lips take the shape of a faint smile.

Just as Gabriel turned the corner and arrived at his street, he stopped dead in his tracks. He saw his brother stepping out of the house. He slipped back onto the street he had come from, before carefully peering out from the corner. He watched his brother lock the door before descending the front steps. Instead of getting into a carriage, his brother started walking. Gabriel frowned as he took a step towards him. He could not be going to the docks; it would take him at least two hours to walk there. As he looked closer, he

spotted something in his brother's arms. Something solid, brown. He squinted his eyes. It appeared to be a chest or a small trunk of some sort, made of leather. And so, he tailed his brother through the streets of London, until they ended up in Mayfair.

Gabriel halted as he finally saw where his brother stopped. His throat had gone dry, his bones felt brittle beneath his skin and flesh. His insides churned, acid pooling in his stomach and sloshing through his veins.

The Silverton Club.

Gabriel blinked, making sure he was not hallucinating, that he wasn't just unconscious in an opium den and that this was all a terrible nightmare. They must have missed the Erebus. They hadn't had the time to check at the bottom of the crates, where they must have stored them. His nails dug into his palm as he watched his brother, looking at the exterior of the club with curiosity, before he disappeared inside.

Water surrounded him. Dark, deep waters. Mist hovered above it, caressing the onyx waters like a lover's taloned hand. Spiked mountains stretched out into the distance, sharp as blades. The sun was setting, colouring the sky a scorching blood-red. Gabriel could feel the thick, murky water snake around him. And then he was pulled down. Gabriel didn't thrash against the arms and legs that were wrapping around his body. Instead, he let them drag him under, to the deep, muddy depths of the river until his breath ran out and the seaweed-filled water finally entered his lungs.

Gabriel's head lolled to the side with a vehement traction. His vision spun, before slowly focusing in on a

blurred, dimly lit room. Shades of red and lamps casting orange light surrounded him. The smell of ammonia wafted in the air, filling his nostrils as it tried to fight its way to his throat. Gabriel coughed. The sound was muffled. A figure stood before him, features unrecognisable. Gabriel could faintly hear his breathing, as if it were coming from some deep ancient pit in the ground. It was shallow. Too shallow.

His head snapped to the side again, his cheek prickling as his vision dotted with black spots. He heard his name being said. Over and over.

'*Gabriel. Gabriel!*'

Gabriel coughed again, before automatically reaching for his pipe. His hands only met the empty space of the sofa. The voice spoke again, but this time Gabriel did not hear it. He felt pressure on his shoulders, shaking him. Then, his vision started clearing. Before him stood a man, a tall, broad man.

'Hugo?' breathed Gabriel. The man's outline morphed into his brother, his own features staring back at him, just like he had done many nights long passed. The green in his eyes gleamed under the candlelight, shadows pooling beneath them. He heard another voice behind him, but he could not comprehend the language. A hand flashed past his vision and then another sting. He was looking at the wall beside him, the blood-red colour almost spilling onto him. The skin on his left cheek prickled incessantly. Gabriel put his palms down on the sofa, forcing himself upright.

He forced out another deep breath, gathering the words stuck in his throat and spitting them out. 'You *bastard.*'

He heard his name again, muffled. 'I loved you.' Gabriel panted. 'I loved you so much, you bastard.'

'Gabriel, it is me, Alexander!'

Gabriel frowned as he watched his brother fade away, morphing into someone else entirely. And then, he recognised him. He recognised the steady grey eyes, the tousled brown hair, the reassuring smile and dotted freckles. He attempted to turn away, crawl into a hole and be hidden from view forever, because with each second that passed Gabriel, despite the total numbness in his body, could feel shame threatening to devour him whole.

'Leave,' he managed to hiss, as he forced his muscles to work and heaved himself upright. He did not remain standing for long before his legs gave out. Alexander caught him by the arms, holding his limp body upright. Gabriel thrashed against him. 'Let go of me!'

'How much have you had, Gabriel?' demanded Alexander. 'How much?"

'How much?' sighed Hugo as he set Gabriel down onto his bed. He held his neck straight, stopping it from lolling back.

'Not that much,' muttered Gabriel slowly, his eyes slowly cascading over the room. 'Is this my room?'

'Yes, Gabriel, it is.'

'How did I get back? What day is it?'

Hugo drew his lips in a fine line, his jaw tense. 'It is Thursday.'

'What time?'

'Six in the morning.'

Gabriel raised an eyebrow as he slowly fell onto his side. His cheek hit the cold surface of his pillow. His eyelids felt heavy as they started drooping, and just as Gabriel thought the mercy of sleep would carry him away, a sudden, extreme wave of nausea washed over him. He heaved himself upright as he started gagging, his Adam's apple bobbing up and down his throat. Hugo was quick. He grabbed a bowl from the floor, holding it before his brother's mouth, just as Gabriel vomited. Gabriel groaned as his chest heaved up and down. The sour smell filled the room. Gabriel let out another low groan as he continued vomiting, gripping on to his brother's forearm. Hugo rubbed Gabriel's back.

'It is all right, just get it out.'

A creak sounded. A creak awfully loud at the crack of dawn. Gabriel's eyes shot to the door. He let out a low sound from somewhere deep within him.

'Get her out,' he said, before having to turn his head towards the bowl once more.

'Adelia, return to your chambers.'

Adelia looked at her brothers with furrowed brows and eyes filled with concern. 'Is Gabriel hurt?'

'No, Gabriel is fine, he just got ill. Please, return now, I shall be there shortly.'

'I do not want to. I can see shadows in my room, and I miss Mother and—'

'Adelia, for God's sake, just leave!' hissed Gabriel, ignoring the spit and vomit that was dripping off his chin. Dismay flashed over her features as she took a step back, still lingering in the doorway, until Hugo closed the door.

'How did you find me?' Gabriel finally fought himself free of Alexander's iron grip and propped himself up against the wall. Sweat beaded at his temples, making his hair stick to his forehead. Droplets of it ran down his back.

Alexander turned to the workers behind them, a Chinese man and woman, clearing up pipes from the floor. 'How much has he had?'

They looked warily at Alexander.

'I asked *how much*?' demanded Alexander fervently.

'How would they know?' said Gabriel, waving his hand. 'Sing has many customers.' He turned towards the man. '*Nǐ jiào tā guěn.*'

Sing shook his head. '*Nǐ yīng gāi huí jiā*, Gabriel.'

Gabriel scoffed. He tripped over his own feet as he took a step forward, catching himself just before he hit the floor.

'What did you say?'

'Nothing you should concern yourself with.'

Alexander sighed as he moved to Gabriel's side, slipping his arm into his. Gabriel snatched his arm back, shooting Alexander a glance he had not given him since the first time they had met. Alexander pretended he did not see it, willed the look of hurt flashing across his face to disappear.

The icy air shot through them like a bullet. Gabriel stumbled out of the opium den, his vision still hazy. He shivered, realising he was only wearing a shirt. The ground was covered in a layer of snow, crunching with every step they took. Gabriel's stomach churned. He steadied himself against a wall with his palms, arms outstretched, his head bowed forwards. He felt something warm wrap around his

shoulders. When he looked up, he realised Alexander had given him his coat.

'Are you all right?' he asked, looking at Gabriel with concerned eyes.

Gabriel resisted the urge to groan again. 'Perfectly fine,' he managed, before shrugging the coat off. It fell to the floor, burying itself in the snow.

'Oh, come on, Gabriel, it is bloody freezing,'

'I do not want it.'

Somehow, Alexander managed to haul Gabriel into a carriage. Gabriel rested his head on the window, letting the rocking and the sound of hooves pull him back into a trance, desperately trying to reach that state of blankness, solitude, again. It was as close to peace as he could get. He could feel Alexander's eyes on him.

'What happened, Gabriel?' he asked in a low voice.

Gabriel remained silent, watching fresh snow fall out of the midnight sky.

'You could have come to me.'

At that, Gabriel let out a bitter chuckle, sharp and twisted. 'Oh, really?'

'Yes!' exclaimed Alexander. 'I have told you so—'

'You are a liar,' seethed Gabriel. His surroundings started spinning again. Gabriel resisted the urge to vomit. 'You would just leave the second things got difficult, just like they all do.'

'No, I would not, for God's sake!' Alexander flushed, his cheeks blotting with colour. 'You have become my friend. A cherished friend. My only friend.'

Gabriel's lips formed a venomous grin. 'Are you that lonely you wish to be burdened with others' problems?' he slurred. 'I find that quite pathetic.'

Alexander's lips thinned, the muscle in his jaw tensing. '*You* are pathetic.'

Gabriel chuckled, his voice echoing into the depths of the night.

'This is not my house,' protested Gabriel as the coachman opened the carriage doors.

'No, indeed it is not,' said Alexander coldly as he appeared from behind the man. He grabbed Gabriel by the arm, pulling him out of the carriage. Gabriel was too disorientated to fight against him. 'It is mine and you are staying here for the night.'

'How torturous,' muttered Gabriel as he stumbled out. 'I do hope that is not an invitation to your bed...' Gabriel panted at the exertion, before continuing, slurring the ends of his words. 'You might not be aware, but I am not a homosexual.'

Alexander's expression remained stone-hard, unamused. 'Neither am I. Now get inside.'

The front door was opened, spilling bright light out onto the dark street like golden paint. A silhouette of a short man stood before it.

'Cyril, we shall be taking Mr Ashmore up to the guest bedroom.'

'Very well, Mr Wakefield, may I ask which one?'

'The one on my floor.'

'Do you intend on keeping me prisoner?' Gabriel slurred.

'No,' said Alexander dryly. 'Are you also drunk by any chance?'

Gabriel did not respond as he let Alexander half-carry him up the stairs. He felt his momentary consciousness slipping, making his legs weak. Alexander, now carrying all of Gabriel's weight, grunted as they reached the door, before dropping him onto a large four-poster bed. The room was dark. Gabriel's eyes had closed. He heard Alexander's footsteps recede, and just as he thought he had left him, feeling a strange, secret disappointment within his chest, he returned. Gabriel forced his eyes to open, fighting the extreme drowsiness that was threatening to consume his consciousness. Alexander had set down a crystal decanter full of water, alongside a thick glass.

'Drink all of this. I shall check up on you in the night.'

'To make sure I am not dead?'

Alexander's face turned grim. 'Do not joke about such things.'

Gabriel sighed, reaching to take off his shoes. He fumbled with the laces. His arms felt like lead, his fingers slipping with each movement he made.

'Just let me do it,' said Alexander, pulling off Gabriel's shoes in one swift motion.

'Are you thinking of undressing me too?'

Alexander scowled. 'You can do that yourself.'

'Pity.'

'You seem to be seconds away from losing consciousness, yet your sarcasm remains untouched. Unbelievable.'

Gabriel chuckled dryly. His chest hurt at the act.

Alexander hesitated before speaking. 'What happened, Gabriel? You mentioned Hugo.'

The smile upon Gabriel's lips faded. He cleared his throat, which made his ears ring. 'That is between him and I.'

Alexander looked at him warily. 'Does it have something to do with the investigation? You ought to tell me if it does.'

Images flashed before Gabriel's mind, laughter and joy, tears and pain. He saw rolling hills, his brother's face a canvas of merriment against the deep green. And even now, when he looked into those emerald eyes, he saw despair and hatred, but he also saw the past. He saw the faint glimmer of an age of happiness, innocence. And that is why Gabriel did not say anything as he watched his friend's eyes beg him to confide in him. He saw the desperation, so like his own; the need, the desire to succeed in something. And yet, he did not say anything, and let unconsciousness finally carry him away.

CHAPTER XXXVII

Dawn of Dismay

The morning was unforgiving. Gabriel was awoken by the sound of clattering plates. Daylight shone into the room. He winced, covering his eyes with his forearm. When he opened them again a few seconds later, he saw the blurred image of multiple people coming in and out of the room. He frowned as he heaved himself upright. Every muscle in his body burned with the flames of a thousand suns. His mind felt diluted, muddled, as if he were trying to look through swamp water.

'What are you doing?' muttered Gabriel to the room of people, massaging his neck.

A short man dressed in a black suit bowed. 'Readying breakfast, Mr Ashmore.'

'Cyril,' said Gabriel. He blinked, looking around the room. Plates full of various breakfast items, which Gabriel could not yet make out, had been laid out on the table at the

far end of the room. He focused his eyes, and realised it was only for one. 'Where is Alexander?' he asked as he hoisted himself out of bed. He was still dressed in his clothes from the night before: a wrinkled shirt and black trousers.

Cyril pursed his lips. 'Mr Wakefield shall not be joining you.' He said it in such a tone that indicated he must know about last night's occurrences. Gabriel could not remember if he was present or not.

'Where is he?'

'He is working,' was all Cyril said, before he turned on his heel and swiftly exited the room, the servants following him. The door slammed shut, the sound of it echoing through the room. Gabriel stepped towards the table. He felt a tightness in his chest. Alexander had ordered an elaborate meal, complete with cooked bacon, potatoes, porridge, pastries and even various sorts of meats and cheeses. The room was eerily quiet, a new sort of solitude settling over it. The thought of getting the food down his throat made his stomach churn. The daylight streaming in was too bright, the colours of the walls too red, the silence too loud. He had to get out of there.

Gabriel charged out of the guest room, taking long strides before heading down the stairs. He had reached the foyer, halfway across, almost at the door, until a voice stopped him.

'Leaving already?'

The voice was cold, devoid of the usual passion that radiated from his friend.

Gabriel turned to face Alexander. He was leaning against the doorframe of a study, his arms crossed over his

chest. His hair was dishevelled, dark circles forming under his eyes. Gabriel did not say anything as Alexander held his gaze. 'I assume breakfast was displeasing, then.'

'I am not hungry.'

'You ought to eat,' retorted Alexander sharply.

'I said, I am not hungry. But I thank you for the efforts of—'

'Do not lie; you are not grateful.'

Gabriel inhaled sharply. He opened his mouth to speak, which, with no doubt, would have included a sharp remark, but he closed it again.

'You are keeping something from me.'

Gabriel's eyes narrowed slightly, his shoulders becoming even more rigid than they already were. 'No.'

'Yes. What is it?'

'I am not keeping anything from you.'

Alexander's jaw tightened. 'It is about your brother, is it not? What have you found out?'

'Look, just leave it—'

'Leave it alone?' Alexander laughed bitterly. 'Really, Ashmore? Leave it alone, whilst the people of this city are dying? Whilst criminality devours us whole? Do you not realise what this is doing to me? What this is doing to *everyone*?'

Gabriel sighed, remaining quiet as his friend looked him in the eyes.

'You are a selfish bastard,' said Alexander.

Gabriel inhaled sharply. 'I have never asked anything of you.'

'No, but I gave it to you nevertheless.'

'Then stop giving.'

Alexander's lips thinned. Gabriel sighed. 'What do you want from me, Wakefield?'

'Nothing! I do not want anything from you except your bloody friendship. Perhaps it sounds mad to you, but I see you as my friend. And what you did last night…' his breath quivered, 'it scared me. But most of all, it disappointed me. That you gave up so easily.'

Gabriel spoke in a small voice. 'I did not give up.'

Alexander scoffed. 'We both know that is a lie. God knows what would have happened if I had not found—'

'I did *not* give up,' hissed Gabriel. They stared at each other in silence for several seconds before Gabriel spoke again. 'Sometimes… things get too much, and I just need… I just need to forget it.'

Alexander stared at him with that same stern expression, but something flickered in his eyes.

Gabriel cracked his knuckles behind his back, glancing away from Alexander. 'I must depart now.'

'What happened between you and Hugo?' asked Alexander suddenly, stepping forward. Gabriel halted.

'Nothing you should concern yourself—'

'Stop that,' snapped Alexander. 'For once, tell me something true.'

Gabriel's jaw tensed. He shifted, feeling his limbs grow heavier with each passing second. His lips parted slightly, before closing again. The foyer went quiet, so quiet Gabriel could hear a distant clock ticking.

A bitter scoff escaped Alexander's lips. 'You cannot do it, can you?'

'Thank you for breakfast,' said Gabriel, before he turned on his heel and exited the Wakefield residence, leaving behind an impenetrable silence that settled throughout the entire house.

The same silence engulfed him as he stepped foot in the Ashmore house. It was cold, but Gabriel did not shiver, nor did he light a fire. Instead, he headed upstairs. The wood creaked beneath his feet, ancient and worn. He passed by portraits of elderly family members, their colour no longer maintained, fading with each passing day. He peered into his father's study, and, to his luck, he was not in it. Gabriel did not even stop to wonder where he might have gone as he pushed open the door, heading straight for the desk. He pulled open the last compartment, rifling through a thick stack of letters until his hand finally found its target. A small, velvet pouch. Gabriel pulled its strings, by which it was fastened, open, his fingers impatient. Within it laid a singular gold-coated opium pill. His father's own collection, reserved for special occasions of the past, occasions which no longer occurred. Gabriel did not hesitate as he put it in his mouth.

The ice-cold water that filled the bath pressed down on him like a heavy weight, constricting his breathing, squeezing the air out of his lungs. He did not continuously gasp anymore, like he had done the first few months they had run out of hot water. He remembered how he used to use the little gas they could afford to heat the water Adelia bathed with, carrying large bowls of it up and down the stairs. He'd become used

to it now, used to the water numbing his muscles, turning his blood into ice. Occasionally, if he was lucky, it would numb his mind too. He let his body slide deeper into the tub. The water had reached his bottom lip, then his nostrils, until his entire head went under.

Gabriel barely felt the effects of the single pill as he dressed himself. He looked at his reflection, and all he saw were purple smudges beneath his eyes, the dullness of his skin, the fading brightness of his eyes. His lips were dry, flaking at the edges. He closed his eyes, inhaling deeply.

Evening had fallen, spilling an obsidian darkness into the house. Gabriel set foot in the parlour, the entire house suspended in silence, frozen over with bleakness. The faint outline of the furniture hovered in the air, as if they were nothing but mere apparitions.

His father returned at midnight. Gabriel's head snapped towards the door, before he scrambled to bunch together the parchments on which he had been writing every single clue they had found. He put the quill down whilst rising from the desk positioned at the edge of the parlour. Cassius did not notice Gabriel's presence as he slowly walked into the foyer.

Gabriel cleared his throat. 'Father.'

Cassius looked up, his manner disinterested as his eyes fell on his son before him. 'Ah, you.'

'Where have you been?'

'Out, boy,' muttered his father as he took out a crumpled newspaper he held between his arm and his side, discarding it on the table.

'Out where?'

'Must I explain myself to you?'

Gabriel bit the inside of his cheek. 'Well, since I am tasked with taking care of you, I believe it is my right to—'

Cassius grunted. 'Am I a child?'

'Until you stop acting like one, apparently so.'

His father's eyes narrowed, brows furrowing at Gabriel's words. Gabriel had thought he would fire a retort at him, tell him how disappointing he had become, how unlike his mother; yet all his father did was shake his head, turning his back to him, before disappearing up the stairs. And for some reason, the sense of indifference hurt Gabriel more than the vile words he normally uttered. He remained standing in the dark foyer, the flickering light of the streetlamp barely penetrating through the windows. His eyes fell on the newspaper his father had left behind. Gabriel grabbed it, taking it towards the candles he had lit earlier. Shadows danced against the walls as he lowered the newspaper to the oak desk. And then he stopped breathing. The letters danced with each flicker of the candlelight, yet they stood out like blood upon white flesh.

FIFTEEN MORE DEATHS RAVAGE LONDON.

Gabriel did not continue reading the article as he swallowed hard, willing oxygen into his lungs. He staggered back, hitting the bookshelf behind him. Pain shot through his back, pain which he barely felt. His chest had become tight. He ripped open the first few buttons of his shirt, attempting to steady his breathing. The buttons bounced on the floor, rolling under the sofa. He gripped onto the armchair, his knuckles white and strained, before he shot

to the front door. He threw on a coat, taking nothing with him but his rage and anguish as he headed for the streets of East London.

CHAPTER XXXVIII

Smoke and Madness

The air smelt of sour fish and smoke. Gabriel could feel the breeze of the river as his boots squelched in the mud wedged between the cobbles, hear the distant cries of sailors having just arrived from faraway voyages. He walked quickly, fervently, through the narrow streets, in search of just one thing. The Erebus. There must have been others spreading it, now all he had to do was find out who. Perhaps he could find suppliers in certain opium dens, Gabriel thought, as he headed towards Chinatown. The sky rumbled above him, warning of an impending storm. Women of the night attempted to approach him, but he charged past them before they could get a word in.

He barged into the first den he saw. It was not his usual, but he had been there once before. It was one of the worst, with no furniture but only mattresses on the mouldy floor. Insects crawled on the bare walls, however, it was nothing

compared to the diseases that those who frequented it brought. The smell of opium was stifling, mixed with other scents Gabriel did not wish to ponder on. Gabriel analysed the room. Nobody was conscious, and no trace of the Erebus. He walked further in. The scent of urine suddenly bit at his nose. Gabriel resisted the urge to gag as he continued on his path. He was met with nothing but unconscious, drooling men, who all had an opium pipe in hand. None of the midnight powder in sight.

'Fancy a night together?' a voice purred as Gabriel stepped out of the den. He took a large breath, savouring the cold air. Gabriel ignored the woman, did not even look at her as he continued down the street. The clacking of heels sounded behind him. 'With a face like yours, I'd do it for free.'

'Leave,' said Gabriel coldly, keeping his eyes on his next destination just ahead.

'Are you sure? You look quite stressed, sir. I'd be happy to relieve you of—'

Gabriel turned around sharply, grabbing the woman by the arms. She flinched at the movement, her blue eyes wide. Curly, blonde hair cascaded down her shoulders. 'Leave right this moment. I do not wish for your pathetic services,' spat Gabriel, before releasing the woman. She trembled slightly as she staggered on her heels, before turning away and disappearing into the darkness, the smog consuming her figure whole.

Gabriel had entered four more dens by midnight. His limbs tingled with nerves and fury at his fruitless

endeavours. He clenched and unclenched his fists as he paced around a square. The cold had started biting at his skin, knives and needles taunting him. He approached the last den of the area. A bigger one, slightly better kept than the first. Occasionally frequented by noteworthy figures, those who liked to pretend they were something they were not, a sick escape from their privileged pressures of the day.

The aroma of ammonia circled his nose as he entered the den. It had been a former townhouse, by the looks of it. Vast ceilings rose to the sky, a broad staircase leading up to the upper floors before him. The wallpaper, a metallic shade adorned with flowers, which once could have been considered beautiful, had started peeling off at the edges, crumbling onto the creaky wooden floor. The foyer was filled with sofas, and the sofas were filled with men and their long pipes. Gabriel had refrained from watching them too closely, ripping his eyes away the minute he realised the Erebus was not there, but now, as the night closed in on him, and the futility of his endeavours became apparent, he watched them for a bit longer. Watched as some heated their pipes upon fires, listened to it bubble, felt how they inhaled it. He cracked his neck, running his hands through his hair as he exhaled. He let his hands fall to his side, his nails digging into his palms. He forced himself to move, drawing blood from his hands as he slowly stepped further into the house. He did not feel the sting, nor did he feel the blood drip onto the floor. His eyes were fixated upon the pipes, one part of his brain searching for any sign of the Erebus, and the other desperate to succumb to blissful oblivion.

He found himself on the upper floors. A deep ache settled into his head, expanding with each passing minute. Gabriel knew he had to get out of here, knew that if he didn't he would end up just like all the other men. He found himself before a window, its panes fogged up at the corners, looking out onto a misty courtyard. The room, a former bedchamber, was lit by candlelight. Gabriel caught sight of his flickering reflection. He turned away quickly. His head spun at the movement, and suddenly he could not remember where he was. He stumbled out onto the hallway, his breathing thickening as he looked around, but only saw four empty walls facing him. He cursed, stepping back until he was pressed up against one of the walls. His eyes frantically searched the room, looking for a way out. He tried to steady his breathing, clenching his hands into fists. He closed his eyes, breathing out slowly.

When he opened them again, the landing had returned, alongside the armchairs and men within them. Gabriel rubbed his temples, exhaling loudly, before he started charging towards the stairs. And just as he put his foot down on the first step, he halted. He turned around, facing another hallway he had not yet ventured into. It was dark, shadowed in obsidian. It appeared almost deserted, and just as Gabriel was about to turn away, he saw the faintest trace of illumination. It peeked out from the corner of the hallway, easily mistakable for a mere discolouration of the wooden floors. He hesitated before entering the hallway. No matter how badly he wished to solve this investigation, another part of him, a deeper, more primitive part, screamed at him to leave.

He swallowed hard, blocking it out as he stepped into the darkness.

The air, somehow, felt heavier, damp, as he continued down the long hallway. There were no windows lining the space, no escape. Mould grew on the corners of the wall, slowly infesting its way upwards until it devoured the entire house. Gabriel struggled to breathe, the walls closing in on him with each step he took. Finally, just as he thought about turning back, he reached the door. The light was brighter as he stood before it. He placed his hand upon the doorknob, and before his mind could tell him anything different, he twisted.

The room was dark, like the hallway, except for two candles burning beside the door. Gabriel took one of them, extending it before him. The room, another previous bedchamber, was mainly empty, save for two mattresses upon the ground. One right in front of him, and the other in the far corner. A man looked up at him, shooting him a sharp smirk. He was dressed in a tweed suit, with sharp, delicate features. His dark hair was neatly trimmed. He could not have been older than thirty.

'This is a private residence,' he teased, waving his hand around the room, before it fell back down his side. His voice was articulate, posh almost, although Gabriel suspected he was trying to hide it. He did not await Gabriel's response as he brought his pipe to his mouth, inhaling deeply, and sprawled on the mattress. His chest moved up and down slowly, as if at any time it would just stop moving altogether. Gabriel turned away, his head spinning, sweat dripping down his back as he neared the second mattress. His heart boomed

in his chest. Upon it was a man, head turned towards the window, breathing slowly. His skin was beaded with sweat, and as Gabriel looked closer, grey in colour. His eyes fell on the mattress he was seated upon, searching for just one thing. After half a minute, the man, noticing Gabriel's presence, turned his head towards him. He looked of similar age to Gabriel himself, with golden brown hair that was now plastered to his forehead. He had narrow eyes, coloured an absolute black. Gabriel sighed, and just as he was about to turn away and leave the doomed place behind forever, he saw it. The faintest trace, nestled right on the inside of his nostril.

Black powder.

Gabriel's eyes widened, the mist in his head disappearing as his body gathered all the focus left within him and shot it at the man sitting before him. He fell to his knees before him, grabbing the man by his bony shoulders.

'Where did you get that from?' demanded Gabriel, eyes flaring with urgency. His heart pounded in his chest, so loud he thought he could hear it echoing in the room.

The man's eyebrows furrowed together as he attempted to withdraw his body from Gabriel's grip. 'What are you on about?' he exclaimed.

'The Erebus. *Where?*' hissed Gabriel.

'I... I...' the man stuttered, fear forming in his pupils. 'If... if you would like some, just take it, I have some left—'

'No, you *idiot*, that is not what I am asking. Who did you obtain it from?'

'Who?'

'Yes, *who*! Now answer me!'

'A... A man, he was just in here several minutes ago.'

'What man? What did he look like?' Gabriel's chest moved up and down rapidly, his nails digging through the man's shirt into his flesh.

The man winced, still squirming to get free of Gabriel's grip. 'I do not know; I did not see! He was wearing a black hood!'

Gabriel released his grip, shoving the man against the wall before he rose to his feet, storming out of the room. The world spun around him as he dashed down the stairs, taking three steps at a time, landed in the foyer and sprinted towards the exit. He stumbled out onto the dark street, head whipping left and right. He squinted his eyes, willing them to adjust to the dimmed gaslights. He could follow the narrow street for a reasonable distance until it curved to the left. He stepped forward, his carotid artery pulsing in his neck, his breath misting in the air, and then he saw it. A dark silhouette, disappearing around the corner. Gabriel felt his body break into a run, carrying him with a vehemence he did not know he possessed. The cold air burned his throat and lungs as he panted heavily. And then, he reached the corner.

It was a man walking before him, dressed in a long, dark cloak. Moonlight shone down on them, illuminating the street in silver light. Gabriel pounced, grabbing the man by his shoulder and slamming him into a wall. A loud wince escaped him, just as his hood fell back. The first thing Gabriel noticed was his eye-bags, coloured a deep grey. Exhaustion dripped from his young features, as he stared at Gabriel with wide eyes, his mouth opening and closing as he stammered incoherently.

Gabriel's lips twisted into a sneer as he looked at the man. 'Where is it?' he hissed with such vehemence that it made the man stutter even more.

'W-what... whatever do... whatever—'

'*Speak*, for God's sake!'

'W-whatever do you mean?'

'The Erebus; where did you get it from?'

The man hesitated for a moment, eyes flickering down to his pocket for a mere second, before looking back up at Gabriel. 'I... do not know what you are speaking of.'

Gabriel let out a sharp sigh, before moving the man forwards and slamming him back into the wall. He groaned as his head collided with the bricks, blinking rapidly as if trying to ward off unconsciousness.

'Do you take me for a fool?' growled Gabriel, his gaze brimstone and fire. He tightened the grip he had on the man's shirt.

'No, no, of course not!' exclaimed the man, on the edge of a whimper. 'It is in my pocket, my left-hand pocket! Take it, it is yours—'

'I do not *want* it; I want to know where you *obtained* it.'

The man frantically shook his head. 'I don't know... I don't know—'

Gabriel's lips thinned as all noise muffled around him, until it was just him and his quick breaths, and then his fist collided with the man's face. Pain flared in Gabriel's knuckles. The man staggered sideways, clutching his nose, before he fell onto his knees. Blood ran through his fingers, a stark scarlet against his pale skin, dripping onto the ground. A sound escaped him, something between a sob

and a curse. Gabriel knelt before him, grabbing his collar as he pulled the man's face up towards his own.

'*Where. Is. It?*'

'Please… I just deliver it, I do not know—'

'Just tell me where, God damn it!'

'I do not know! I obtain it from different places – in public – I do not interact with anyone, I only just started this!'

Gabriel clenched his jaw as he slowly dropped his hands to his side, balling them in fists. The man let out a breath, body still slightly quivering. Gabriel put a hand on his shoulder, pressing his lips into a fine line as he looked down at the ground and then back up at the man. His bark-coloured eyes shimmered under the gaslight, lined with tears. Gabriel's throat constricted as he struggled to swallow, because at that very moment he saw himself, just as he had been several years ago. Desperate, frightened; a fool. Disgust pooled in his stomach like acid, disgust so strong it made his hands twitch, and before he knew it he had delivered another blow to the man. He grunted as he slid down to the floor, head lolling back. Everything around Gabriel was starting to become a blur, except for the person before him. Blood dripped out of the man's mouth as he attempted to heave himself upright. Gabriel grabbed him by his shirt, tangling it into his fist as he pulled the man up to face him.

'*Where*,' was all he snarled, and it was no longer a question, but a mere primitive exclamation of anger containing years' worth of fury and rage.

The man merely let out a low, gargling sound as a response, unable to articulate any words. Gabriel looked down at him

with a sneer, and once again the man fell back and the same sharp pain shot through Gabriel's fist. He breathed hard, chest rising up and down vehemently. His mind was blank, emptied, save for that feeling of resentment burning deep within him, rising higher to the surface with each passing second. Blood dripped from his knuckles as he grabbed the half-unconscious man off the ground, lifting his fist…

'What are you doing?'

Gabriel blinked rapidly, head whipping towards the source of the sound. The man dropped down to the ground behind him, groaning softly.

Before him stood a little boy, no older than six. His cheeks were covered in soot, his attire worn down. His head was shaved. Gabriel frowned at the boy, looking around the street for any sign of his mother.

'Is that man okay?'

'Yes,' muttered Gabriel, clearing his hoarse throat. The boy stared at the man on the ground, brows furrowed together in concern. Gabriel took a step towards him. He put his hands on the boy's bony shoulder, turning the boy's back to the man. 'He shall be fine.'

'What happened?' the boy asked again, bright blue eyes staring up at Gabriel with determination.

'He got ill.' Gabriel put his hands in his pocket.

'That is a lie. I saw you hit him.' The boy crossed his thin arms over his chest. 'What did he do to you?'

Gabriel narrowed his eyes. 'Do not question me.'

'Why not?'

'Because I said so.' Gabriel looked around the street. 'Where are your parents?'

The boy shrugged. 'What are you doing here?'

'My affairs are none of your concern.' Gabriel eyed the boy, observing the thin material of his clothes. 'Are you not cold, boy?'

The boy shrugged again, but Gabriel could see the shivers he was trying to hide. Gabriel sighed, reaching to take off his coat, before he realised he did not have it on. He frowned as he looked down at himself, dressed in a mere shirt. He must have lost it at one of the opium dens.

'Where do you live?'

'I lived at a workhouse. But I escaped.'

'Why?'

The boy hesitated before answering, looking down at the ground, before muttering: 'They beat us there,'

Gabriel's lips thinned. 'I see.' He reached into his pocket, pulling out whatever shillings were in it. He handed it to the boy, who stared up at him with wide eyes.

'Is this for me?'

'Yes, it is. Go buy yourself a coat first thing tomorrow morning. Use the rest for your admission to an orphanage.'

The boy's eyes turned glassy as he stared up at Gabriel, as if he couldn't quite comprehend what had happened. Gabriel could see the renewed hope sparkling from them like falling stars. He straightened his back, nodding. 'I thank you greatly, sir.'

'No need to thank me,' said Gabriel dryly. 'Now be off.'

As Gabriel watched the small boy scurry away, he saw his own innocence. The innocence he had lost so long ago, running away from him yet again.

CHAPTER XXXIX

---•- •-----

The Prison in Scotland Yard

Gabriel did not let his mind linger on the events of last night, nor on his failure. His body had been aching with exhaustion as he arrived home, and so he fell asleep on the sofa within several seconds of putting his head down.

Gabriel jumped awake at a booming sound echoing through the house. He blinked rapidly, wincing at the daylight streaming in through the windows. He heaved himself up, looking around the room. Empty. Just as he thought he might have been dreaming, the sound occurred again. It was coming from the door. Someone was knocking on it. With great urgency.

Gabriel got to his feet. His head pounded at the movement. He headed towards the door, placing his hand upon the doorknob. He paused as he saw his knuckles. Cut

and bruised. His breath quivered as the memories from last night flooded back into his mind, but he pushed them to the side. Not now. He opened the door.

Gabriel frowned. 'Cyril?'

'Yes, Mr Ashmore, it is indeed I.' Alexander's butler stood before him, dressed in his usual smart attire, yet the man looked frantic. 'I require your help.'

'Whatever for?'

'Mr Wakefield has been imprisoned.'

Gabriel's eyes widened. '*What?* How on earth did this happen?'

'Mr Wakefield went to investigate someone last night. At the docks,' explained Cyril frantically. 'I just received word of it this morning. I believe he was arrested for trespassing.'

Gabriel swore. Alexander had gone to investigate Hugo. Of course he did. Gabriel should not have left him alone, should have known his friend would not give up. 'Well, did you see him?'

'I did, sir, I brought a large sum of money to bail him out, but the commissioner refused. Outright refused. I offered an even larger sum, a sum large enough to excuse even the most grotesque of crimes, but they would not have it.' His eyes widened suddenly. 'He told me something regarding a shipment, a shipment set to come in. He suspects his knowledge of it was the very reason for his imprisonment.'

'What shipment, Cyril?'

'I do not know, Mr Ashmore. Mr Wakefield was frantic—'

'I must go to the docks.'

'No!' exclaimed Cyril. 'You must go to Mr Wakefield first. He was not in a good state, I fear they may harm him.'

Gabriel's nostrils flared as he ground his teeth. 'We shall depart straight away.'

The carriage came to a halt in front of Scotland Yard. His eyes widened as he stepped out. A massive crowd had gathered before the building, all with the same red and white banners he had seen before.

'*Reform Scotland Yard! Reform Scotland Yard!*' they all shouted, raising their banners into the air. Gabriel pushed through the crowd, which was composed of all manner of people: women, men, upper class and middle class alike. When he finally reached the doors of the reception, he was held back by an officer. Gabriel cursed under his breath, craning his neck to look for an alternative entry. Then, the crowd behind him started pressing further into the building. The officers were engulfed in the crowd, giving Gabriel a chance to slip in.

The reception hall was packed with officers. They were all talking intently, attempting to figure out how to deal with the situation outside. He spotted the same clerk as before behind the main desk, who Gabriel quickly approached.

'Where are the prison cells?'

The thin, mousy man looked up with an unimpressed expression, raising an eyebrow. He appeared oblivious to the commotion that was taking place outside. Gabriel sighed frustratedly, pulling out two pounds from his pocket, from what Alexander had recently paid him. The

man's bony fingers immediately snatched the money off the table. He pointed to the left.

'Down the hall, in the basement,' he said curtly.

The crowds had started pushing against the doors, which were barely holding. Gabriel pushed through the crowds of officers, who barely noticed him, as he headed towards the cells. As he ran through the hallway, an officer appeared before him. Gabriel slowed, attempting to behave normally, but the officer was already frowning, calling out to him.

'Who are you? You are not supposed to be back here,' he said, pointing down the hall. 'Go back outside.'

Gabriel sighed. 'I am truly sorry, but I have no other choice,' he said.

The officer frowned, before Gabriel punched him in the face. The officer let out a groan, stumbling back and crashing on the floor. He blinked a few times, before his eyes closed and he fell unconscious. Gabriel grabbed the officer by the arms, dragging him into a nearby interrogation room. He quickly stripped him of his uniform and pulled it on over his own clothes. He buttoned up the navy blazer and put on the helmet. He rushed back out to the hallway and continued his way to the cells.

The prison was located in the basement. As he descended the stairs, everything became darker. When Gabriel reached the bottom, he could barely see his surroundings. He blinked rapidly, letting his eyes adjust to the darkness. He could now see the faint outline of two cell doors, and, on the ground, a lantern. He picked it up, taking out a match from his pocket and lighting it. He held the lantern

to the first cell door, peeking in through the small hatch. He saw a bearded man, sprawled upon the ground, sleeping. He moved on to the second one, and gasped.

Alexander was lying on the ground. Purple bruises covered one side of his face, his hair dirty and dishevelled. Most of his clothes had been taken away, so he was only left with his trousers and a ripped shirt covered in filth.

'Alexander!' Gabriel called out. Alexander did not stir. Panic rose in Gabriel's chest, panic mixed with red-hot fury. 'Alexander!'

Alexander shifted slightly. He blinked, opening his bruised eye. He looked around the room as if he were disorientated, and then his eyes fell on Gabriel. His lips trembled.

'Ashmore?'

'Yes, it is me!' said Gabriel, a smile of relief creeping to his lips.

'You… you—'

'What is it?'

'You look ridiculous.'

Gabriel chuckled, shaking his head. 'Hold on, I shall get you out of there.' He searched the room for a sign of the keys. He spotted a wooden chair in the corner of the room, where the officer guarding the cells must have been usually sitting, and above it, hidden in the shadows, a set of keys hanging on a hook. Gabriel quickly unlocked the door, falling on his knees before Alexander.

'What on earth happened? Cyril told me about a shipment – why did you go there alone? You should have told me, you *idiot*.'

Alexander chuckled, before wincing. 'I found an office. A merchant's office on the docks. I broke in and read through the hidden documents. I found out about a large, confidential shipment set to come in today, from Guangzhou. I suspected it to be the Erebus, but before I could find out more an officer found me. He gave me a beating before he took me in.'

'Bastard,' said Gabriel under his breath. 'They are all disgusting bastards—'

'Why are you here?' asked Alexander. 'Did Cyril not tell you about the docks?'

'He did – but he also mentioned you were in need of help.'

Alexander raised an eyebrow. 'Therefore, you chose to come here instead?'

'Well, yes.'

Alexander sighed. 'Well, I guess that makes two idiots.'

'I can lock you back up in the cell if you wish, Wakefield.'

'No, no. Please, carry me out.' He looked back at the other cell. 'This strange man has been whispering things to me all night. I fear I shall lose my mind if I spend one more minute in here.'

Gabriel put Alexander's arm around his shoulder, carrying him to the exit.

'How do you expect to get me out without anyone noticing?' asked Alexander, wincing at the movement.

Gabriel chuckled. 'You should see what is happening outside.'

CHAPTER XL

———. .———

The Shipment

They had arrived back at the West India Docks, greeted with the familiar smell of spices and smoke. Gabriel had gone home and changed into his own clothes. He had treated Alexander's wounds, which included several cuts on his cheekbones and bruising on his stomach. He had insisted that Alexander stay home, but he had refused.

They ran towards the ships, looking for any sign of a new docking. There were large crowds in the docks as well, the whole of London plunged into chaos in a matter of a few days. Several merchants unloaded their small ships. Gabriel and Alexander looked on as they opened the crates. It was all wool or silverware, no sign of the Erebus.

They inspected the warehouses, attempting to peek in through the cracks. They went back to warehouse number seven but found it empty.

'We ought to return to the office,' said Alexander. 'Perhaps it can provide us with more information—'

Gabriel cursed loudly. 'Peelers,' he said, pointing at the end of the docks. They had come to break up the crowds. 'We must depart. Now.'

*

When they arrived back at the Wakefield residence, Gabriel told Alexander about Hugo.

'The Erebus must have been concealed within the tea shipments,' said Gabriel, his voice tense. 'I saw him deliver it to the Silverton Club, personally.' Gabriel looked away, his eyes prickling.

'His ship came directly from China,' said Alexander. 'Meaning that is where the Erebus must be produced.'

Gabriel sighed defeatedly. 'So, whatever do we do now? Arrest my brother? Send him to the gallows?'

'No, you *talk* to him,' said Alexander. 'It is evident that he is not the one orchestrating it. He is merely carrying out a part of it. If you talk to him, and he helps us find the real culprit, we can leave him out of it.'

'You and I both know that will not hold up. The police shall ask us every last detail of how we came to such a conclusion.' Gabriel rose from his seat, folding his arms behind his back as he stared out the window of the library. Frost had gathered in the corners. He stared at the intricate designs, the uniqueness of each one. 'It does not matter,' he said finally. 'This investigation must come before all else.'

'Gabriel, I—'

'Do not say anything.' Gabriel stood deadly still as he watched the falling of the first snow of the day. Several minutes passed, minutes which felt like long hours, before Gabriel spoke again. 'I am sorry. For the other day.'

Alexander looked up. 'It is all right.'

'It is not.'

'I forgive you.'

Gabriel swallowed away the lump in his throat at those words, blinking rapidly. 'The last time this happened – my brother found me.'

Alexander remained still as he watched Gabriel's fingers wrap around each other.

'It was always him that found me. Tried to ensure that my sister did not see me. At first, I thought my father did not even know. But then I realised he did, he just did not care. It was always Hugo.'

Gabriel did not know why he was telling Alexander such things; all he knew was that he could no longer keep it inside of him.

'I am sorry, Gabriel,' said Alexander, understanding.

Gabriel shook his head. 'Save your sympathies. I do not require or wish for them.' He cleared his throat. 'He has brought this upon himself.'

CHAPTER XLI

A Crack in the Game

The sun had started to set by the time Gabriel made his way home. The sky did not swirl with hues of orange or purple, but instead remained a dull, melancholic blue which darkened with each passing second. As he neared the house, he noticed a faint, warm light shining out onto the street from the foyer window. Gabriel swallowed hard, cracking his knuckles as he hovered before the door. His breath misted in the cold evening air. He lifted his hand, his palm against the doorknob. He hesitated. He looked down at his hands and noticed his fingers trembling. He willed his hand to steady, exhaling deeply, before twisting the knob.

The house was warm. The foyer and the parlour fire had both been lit. A voice rang from inside the house.

'Gabriel, is that you?'

Gabriel's muscles stiffened at the sound. He willed himself to step forward, dragging himself along until he

had reached the parlour archway. And there he saw him, Hugo, sitting behind the desk, papers strewn before him. His shirt was folded at his elbows, his blue-patterned vest half undone. His hair was dishevelled, his fingers ink-blotted. A quill rested within his hand as he looked down at a parchment with concentrated brows. Gabriel noticed he had put up a garland above the fireplace, reminding him that it was almost Christmas.

'Yes,' answered Gabriel emotionlessly.

Hugo looked up at Gabriel's voice. His eyes were tired, but bright. 'Hello.'

Gabriel's eyes fell upon the papers, skimming over each one of them. 'Tell me, *brother*,' he started, his tone rancorous as he took a step forward. 'Why are you still in London?'

Hugo filed away a bundle of papers as he answered: 'I told you, Gabriel, a work opportunity presented itself.'

'What work opportunity?'

He looked up at him with a frown. 'I have already told you about this.'

'Tell me again.'

'Selling merchandise, Gabriel. Mainly tea.'

'And pray tell, why is it taking so long?'

Hugo looked up at his brother, brows slightly furrowing as he witnessed his tense demeanour. 'Is there something plaguing you, brother? I know you do not enjoy my presence, but I did not think it aggravated you so.'

Gabriel clenched his jaw, lips thinning as he said: 'Do you really wish to mock me further by acting oblivious? I saw you, Hugo. I am not a fool.'

Hugo's frown deepened as he rose from his seat. 'What on earth are you speaking of?'

Gabriel chuckled bitterly. 'Oh, just stop this charade already.'

'What *charade*, brother?'

Gabriel resisted the urge to hit Hugo's face. He bit the inside of his lip, tasting the metallic tang of blood. 'The Erebus. You delivered it to Harvey Blythe. I saw you.'

Hugo narrowed his eyes. 'What?'

'Do you have any idea what you are doing? Know what effects it has? You are *killing* people, Hugo. Profiting from the very thing that... that has *haunted* me, plagued me with such horrid feelings of regret and deepest anguish for *years*.'

'Gabriel, what are you speaking of?'

Gabriel's breathing had quickened, his chest rising and falling in frequent motions, nostrils flaring as he stared at his mirror image, yet also his opposite. 'I was embroiled in all this, not so long ago. I... I delivered the Erebus, to opium dens and individuals. Ever since our money ran out. It was the only way I could earn anything. The merchants did not wish to be associated with our father. All shops turned me away. I even went to the bloody East End, but nothing.'

'Gabriel, I swear to you, I do not know what you are speaking of.'

'The Erebus, Hugo. The Black Opium. It is concealed within your bloody shipments of tea.'

Hugo frowned. 'That is impossible.' He took a step closer to Gabriel. 'Look, I did go to Harvey Blythe's club. But I did not deliver the Erebus. I have never traded the Erebus in my

life, I swear to you. I was sent a request by my superior, that Harvey Blythe wished to try our premium tea from China to serve at his clubs. If he liked it, it would mean we would have the monopoly of the distribution to his clubs. He ordered me to bring it myself. Usually, we have others to do such things, but he wished to make sure Blythe felt... important.'

Gabriel stared into his brother's eyes, and knew he spoke the truth. Yet, instead of the warm feeling of relief, he felt cold dread. His brother had unknowingly been involved in this business; posing the question, who else was? How far did this really go?

Gabriel's head pounded at the vastness of it, at their minuscular nature compared to this grand plot.

'Hugo, when have you ever heard of gambling dens serving their clientele *tea*? Have you ever properly looked *in* the crates?'

A grave expression formed upon his features. He let out a defeated sigh. 'We were not allowed to do so. They were always sealed.'

'Who told you to do this, Hugo?' asked Gabriel.

'A supervisor.'

'I must see him – must speak to him—'

Hugo shook his head. 'That is not possible, he sailed away to India yesterday.' Gabriel cursed. Hugo took a step towards his brother. 'What on earth is going on, Gabriel?'

'I am trying to find out who is behind all of this. The Erebus.' He ran his hands through his hair, leaving it dishevelled. 'I embarked upon an investigation a few weeks ago.' He sighed. 'Someone tricked you, Hugo. Someone tricked us all.'

'I still cannot believe it. I have always sold tea, it does not make any sense—'

'Who have you sold it to? Has it been multiple people? Or has there always been one buyer?'

Hugo contemplated Gabriel's question, before affirming what Gabriel already assumed. 'A large batch was always sold straight away. The rest was split between two to three different buyers.'

'Do you remember who any of these people were?'

Hugo shook his head. 'No. They always bought it on behalf of someone else. They never used any names.' Hugo cursed. 'God, I have been so foolish.' He looked into his brother's eyes. 'And you, Gabriel – I am sorry.'

'For what?'

'That you had to endure that all by yourself. That I was not more helpful.'

Gabriel remained silent.

'The first thing I did when I came back to the city was visit her grave. Adelia's.' His voice broke at her name, not having spoken it since her death. Gabriel swallowed, firmly pressing his lips together. 'I… I often wonder how she would have been. How she might have looked now. If she would have your temperament or mine, and I… I truly wish I had been better.' The edges of his eyes glistened. 'I wish I had not been so damn *weak*.' Tears rolled down his cheeks. 'I regret it every single second of the day, Gabriel, I really do, and I am so sorry.'

Gabriel swallowed away the lump in his throat, shifting his gaze towards the floor. He rubbed his eyes, sniffing, before looking back up to his brother. He hesitated before

speaking, willing the words to come to his throat, willing his tongue to move. 'I waited. Those first few months you were gone. Every single night I waited. I seated myself right before the door, hoping that door would swing open, and you would be there.' Gabriel exhaled shakily. 'Forgiveness does not come easily to me. Neither does affection. Both things feel foreign. I… I wish it was different, but it is not.'

'I know, Gabriel. Despite your objections, I *know* you. I know you spent all the affection you could give on Adelia. I know that part of you died with her. I knew it the very same day. Felt it. Saw it in your eyes. And I am sorry it happened.'

Gabriel stared at his brother, lips pressed in a thin line, his eyes conveying a kaleidoscope of emotions he himself could not even identify.

'You do not need to say anything,' Hugo continued. 'I shall give you time, however much of it you need, so you may one day forgive me. Now, focus on your investigation. The city is in dire need, by the looks of it.'

'Do you have any more information about who spoke to your superior? Regarding the tea delivery?'

'I would take you to see him, but as I said, he just left.' Hugo shook his head, scratching his jaw. 'I do not know—'

'Please, Hugo, anything?'

Hugo looked at his brother's desperation-filled eyes, something he had only ever seen years ago. 'I still have the documents for it. A letter, written by Mr Davenport, my superior. Details of the shipment. I do not know if it would be of any use, but—'

'I must see them.'

Hugo nodded as he started flicking through the stack of papers upon the desk. Gabriel let out a long breath, running his hands through his hair.

'They are not here. But I could have sworn... ah.' He let out a breath of relief. 'I left them in the library.'

They went up the stairs, two steps at a time, before rushing through the landing.

'Are you certain nobody unfamiliar approached you? Or someone that looked suspicious?' asked Gabriel as he followed his brother to his father's study.

'No. And moreover, how would one even define a "suspicious" person?'

Gabriel rolled his eyes. 'Now is not the time for humour, brother.'

They entered the library. It hadn't been used in years, dust covering everything in the room, except for the large oak desk before the window. 'I worked here several times,' said Hugo, opening the drawer. He rifled through papers. When he was unable to find what he was looking for, he took them all out, dumping them onto the desk. He sorted through them carefully. Gabriel looked at the various documents upon the table, some old and frayed and some new. The corner of a photograph peeked out from between the documents. Gabriel pulled it out. It was a photograph of his father at Oxford. Youth shone from him. He was sat in a chair, dressed in smart attire, smiling at the camera. A sadness formed deep within him, as he stared at an image of lost memories, lost youth. Beside him stood a tall figure Gabriel did not recognise. Yet, he appeared awfully

familiar. Gabriel looked closely at the man's sharp features: his defined jaw and dark hair, his black eyes and broad shoulders.

His body suddenly stiffened as realisation dawned on him. His ears rang loudly, the room spinning around him.

The man he was looking at was Granville.

Granville and his father knew each other. They had been friends.

A suffocating panic rose in Gabriel's chest as he tried to breathe, but no air came to him. He saw Hugo's mouth move, saw his brows furrow with concern but he did not hear him. Gabriel rushed towards the nearest cupboard where he knew his father stored his belongings and started to rip out whatever he could find. He threw out notebooks, pens, books, until he reached a bundle of photographs. He flicked through them, discarding them on the floor, until he found another one.

A photograph of him and Granville, at a private member's club in London. They were older, most probably in their late thirties. Gabriel's hands shook as he continued looking through them, until he came across another one. He felt an ache in his chest as he stared at the photograph. It was of Cassius, Granville and his mother. The three of them posed in front of Christ Church College in Oxford, at what appeared to be a reunion gathering.

Granville's voice sounded in his head, recalling past conversations and occurrences. It hit him then why it was so easy to speak to him. Why he felt like they had already met, why he felt this inexplicable feeling of comfort around him. Because Granville and his father were friends. Dear

friends. Granville had known him before, most probably knew everything about him. But why? Why would he keep such a thing a secret?

Gabriel's eyes landed upon the books that had fallen out. One of them was the *Republic* by Plato. Gabriel picked it up, looking at its cover. It made him remember their conversations, Granville's adoration of the ancient world. He clenched his jaw. At that moment, he detested Granville for tricking him, yet he detested himself more for having been so foolish.

'Gabriel!' Hugo called out, getting on his knees beside Gabriel. 'What on earth is happening?'

Gabriel ignored his brother as he scrambled upright, running down the stairs and onto the street beyond. Gabriel had to get away from the house. He had to ease the storm in his mind and get it to think clearly. He spent the night walking dark streets, surrounded by nothing but the icy cold wind that prickled his skin, or hidden figures that merged with the walls. He walked and walked, until his legs could no longer carry him. He forced himself to stay away from Chinatown, forcing himself until every muscle in his body ached at the resistance. He took up residence at a local inn, yet he did not succumb to sleep. He lay awake, listening to the sound of chatter and clinking glasses until the early morning bustle started to commence.

CHAPTER XLII

Dolos

The next morning, Gabriel visited Alexander, telling him everything he had found out.

'I… I do not understand, said Alexander with furrowed brows. 'Granville *knew* you already?'

'Yes,' muttered Gabriel. 'I saw all of these photographs – photographs of him with my father at Oxford and in London. There were even ones with my mother…' His voice broke.

'But why? Why would he keep such a secret?'

'I do not know,' said Gabriel. His chest burned with an inexplicable emotion. 'I trusted him. I trusted the damned man, and now I do not know what to believe.'

'Perhaps there is an explanation to this all, perhaps—'

'What could it be?' exclaimed Gabriel. 'What could it possibly be?'

As his mind ran wild, a sense of dread rose within

Gabriel. He pushed it away, unwilling to listen to it, but it gnawed at him, getting stronger by the second.

'I do not know, Ashmore, perhaps we ought to ask—'

'The docks,' Gabriel stated. 'If we can find anything, it must be there. That is where the shipment came through, where you were arrested. If Granville had anything to do with any of this, that is where he must have hidden—'

'I have already checked all the dock records for storage space ownerships. I did not see Granville's name anywhere.'

'It would not be under his name,' stated Gabriel. 'Take me to it.' Gabriel was determined to find out who was behind this once and for all. He had to know if Granville was guilty, if he had any involvement in this whatsoever, although a part of him, a large part, wished desperately that he wasn't.

'Ashmore, there is no—'

'Take me to it, Wakefield.'

They found themselves back in the familiar land of the docks. Luckily, due to the number of rallies going on in the city, all of the Peelers had been stationed in the city centre, leaving the docks free. Most merchants were either off work or too busy loading and unloading their ships to notice them as they slipped into the office.

Alexander pulled out a large book from a shelf and opened it before Gabriel.

'The date of purchase or rent is at the top here,' stated Alexander, pointing to the top of the page. The list had been organised in a table, stating the name of the owner, the address of the storage space, alongside information on

its size. They started from four years ago, working their way down the list.

Gabriel read hundreds of names.

Smith. Bennett. Griffiths. Allen.

He continued dutifully.

Alexander stood behind him, tapping his foot on the floor. 'We do not have all day, Ashmore.'

'Be quiet,' said Gabriel, continuing his search.

Parker. Moore. Hughes. Dolos. Green. Lee.

Gabriel halted. He read through the list again and paused at one specific name.

Dolos.

Gabriel's head beat through his rib case, pounding in his ears.

Dolos.

Granville's voice echoed through his head, their endless conversations of the ancient world.

According to Greek mythology, Dolos was the spirit of trickery.

Gabriel's heart sank in his chest. He knew what the word before him meant.

Following the address upon the records, Gabriel and Alexander raced across the docks, towards the storage space. It was located beside the water, on the ground floor of a larger building. The door was locked, but Gabriel had enough rage within him to bash open the door with only one kick.

The room had a desk and various bookshelves within it. Gabriel immediately pulled out the drawers of the desk,

turning it upside down and pouring out all the documents within it. As they both looked through the papers, Gabriel picked up a ticket for a steamboat, with its destination China. It was dated four years ago. They looked further and found multiple letters addressed to the Emperor Guangxu. Guangxu expressed their resentment of the Peking Treaty of 1860, following the Second Opium War, under which they lost a large amount of land. Granville promised to repeal it if he were to become prime minister, in return for financial and military support. Further letters state that the Erebus was formulated by Dr Wagner, produced in China and then transported twice a year to London.

It was Granville. It had been Granville all along. He had caused the spread of the Erebus, the rise of criminality.

'Why would he do this?' questioned Alexander. The colour had drained from his face. 'Why be the cause of the exact thing he is working against?'

Gabriel's mouth twisted in contempt. 'To garner support for his party. Promising a solution to a problem he himself created; a problem only he knows how to solve.' Gabriel let out a shaky breath, leaning back on his chair. 'Christ. This is treason, Wakefield.'

Alexander nodded, brows furrowed as he read another letter. 'Treason of the worst kind. They shall hang him for this.' He glanced at Gabriel. 'Now, the question is, how on earth are we going to convince anyone of this?'

'I believe I may know a way.'

CHAPTER XLIII

Percival Edgerton

Gabriel and Alexander made their way to Percival Edgerton's residence in St James's. Gabriel had remembered Robinson mentioning his address, which he'd luckily remembered. Edgerton was a private advisor to Queen Victoria. He knocked upon the thick oak door and stepped back.

The door opened, revealing Edgerton. He narrowed his eyes as he tried to recognise who was standing before him. 'Mr Ashmore?' he called out in surprise. 'What on earth are you doing here? This is most inappropriate—'

'I need your help, Mr Edgerton.'

Edgerton looked him up and down, before glancing at Alexander. 'With what, may I ask, young man?'

'The Conservative Justice Party,' he stated. 'I believe they are committing a grave act of treason. We need to see the queen.'

Gabriel knew the queen was involved in politics. Even at an early age, she never failed to make her opinions clear, especially evident in the Bedchamber Crisis of 1839.

A solemn look passed over Edgerton's face. He had been suspecting it too. Gabriel had known Edgerton was different, not quite fitting in with the rest of Granville's entourage. 'Do you have evidence, boy?'

Gabriel held up the stack of letters and tickets they had collected from Granville's storage office. A small smile, so faint Gabriel thought he may have imagined it, played upon Edgerton's lips.

'I shall deliver these to the queen myself,' started Edgerton, reaching greedily for the papers. Gabriel held them back.

'No, no,' he said. '*We* shall deliver them to the queen.'

'I cannot just get two commoners a private audience with Queen Victoria!' exclaimed Edgerton.

'Commoners?' questioned Alexander.

Gabriel almost chuckled at the irony. There was no such thing as good men, only those looking to further advance their own interests. 'We either get a private audience, or you never see these letters again.'

'That is absurd! You two fools are wasting precious time—'

'If you take us to the queen, we shall make sure she knows of your participation. I am certain you shall be rewarded handsomely,' stated Alexander. 'Far more handsomely than us.'

Edgerton considered Alexander's proposal, distasteful eyes darting between them, attempting to find any sort

of weakness he could utilise to still get his way. He found none.

'All right,' muttered Edgerton. 'Then make haste. We must depart straight away.'

CHAPTER XLIV

Queen Victoria

Alexander stood fidgeting in the drawing room of Buckingham Palace. He tapped his foot upon the floor, eyes darting around the golden room.

'Will you stop that,' snapped Gabriel. 'Look professional.'

Gabriel held tightly onto the bundle of evidence. Edgerton was seated in an armchair at the far end of the room.

'It is not every day that one gets to meet the queen and has to convince her that the greatest act of treason the country has ever seen is taking place right this second,' said Alexander. He turned to look at Gabriel. 'What if she arrests us for conspiring against the soon-to-be government?'

'She will not,' Edgerton called out from his seat. 'Queen Victoria distrusts Granville as much as you two.'

'I do not trust him,' whispered Alexander, eyeing Edgerton.

'Neither do I,' muttered Gabriel. 'But he is all we have got.'

The queen's servants came into the room. They bowed. 'Mr Edgerton, please proceed to the audience room.'

Edgerton rose from his seat, gesturing for Gabriel and Alexander to follow. They trailed behind him as they walked through the hallway. Beautiful paintings with golden frames adorned the red walls. Gabriel looked up at them, before they entered another room. They made their way before two white double doors and were told to take a seat. The queen would call them when she was ready.

Gabriel clenched and unclenched his fists. Alexander tapped his foot, before realising what he was doing and stopping, and then continuing again.

After several minutes, the white doors opened. A guard with a bright red blazer appeared in the doorway, stepping to the side.

'Your Majesty, may I present to you, Mr Edgerton, Mr Wakefield and Mr Ashmore.'

Gabriel walked into the audience room: a grand space painted a golden colour. They saw the queen sitting on a chair, dressed entirely in black, a distant expression upon her face.

'Your Majesty,' said Edgerton, bowing deeply. Gabriel and Alexander followed suit.

'What is so important that it could not wait, Percival?' she said. Her voice was cold and reserved. She barely even glanced at Edgerton. Her hands were crossed upon her lap.

'Your Majesty, I must inform you of the gravest and most urgent news,' started Edgerton. 'It concerns Lord Benedict Granville and his party.'

Her eyes met his, a flicker of interest shining through their clouded indifference. 'Oh?' Her eyes fell on Gabriel and Alexander. 'And who might you two be?'

'These are my companions, Mr Ashmore and—'

'I did not ask you, Percival.'

Queen Victoria's eyes fell back on them. Alexander stood speechless. Gabriel cleared his throat, quickly introducing themselves. 'My name is Gabriel Ashmore, your Majesty. This is Alexander Wakefield.'

'And what do you two have to do with all of this?'

'We have been investigating the countless murders that have plagued our city, your Majesty, alongside the distribution of a new opium variant, named the Erebus. We have reason to believe that Lord Granville orchestrated this, committing illegal acts in order to gain favour for his party. We have found proof of a conspiracy he is undertaking with Emperor Guangxu.'

'Goodness,' she muttered. 'Do you have a copy of this evidence, Mr Ashmore?'

Gabriel nodded, handing the queen the stack of papers. Edgerton looked on with a sour expression.

Queen Victoria read through the letters, her eyes widening as she took in the details. When she put the papers down, her blue eyes were hot with rage.

'Thank you, Mr Ashmore and Mr Wakefield.'

Alexander only managed to nod.

'I shall handle it from here,' she said, rising to her

feet. 'Rest assured, your brave endeavours shall not go unnoticed.'

'May I remind you, your Majesty, that I brought them here, I—' started Edgerton, before being cut off.

'Do be quiet, Percival,' snapped the queen. 'We must act before the general election takes place. Gather my council and the royal guard,' she instructed the guard at the door. 'Granville shall not get away with this.'

CHAPTER XLV

———•‒ •——

The Game Falls

Gabriel exhaled steadily. Snow fell in thick chunks, clinging onto his hair and blazer. He adjusted his tie, his palms damp. He straightened his back before knocking on the door. Several seconds passed before it swung open. Gabriel's breath caught in his throat.

'Ah, Gabriel, what a lovely surprise. Come on in.' Granville left the door open as he walked through the foyer. Gabriel trailed behind him, limbs stiff. 'I have something to tell you, something I believe you shall be delighted at. I have managed to obtain the original Aristotelian Constitution of the Athenians.' His face beamed with satisfaction. 'It was discovered around ten years ago, in Fayum, Egypt. I have been trying to get my hands on it for several years now, but, of course, they had to first translate it, and do with it whatever historians do.' He chuckled. 'I would like to gift it to you.'

Gabriel cleared his throat, ignoring the burning of his eyes as he came to a halt in the middle of the foyer. Granville kept his pace, until he realised Gabriel was no longer behind him. He halted, and Gabriel could have sworn, from that moment, Granville realised.

'I know,' said Gabriel.

'Pardon me?'

'I know what you have done.'

'I do not quite understand what you are talking about, Gabriel.'

'Do not treat me like a fool. You have done enough of that.'

Granville let out a long sigh. 'I did not mean for you to find out this way.'

Gabriel's nostrils flared. 'Why?'

Granville turned to face him. His eyes were shadowed, his features sterner, as if this entire time they had been covered by a mask of amiability. 'To protect our future.'

Gabriel did not hide the disgust that shot from his eyes. '*Your* future.'

Granville shook his head, his lips curving into a slight smile, a smile that held the knowledge of a thousand years, a smile that knew more than any other living being on this earth. 'No, Gabriel. Ours. This future is for everyone.'

'This *future* that you speak of is based on *lies*. Are you not ashamed of deceiving those who trusted in you?'

'No. I am not. I *created* our future. Ensuring an optimal method of governing, enhancing order, controlling crime—'

'*You* were the one that spread this crime in the first place!'

'A *necessary sacrifice*, Gabriel. The people needed to be shown what would inevitably happen if the city continued as it did. It opened the people's eyes to the problems that were already deeply rooted, infesting everything and everyone.' His face turned grave. 'I took no joy whatsoever in facilitating the spread of the Erebus. It was merely a means to an end.'

'How?' asked Gabriel. He needed to hear it from him.

Granville took a step closer. 'I cannot tell you the details of that, yet, Gabriel.'

'How did the Erebus work?' continued Gabriel. 'I made hundreds of Erebus deliveries until those first deaths. Why did it only kill certain people?'

'I released a lethal batch alongside the normal product.'

Gabriel's features twisted into a scorn. 'To spread even more chaos? Was it not enough for you?'

'Yes, to hasten the progress,' answered Granville unapologetically. 'Time is of the essence, Gabriel.'

'And Harvey Blythe? Heinrich Wagner? Were they in on this scheming plot of yours? Was everything a mere lie?'

'I knew you were too clever to be completely misled, Gabriel. What you investigated was not a lie. I chose to divulge only a small part of my plan: Harvey Blythe. He was a mere means to an end, distributing the Erebus, helping it gain a reputation.' He tilted his head slightly, taking a step closer. 'I expected it to lead to a dead end. I expected you to become too puzzled, unable to proceed further. What I did not expect was that you would somehow succeed in obtaining more information, somehow breaking into one

of the most well-guarded buildings in all of London.' His eyes shone. 'How did you do it?'

Gabriel remained silent as he held Granville's stare.

'Anyhow, Harvey's enterprises will be no longer once I am elected.'

'And Heinrich Wagner?' questioned Gabriel, his voice shaking with fury. 'He tried to *kill* us.'

Granville shook his head, frowning. 'I never intended for that, Gabriel.'

'What was his role?'

'Dr Wagner helped me with the initial formulations of the Erebus. You were never meant to find him.'

Gabriel let out a slow breath. 'What shall happen to them?'

'They shall cease to be.'

Gabriel scoffed. 'You used them and are now going to kill them?'

'Everyone uses each other, Gabriel. That is the way of the world. Their immorality has no place in the England I wish to build.'

'And you truly believe that is fair? Just?'

'How would one define "just", Gabriel? How would one define fairness? Is justice not all about balancing the scales? Harvey has taken too much of this city, of these people. Now, this city must take back from him. Wagner is a deranged man who must be eliminated. That is what I believe is just.' Granville sighed, his features softening. 'I do not wish to terrorise this city, Gabriel. On the contrary, I wish to make it better. Under my leadership, stricter measures will be implemented. The police force shall be

expanded, every part of the city shall be monitored to ensure crime can never occur again. The passing of laws will be made more efficient, the method of governing simplified. The House of Commons and Lords shall be reformed, focusing power on a singular source rather than spreading it out.'

'You wish to obtain absolute power? Envisioning yourself as an eleventh-century monarch?'

Granville shook his head. 'Not quite. Monarchs are born into their power, making them terribly incompetent. I shall be *chosen* to lead. And I shall not answer to lesser powers, to those who are mentally inferior. This country needs a single, strong vision. A vision that will power through, a vision that will succeed. A vision that is not to be muddled by the incoherent ideas of others.'

Gabriel inhaled deeply. 'Why did you not eliminate us? Why did you help us? Why did you *befriend* me, if this entire time it was you behind it all?'

'Control, Gabriel. Involving myself in your investigation would ensure I could guide you where I wished, I could follow every step. But that was not the only reason. It was not the reason why I befriended you.'

'What was it then?' hissed Gabriel.

Granville smiled then, an odd smile which shone with sinister sincerity. 'Because I saw myself in you.'

'No,' protested Gabriel immediately. 'I am *nothing* like you.'

'Do you truly believe that, Gabriel?' He stepped closer. Gabriel saw his reflection in the darkness of his eyes. 'Can you really say you felt nothing, hearing these ideas? Not

a glimmer of hope? A hint of consideration? Did you not support my party?'

'My father,' said Gabriel, barely managing to force the words out of his throat. 'You knew me all along. And those Erebus deliveries—'

'I apologise for that. I tried to directly help your father financially, but... he is a proud man. Too proud... He refused my help each time. I sent Rufus after you. Did you never wonder why you got paid such a large amount for being a mere delivery boy?'

Gabriel clenched his teeth. 'You could have just given me the money instead of subjecting me to *that*.'

'Yes, I could have. But you did not see what you had become. Empty. Lost. You needed something to keep you grounded, to stop you from losing yourself completely. Even if that something was the thing you hated above all else. I find that nothing keeps one more alive than hatred. Deep, burning hatred for something.'

Gabriel sneered, his nails piercing the skin of his palms.

'I knew your father from our time at Oxford. He was my closest friend. Someone I cherished above all else.' He looked Gabriel up and down. 'I remember the time you were but a mere boy.' Granville smiled. 'Only three or four years of age. I used to gift you toy soldiers.' He sighed melancholically before continuing. 'It was your father who inspired me. Well, your mother, actually.'

Gabriel's heart sped up, pounding in his chest. 'What?'

'Your mother's death. That terrible, awful time.' He turned away, folding his arms behind his back. 'Her death was caused by criminality. Criminality that the government

allowed to thrive. Criminality that the government did nothing against.' He stared at a painting hanging on the wall, depicting a castle perched on the top of a cliff, with glimmering waves beneath it. 'This is what weakness in those who rule causes. Seeing your father's despair, seeing him unravel, it spurred me to act. Your father even helped me in designing my plans, my goals.' He turned back to Gabriel, his eyes shining with promises. 'I wish for you to join me, Gabriel. I see the same vision within you. Together, we can build greatness within this city.'

Gabriel felt a stab in his chest. He had not only been betrayed by Granville, but also by his father. He hesitated before answering, grinding his teeth in anger. 'You caused the death of countless people.'

'Again, necessary sacrifices. The ends justify the means, no matter how horrible they may be. You know this, Gabriel. I apologise you had to play a role in it, but now you have witnessed first-hand just how easily criminality can thrive within this immoral city, how the law, how authority, has no meaning. Government, society, hold themselves back with trivial fears of radicalism, but it is undeniable that someone must finally act. Someone who is not afraid of criticism, someone who can eliminate doubts and questions. A new age is coming, Gabriel. The question is, will you take part in its making?'

Gabriel did not answer as he looked at Granville, his dark eyes steady upon his own. He had always had a clear idea of good and bad, the two concepts as separate as the sun and moon, but now they had started to combine, merge into one, forming a perfect eclipse.

'Do you not wish to get justice for your mother? Your father? Your sister?' His dark eyes pierced into his own. 'I wish for you to join me, Gabriel. Aid me in restoring peace and justice to this country.'

Before Gabriel could answer, a boom echoed through the foyer, and the front door was knocked down. A group of Peelers marched in, followed by George Goschen, the Chancellor of the Exchequer, with a man unknown to Gabriel, dressed in royal uniform, beside him.

'Lord Benedict Granville, you are under arrest for treason,' said the head Peeler gravely.

Goschen stepped forward, his features scornful. 'How dare you, Benedict,' he spat. 'When we all trusted you so dearly.'

Several seconds later, Alexander emerged from the doorway. His hair was windswept, his tie askew. His eyes landed on Gabriel, looking him up and down to make certain he was well, before nodding. Gabriel pressed his lips into a tight line, before letting his gaze fall back upon Granville.

Granville's expression did not even sport the faintest of surprise. Instead, a smile formed upon his lips as he looked at Gabriel. Gabriel resisted the urge to apologise, and instead kept his head high.

'How?' Granville simply asked.

'We located your warehouses.'

'None of them were under my name,' stated Granville, raising an eyebrow.

'We searched the entire docks, until we came across one under the name Dolos. The Greek spirit of trickery.

Perhaps we would have overlooked it, if it was not for the fact that you had indulged me in your interests in the ancient world. You see, this was the one weakness in your game of deceit. Whilst you used the words I told you in confidence, I also used yours.'

Granville's smile had widened. 'Well done, Gabriel.' The guards started to close in. Granville raised a finger, tutting at the guards. 'Just one more minute.' He stepped closer to Gabriel, arms folded behind his back, his face the perfect portrait of intrigue. A part of Gabriel felt alarmed at Granville's calmness. 'How did you manage to convince the authorities?'

'We did not,' said Alexander, stepping forward. 'We convinced the queen.' Granville's eyes shone brightly at Alexander's words. Alexander continued, 'She is not really that fond of you, apparently.'

'Brilliant. Truly brilliant. I knew you two had potential.' He tilted his head. 'But all the evidence you have gathered must have been circumstantial, it shall never hold up in a court of law.'

'You shall not be stepping foot in a court of law, Benedict,' hissed Goschen. 'Your status in society and politics is the only thing that is preventing us from hanging you!' He gestured for the officers to move forward.

Granville remained quiet as the officers handcuffed him, his features calm, his posture relaxed. 'Virgil's Proteus,' muttered Granville. 'Art truly is a reflection of life, is it not, Gabriel?'

Gabriel swallowed hard. Granville was speaking of Virgil's poem, in which Aristaeus captured the sea

god Proteus with handcuffs, one of its earliest literary allusions.

Everything appeared to be solved, yet something gnawed at Gabriel. Like that faint tickle in one's throat, that would only fester and grow, but this time it was a gnawing at his skull, his brain, his very being.

'*The devil is not as black as he is painted.* Remember that, Gabriel.'

Granville's eyes met his own, black and green connecting, and as he watched Granville being escorted away, he could no longer discern if he had prevented evil, or good.

THREE YEARS LATER

———• •———

Snow fell outside. A Christmas tree stood in the corner of the dining room in the Ashmore residence, adorned with red and gold baubles. The fireplace roared, filling the room with a velvet warmth. Christmas carols sounded faintly from the street.

Gabriel stood in the corner of the room, taking a sip of his mulled wine as he watched Xing bring in a large turkey, setting it down in the middle of the table. The rest of the table was filled with various dishes including fish, sweetbreads, mutton cutlets, roast vegetables and many more things that made Gabriel's stomach growl. It filled the room with a savoury aroma, which circled his nose, tickling his senses. She moved the flower arrangement Hugo had placed earlier and set it down on the centre of the table. She turned to head back into the kitchen, before spotting Gabriel.

'Hungry?' she asked, dark eyes gleaming.

'After witnessing that work of art,' he nodded towards the turkey. 'Certainly.'

'Good,' Xing said. 'I would not have accepted any other answer.'

After Granville was captured, Gabriel had arranged for Hugo to meet Xing. He accompanied her on the journey to China with the aim of establishing new trade relations, and ended up falling in love with her during the six-month journey. They had married in Guangzhou, in Xing's family home. Xing had told him how she was taken from her home at the port when she was only four years old and had been looking for a way back ever since. Once she was reunited with her family, she soon realised that over the course of half a year together, Hugo had become her home. They had stayed with her family for a month, before returning to London together. Hugo decided to take on a permanent role in the city.

Gabriel heard his brother laugh again; he saw the life return to his eyes. In many ways, as he got to know Xing better, he realised she was a copy of his brother. She was humorous and clever, never failing to bring joy to an occasion. They had found each other when they both needed it the most.

Xing had her dark hair braided back, the sleeves of her dress rolled up to her elbows. She had insisted they prepare the entire meal themselves.

'I do hope everyone shall enjoy it. I have never had a Christmas dinner before.'

'I am certain it will be great,' said Gabriel.

'If not, I shall still force you all to eat it.'

Gabriel chuckled. She always managed to extract a laugh out of him and, most of the time, focused on doing

so. He was convinced she could sense something in him, the lingering sadness, the hollowness he still felt within his chest, and took it upon herself to minimise it each time they shared each other's company.

A loud, incessant knock sounded on the door. It continued until someone finally opened it.

'Christ,' muttered Hugo. 'You never fail to make an entrance.'

Alexander strutted into the Ashmore house. He put down his thick briefcase, bits of paper sticking out from the edges. He shot Hugo a wink. 'Of course not.'

Hugo rolled his eyes.

'It smells rather delicious in here,' remarked Alexander, hanging his coat. 'Do not tell me *you* cooked for us, because I would not believe it.'

Hugo narrowed his eyes at Alexander. 'I did help, actually.'

'And with "help", do you mean you idly stood by whilst others prepared it for you?'

'Stop bickering you two,' said Xing as she appeared from the dining room. 'Hugo, would you mind helping me bring the wine?'

'Certainly, darling.' He shot Alexander another look before he disappeared into the kitchen with his wife.

Alexander's eyes eventually fell on Gabriel, who was standing by the doorway of the dining room. 'Ashmore. I was wondering where you were.'

Gabriel raised his arms. 'Here I am.'

Alexander raised a brow. 'Were you eavesdropping, old fellow?'

'Perhaps.'

Alexander's lips curved into a wide grin as he opened his arms. Gabriel smiled as he embraced his friend.

'How is Oxford treating you?'

'Rather wonderfully,' answered Gabriel. 'Thank you for your recommendation.'

Alexander shot him a dismissive wave. 'It was nothing. Your application was most excellent anyway, you certainly did not need it. It is only good that they know who your friends are.' Gabriel had started his third year of studying Jurisprudence at Oxford, something he had dreamed of for many years.

'How is Scotland Yard, Detective Wakefield?'

'Excellent. We are working on expanding the Criminal Investigations Department. Alongside my detective work, I am currently in charge of recruiting the finest officers England has to offer.'

'Yes, Scotland Yard is certainly in dire need of it.'

'Indeed. I have become somewhat of a celebrated person, after our success with Granville. After I completed my training, the commissioner tasked me with great administrative duties over the Criminal Investigations Department. Finally, this country shall receive the change it needs.'

'I cannot think of anyone that deserves such responsibility more, Wakefield.'

'God, I never thought I would hear those words from you, Ashmore,' said Alexander with a grin.

Gabriel chuckled. 'Have your parents returned, then?'

'They indeed have. However, I am not seeing much of them.'

'Oh?'

'I have moved out of the Wakefield residence. Moreover, it suddenly occurred to me that I do not actually need my father's approval. In light of all we have achieved, his admiration seems rather inconsequential.'

Gabriel smiled. 'My thoughts, exactly.'

They soon all sat down to eat. The sky was swiftly darkening outside. Candlesticks were lit in each section of the large room, illuminating the table in a warm light. They had reinstated the Ashmore residence to its former glory, renovating the entirety of the house with both Gabriel and Hugo's earnings. No longer did the stairs creak malevolently, or did the thin windows let in any cold air. They even hired their old servants again, but Xing had sent them off to enjoy themselves in town for the night. They even had a nurse reside in the house to care for their father. Occasionally, Gabriel would hear his father's frantic footsteps. He had been devastated at the news of Granville's arrest, and had barely spoken a word to either Gabriel or Hugo since then. Although Gabriel understood his father's actions in supporting Granville, aiding him with designing his plans, he had not been able to forgive him. Hugo was convinced it would come with time, but Gabriel was not so certain.

The evening was better than Gabriel could have hoped; yet, ever since that day, Gabriel felt that same gnawing. He had pushed it under the surface, ignored it to the point he sometimes forgot it existed, but it always came back to haunt him. He saw it when he looked in the mirror for too long, like a shadow wrapping itself around his face until

all he saw were those black eyes. At times, it took him everything not to obliterate his thoughts, cast away the sins of the past to make room for sins of the future; but he had not touched it. Not since the night Alexander had found him, and he had vowed to never touch it again.

He pulled himself back to the present. Xing's laughter sounded through the room. He looked at Alexander, whose eyes were already on him. His eyebrows were slightly furrowed, a questioning look upon his features, as if he knew. Gabriel only quizzically raised an eyebrow at his friend, with the purposes of easing his doubts, but Alexander did not appear convinced. Nevertheless, he let it go, as Hugo served everyone a selection of the meat they had prepared.

'Dear Xing, do tell me, did you have the kitchen maids prepare some of these?' asked Alexander, sporting a sly grin.

She furrowed her brows. 'You offend me so, Alexander.' She started loading potatoes upon everyone's plates. 'But yes. Hard work and determination can only take one so far when you have Hugo in the kitchen.'

Hugo chuckled. 'Do you truly take such pleasure in insulting me?'

'I believe everyone takes pleasure in insulting you, Hugo,' commented Alexander, taking a large gulp of his wine.

'It is indeed rather gratifying,' added Gabriel.

For the first time in years, Gabriel felt joy. He felt a sense of belonging he had never experienced before; felt all the things he had ever wanted. Yet, he also felt *him*. He was still there. Hiding. Gnawing. *Waiting*.

To my dearest Mama and Papa –
Thank you for making every day so wonderful

GAME
—·OF·—
INIQUITY